DIRTY HOLY WATER

Science Traveler Series

Book 8

DIRTY HOLY WATER

Science Traveler Series
Book 8

J. L. Greger

Bug Press
Bernalillo, New Mexico

Dirty Holy Water

Bug Press
An imprint of IngramSpark
Bernalillo, New Mexico 87004
http://www.jlgreger.com

ISBN (paperback): 9780960028580
ISBN (EPUB): 9780960028597
Library of Congress Catalogue Number: 2020913030

DEDICATION

I want to honor three individuals:

Bug—my faithful and loving companion.

The diffident tour guide who introduced me to India.

Elizabeth Jennings, my sixth grade Sunday school teacher. When a student was shocked that the water in the baptismal font was from the tap, Mrs. Jennings replied, "All water is holy."

ACKNOWLEDGMENTS

I want to thank John Byram for editing this manuscript. I also want to thank Barbara Hodges for her patience and creativity when designing covers for my books.

I appreciate the staff at the FBI Field Office in Albuquerque for allowing me to tour their facilities.

CHAPTER 1: Sara Almquist in Early October

Lurleen Jansen must have been a pretty woman once. Now Sara Almquist could see little attractive about Lurleen, except her expressive green eyes. Lurleen had called Monday and almost demanded that Sara drive her to El Santuario de Chimayó this week. Sara had hesitated but finally agreed to the field trip because Lurleen needed a friend.

Although Sara had pushed the front passenger seat of her Subaru Forester back to the maximum, Lurleen looked like she was a piece of pimento stuffed in a green olive. Her face was red as she tried to close the clamp shut on the seat belt that strained around her green camouflage cargo pants and T-shirt. "Should have brought my seat belt extender along. Too much work to walk back inside for it."

Sara felt a twinge of guilt. She considered volunteering to get the seat belt extender but knew she wouldn't. Lurleen had been her neighbor in the adults-only community of La Bendita until Lurleen and her husband Pete decided about five years ago that the two- and three-bedroom houses of the gated neighborhood were too small to meet their needs. It wasn't jealousy that kept Sara from looking for the seat belt extender in Lurleen's large house. Her reasons were simpler—she knew it would be difficult to locate something small, like a seat belt extender, among the stack of boxes and piles of junk in the house. She was also afraid what she might find. Lurleen didn't waste time cleaning her house and only hired someone to clean it when a new infestation problem appeared. Some sort of pest, usually bigger than ants, appeared every year.

Lurleen appeared to hold her breath and clicked the seat belt shut. "Pete's being tight with me." She smiled. "But I'll get what I want."

Before Sara could make a catty comment, such as *you must have asked for the moon this time*, Lurleen changed the subject. "Thanks for agreeing to take me to Chimayó to get some holy dirt for Matt. He's talking less these days."

Sara gave a soft sigh because Lurleen had reminded her why they were making this trip. Lurleen's daughter Mitzi had become a foster parent for a one-year-old girl named Kayla almost twelve years ago. About that time, Kayla's biological parents had another child Matt. He was born addicted to cocaine and quickly displayed developmental delays. The New Mexico Children, Youth, and Families Department, better known as CYFD, had decided the two children must be kept together, and Mitzi had reluctantly agreed to become Matt's foster care mother, too. When she was five, Kayla had been diagnosed with attention deficit disorder. Eventually Mitzi had adopted both children. Lurleen had been supportive of Mitzi and her two adopted children during the long adoption process.

Sara admired both women because it took guts to adopt special needs children. Although Sara doubted the holy dirt dispensed from a small pit at El Santuario de Chimayó had curative properties, she recognized faith was sometimes effective in helping patients.

Chimayó was north of Santa Fe, almost a two-hour drive from La Bendita. Since 1816, pilgrims had claimed the dirt there had healing powers. Now the adobe chapel built around the pit with holy dirt was probably the most important pilgrimage site in the United States.

Sara had visited Chimayó several times because the drive in the foothills of the Sangre de Cristo Mountains was scenic and a nearby restaurant was excellent. Sara also recognized Lurleen needed a chance to vent her feelings more than Matt needed the holy dirt. So, she drove north and mainly listened.

***

The doorbell rang. Bug, Sara's Japanese Chin dog, didn't bark. He just glided to the front door, waved his luxurious tail, and waited for Sara to move from her computer. She was slow in getting to her door because she was working on one of her continuing scientific consulting projects for the U.S. Agency for International Development, better known as USAID. Her current project was based in Cuba.

Sara gasped when she saw her visitor—Gil Andrews, the Mercado police chief. He had police jurisdiction over the community of La Bendita and had been a frequent visitor to her house as she had helped him and the FBI solve crimes in the area. Today he looked paler and more tired than usual. It wasn't surprising. She'd been told his wife was losing her battle with breast cancer. Sara doubted he'd mention his personal problems. He seldom did.

"Sara—tell me about Lurleen Jansen?"

She was surprised by the abruptness of the question. "She used to be my neighbor."

His big shoulders sagged.

Obviously, he expected more of an answer. "Why don't you come in? I'll pour each of us a glass of iced tea. Why do you want to know about Lurleen?

"I'll get to that in a minute." The big man sat on the oak stool and hunched over her kitchen island. "I'm going to record our conversation."

Sara didn't rush to start any conversation as she poured two glasses of tea. Usually Gil outlined the situation first when he sought her professional advice on a case. Now he was treating her more like a suspect. She decided brevity with no, or at least few, smart-aleck remarks was best until she learned more. "Lurleen can be quite determined as long as it doesn't include following a diet, exercise, or cleaning her house."

He sipped his iced tea. "You're still a Northerner at heart. You don't sweeten the tea."

She laughed, pulled the sugar canister from her cabinet, and handed him a spoon. "I know I'm repeating myself, but why do you want to know?"

He ignored her as he stirred his sweetened tea.

Sara was surprised at his silence. "Er... er... I guess this is an official crime investigation. This might interest you, Gil. She's in the process of divorcing her husband of thirty-eight years."

"Is that a recent development?"

"Not really, but I just learned about it yesterday at lunch. We went to Chimayó."

"I wondered when you'd mention the trip. The only item on her calendar for this week was 'Chimayó with Sara' on Tuesday. That was yesterday."

Sara stopped sipping her tea. "What happened?"

"First, tell me about the couple."

Gil didn't usually take such a serious, no-nonsense approach with her. Sara was concerned. "When I moved to La Bendita nine years ago, Lurleen was already here, but her husband wasn't. She said he was in the process of retiring, and she was getting their post-retirement life set up in La Bendita." Sara paused to think. She suspected Gil was asking these questions because Lurleen was in trouble. There was a lot to say about Lurleen, and she didn't want to get Lurleen in more trouble.

"When did he join her in La Bendita?"

"He didn't. He visited about twice, maybe three times, a year. Each time for a week or two. Until five years ago. Then he stayed six months before he left to set up a new chemical processing plant in Aruba for Dow Chemical Company."

She noticed Gil's frown. "He's a chemical engineer and had set up and managed plants in other countries before. Anyway, Lurleen announced that she was moving immediately after he left. They'd bought a larger house, like double the size of their house here. About five miles away. They also built a two-thousand square foot man cave with a workshop for Pete in the backyard."

"Chimayó is a pilgrimage site. Why did you go there?"

Sara was surprised when Gil abruptly changed the topic. She figured Lurleen must have really done something dumb this time. "Not until you explain this quiz."

Gil shifted his weight on the stool. "Her daughter…"

"Mitzi?"

"Found Lurleen dead this morning. Looks like a crime of passion. The daughter mentioned her parents' divorce had turned nasty." He stared at Sara as if he expected insights.

Sara gulped. Lurleen had shown an ugly side to her personality yesterday that Sara had never seen before. While Lurleen tended to be outspoken, even flamboyant, her husband Pete had always seemed controlled, not prone to angry outbursts. But anything was possible during a divorce. She decided not to lead Gil into a snap conclusion. "Lurleen was in a bad mood yesterday and complained about everything, but she never mentioned Pete was in town."

Gil nodded. "Daughter said her father could have come and gone on one of Dow's executive jets. The murder scene was bloody… but well controlled. The weapon… isn't clear."

Sara was surprised by his hesitation. He was definitely speaking to her as if she was a suspect not a colleague. "Well… I could be more helpful if you were less stingy with the details."

Gil swallowed hard. "The murderer may have used a large shard of glass." Sara almost fell off her stool. "Didn't Mitzi tell you a story about glass shards?"

CHAPTER 2: Perspective of Gil Andrews, Mercado Police Chief

Gil Andrews thought of his morning before he replied to Sara's question. He knew he should be careful to not say too much. He was at Sara's house not to consult and seek advice but to interrogate her. That would be hard because he considered Sara a friend. To stall for time while he thought about how to proceed, Gil hummed a few bars of "Wichita Lineman."

***

Gil remembered thinking when he first saw Lurleen Jansen a little after nine this morning that she was an ugly corpse, especially for a fresh one. The body was beginning to go into rigor. She was tied in a chair with her head lolling to the side and her eyes wide open. Gil guessed she'd been dead two to four hours. The crew from the medical examiner's office would eventually provide a more precise estimate.

Lurleen was obese—almost three hundred pounds. Hell, that wasn't what made her grotesque. He'd packed on a few extra pounds and had almost two hundred pounds on his six-foot frame. It was her face. It was contorted as if she died screaming. The killer had stabbed her repeatedly, at least six times, around the mouth. He thought the slashes were made before the jugular had been cut because blood had streamed from the cuts. Gil had never seen this pattern of stabbing before, and he'd seen quite a few murder victims. He'd worked in the Albuquerque Police Department and on the New Mexico Drug Task Force before he retired to the easier job of being police chief in Mercado six years ago. Only it hadn't been easier. Mercado had been the scene of several high profile cases during his tenure as chief.

The crews from the medical examiner's office and the crime lab had already noted major problems by the time he arrived at the murder scene. The slashes on Lurleen face and neck were jagged and could have been made by several devices. None had been found yet. The technicians guessed the gashes were too wide to have been made by a knife blade.

Furthermore, no useful prints were obvious in the blood, instead someone had smeared blood everywhere.

Gil left the management of the crime scene to Chuy Bargas, an experienced sergeant in his mid-thirties, and focused on the two young officers trying to interview Mitzi Jansen. She claimed she'd called the police as soon as she overcame her shock. However, a neighbor had recognized Gil as the local police chief when he arrived at the scene and asked why the police were so slow to respond. Mitzi's SUV had almost run over him and his dog around six-thirty this morning when the vehicle was pulling into Lurleen's garage. Gil had checked with the dispatcher. The first police officers had arrived at the scene seven minutes after receiving the call. That was not a great response time, but he was surprised Mitzi had waited more than two hours before she called 9-1-1 around nine in the morning. However, people, especially close relatives, often reacted strangely at murder scenes.

The young officers had wisely moved Mitzi to the living room where she could not see the victim. Gil stood behind the recliner where Mitzi sat and listened for a couple of minutes. Her responses were unusual. They sounded like rehearsed sound bites. She was strangely unemotional considering the situation and seldom answered the officers' questions. In response to most, she said, "They were fighting over the divorce. Dad did it." or "No one could do this alone. Dad had help." Whenever the officers tried to focus Mitzi on a question, Mitzi repeated one of her two responses, unless the question was about her father Pete Jansen. Then she gave coherent, even long, answers. It was obvious Mitzi disliked her father, but she gave no real reason.

She repeated several times, "Everything was okay until DuPont Chemical Company merged with Dow Chemical in December 2015. Then Dad changed." Gil thought it odd she remembered when the merger occurred and suspected a family blow-out of some sort had occurred then. The officers had tried to probe the importance of the date, but Mitzi never lost control of the interview.

He quickly confirmed Mitzi's statement that Pete Jansen now headed an operation for Dow in Aruba. However, he couldn't confirm Mitzi's other comments about her father. She claimed he had easy access to corporate jets and could be anywhere. She seemed convinced he'd flown into Albuquerque, murdered his wife with the help of a woman, and left. However, she could provide no evidence to substantiate her claim.

The officers were probably being too gentle with her. The blood on her clothes and hands indicated she had tampered with evidence. He didn't think anyone would have thought Lurleen was alive and tried to resuscitate her as Mitzi claimed. However, he also thought she was too calm to have been the murderer, especially because the murder scene suggested high emotions.

He walked to the kitchen and called Ulysses Howe, the lead FBI agent in Albuquerque. Ulysses owed him a favor, and Ulysses could locate Pete Jansen quickly. Although the FBI didn't become involved in most murder cases in the Albuquerque area, he was sure Ulysses would be interested in this case because Mitzi had mentioned a name well known to both of them.

He listened again to the officers interviewing Mitzi and asked her whether she'd be more comfortable at the police station away from the crime scene. She turned red and said, "No." He debated insisting that she go to the police station but that would alert her to his suspicion that she was lying or at least withholding crucial information. If she stayed here and kept talking, she might slip and say something useful.

He figured she'd say more if he wasn't staring at her and asked Chuy Bargas to give him a tour of the crime scene. It was an investigator's nightmare. Lurleen was a hoarder. Most of the rooms in the house had multiple piles of junk and stacks of boxes ranging from three to five feet high. Paper plates with half-eaten food were on top of many surfaces. He'd already noted streaks of blood in the kitchen on a box of cookies, on the refrigerator door, and on a number of the stacked boxes.

Gil thought the kitchen looked like one found in the home of an alcoholic because the shelves were empty except for snack foods, mainly microwave popcorn. However, the refrigerator contained no booze—only cases of soft drink cans and half-eaten boxes of carry-out food.

Chuy pointed to the central island in the kitchen, which had been strewn with bottles of pills "The technicians cataloged and bagged the drugs. Nothing unusual, at least for an older obese woman. The medicines were for hypertension, arthritis, and heart disease. Mrs. Jansen appears to have been out of control in several ways, but she wasn't a drug addict per se. Of course, the killers could have taken any high potency painkillers, but look at the photo of this island before the technicians cataloged the drugs. There's no obvious place where several vials could have been removed by the killers. Also, there were no blood streaks but lots of fingerprints. The lab will be busy."

Gil coughed. "So, it's doubtful Lurleen was tortured by drug-inflamed killers."

The Adam's apple in Chuy's throat bobbed, as it often did when he was nervous, and he pointed to a day calendar on the island. "This was the only other item on the island besides an empty pizza box. Note the entry for yesterday."

Gil didn't like what he saw. "I'll follow up on that. Continue with our tour of the scene."

Chuy nodded and pointed out technicians had found blood streaks on the doors to the garage, patio, and the building in back. Gil thought the killer or killers were sloppy, which didn't sound like Mitzi's description of Pete Jansen. Of course, he could have been in a frenzied hurry. Chuy noted all the blood streaks found so far appeared to be swipes from a gloved hand. The swipes were too smooth to be produced by fabric. Gil wondered whether the blood smears were an intentional way to hide evidence. Mitzi's description of her father suggested he was clever.

The biggest surprise during Chuy's tour was the building behind the house. Gil guessed the back building could be called a man cave. It included a clean bathroom, an almost empty kitchenette, a neat bedroom, and an organized office. Even the well-equipped workshop was tidy.

Chuy pointed toward a technician who was picking up pieces of broken glass with a pair of tweezers from a work bench and bagging the pieces. In the center of the broken glass was the remains of what he guessed had been a vase. "This area looks staged to me. Why was the vase here? It couldn't be repaired. I'm having the technicians examine this area thoroughly."

Gil returned to the living room. Mitzi was still in control of the interview. He had nothing to lose. He asked her permission for the crime lab crew to examine her SUV parked in the garage.

She objected. Gil gave her two options. She could stay at Lurleen's house while Chuy got a search warrant to examine her SUV or the young officers could take her home. Mitzi chose the former but refused to answer any more questions. Instead, she played with her phone.

Gil was pleased with Mitzi's choice. He whispered to the two young interviewers and sent them to another assignment after he made a call. He knew he didn't need her permission to inspect her SUV because there were blood smears on the door to the garage but none elsewhere in the garage, except a bit of red, probably blood, on the back hatch of the SUV. However, he didn't want any evidence found in the SUV to be

8   J. L. Greger

declared inadmissible in court because of improper procedures. More important, he thought Mitzi was apt to make mistakes and reveal clues if he made her nervous. As she played with her phone, he doubted he'd fazed her. Or perhaps she was innocent of anything, except stupidly touching her mother's body and getting blood on her clothes. Even so, the young investigators would be more productive at their next assignment.

Gil had hated what he had to do next. The lone entry for the week on Lurleen's calendar said:

Sara—at 9—Chimayó

He guessed the "Sara" was Sara Almquist. Mitzi had mentioned Sara Almquist was a friend of her parents, especially her father.

Sara Almquist was a top-notch epidemiologist who consulted with the FBI and U.S. State Department on cases worldwide but liked living in the Southwest. The tall blonde had put on a few pounds but was still fit enough to do field work as she had when she was a professor of epidemiology at Michigan State before she retired early. Both he and Ulysses Howe had relied on her to help solve several cases during the last five years.

Most of all, he considered Sara a friend. She wasn't the typical university snob, although she seemed to love talking about complex scientific issues. It was obvious she'd worked with men during her career and worked easily with them. However, she wasn't particularly flirtatious and had a boyfriend—a high muckety-muck in the State Department— Eric Sanders. Granted Sanders was often absent and usually seemed aloof. But being Sara's boyfriend couldn't be easy. He had to compete with Bug for her affections.

He replayed the tape of Mitzi's interview with the young officers at Lurleen's home. Early in the interview, Mitzi said, "Sara always takes my father's side. Seems to think he has a right to expect Mother to take care of the house because he's a VP at Dow. That really steams Mother and me." Gil winced as he listened to more of the tape. Mitzi's comments didn't describe the Sara he knew. Moreover, Mitzi's comments about Sara became more caustic and incriminating as the interview progressed.

As he parked his car in front of Sara's house, he decided he shouldn't give her a hug as he often did when he saw her. She wasn't a colleague now but rather a potential murderer, at least according to Mitzi.

Not surprisingly, Sara sensed his reticence. Her conversation lacked her usual candid, funny observations until he mentioned the murderer may have used a shard of glass from a broken vase. Sara bounced on her stool and said, "Didn't Mitzi tell you a story about glass shards?"

***

Sara was staring at him as he hummed the second verse of "Wichita Lineman." She knew he was stalling.

"Why don't you tell me the story?" suggested Gil.

"A couple years ago..." Sara grimaced. "I guess quite a while ago. Kayla, Mitzi's adopted daughter, was six or seven. No, more like five or six. She'd just started school and is thirteen now. Anyway, Lurleen often reported Kayla had temper tantrums." Sara paused.

"That's it?"

Sara reddened. "Of course not. I'm trying to get the details right because the next part is so bizarre. Yes, that's it. Lurleen stopped by one evening. She was alone, and Pete wasn't around. As soon as I offered her a soda, she began to cry. It seems Lurleen had reprimanded Kayla for throwing a ball at an antique, leaded, cut-glass vase and breaking it. Kayla protested that the vase made a good ball hoop. They got into an argument. Can't remember any details except Kayla finally stared at Lurleen and said, 'I could take a piece of the glass and cut your throat.' Then Kayla smiled."

"Was Mitzi present?"

"Yes. I remember because Mitzi's response was so strange. Lurleen claimed Mitzi said something like, 'I've told the social worker that Kayla is often violent after she spends a weekend with her birth parents. Maybe now she'll believe me that those court-ordered visits must stop, and we should finalize the adoption.'"

"Strange response from Mitzi." He frowned. "I don't think most five -or six-year-olds are capable of that reasoning level. Are you sure Lurleen told you the truth?"

"I was never sure of anything with Lurleen, but Kayla is smart and has often shown violent tendencies. She regularly beat up other children at school. Two of her teachers claimed she tripped them, but they couldn't prove their claims. I told Lurleen after the vase incident perhaps the adoption of Kayla and her brother wasn't wise. She about took my head off. Said I didn't understand." Sara picked up Bug who sat at the base of her stool. "Guess she was right. My maternal instincts have limits, except when it comes to Bug. I've held my tongue since then."

"Anything else?"

Sara grimaced. "I think a month later, Lurleen told me that the biological parents had lost their visiting rights and Mitzi had been ordered to take Kayla to a psychiatrist once a week for six months. However, the approval of the adoptions was slow. That took about a year more."

Gil thought Sara had told the truth but he was also sure she'd left a lot unsaid. He checked his phone. His wife Jen should have left a message by now. "Sara, that's all for now. Got to follow up on a few other issues."

***

Gil felt guilty as he drove to his office. He'd planned to go with Jen to her doctor's appointment this morning. However, when Chuy notified him of a murder in his Mercado jurisdiction, Jen had insisted Gil take care of business. This was Chuy's first big case after being out on medical leave for almost a year. Chuy had been critically injured while working for the New Mexico Drug Task Force. Sara had provided crucial clues for that case. It was one of several reasons that he and Chuy knew in their hearts Sara hadn't killed Lurleen. They trusted her implicitly. However, now was not the time to think about work, but about his wife.

He called Jen's oncologist. The last round of chemotherapy had curtailed the growth of cancer in Jen's lungs but not in her spine. The oncologist urged Gill to convince Jen to endure another round of chemo. Gil called his home but Jen didn't answer. He left a message and swung by his house. She wasn't there. He left another message.

Chuy was waiting for him at the Mercado police station with bad news. Chuy had been convinced Mitzi had disposed of bloody gloves in her car because he'd found none in the garbage or in Lurleen's house. A judge had granted the search warrant, but it was bust. Technicians found nothing unusual in the SUV. The small red smear on the SUV's hatch door was blood. The lab would analyze it to determine if it was Lurleen's, but it would prove little.

Chuy had stared at Gil expectantly for several seconds before he said, "I can take care of everything on this case but Sara. You need to pin down Sara's whereabouts last night."

Suddenly Gil's day turned brighter. Jen waltzed into his office. "I went shopping."

Chuy, gulping in his usual nervous fashion, left quickly as Jen held up a gauzy dress with pink, orange, and red stripes It was not her usual conservative style. Gil didn't know what to say and felt heat moving up his neck. He figured that he'd turned red because Jen laughed.

He regained his composure. "Should I make reservations at Prairie Star Restaurant for tonight? Can't think of any other place elegant enough for that dress."

"I thought it was pretty. And... and... I'm not getting younger. Can we go for an early dinner before I wear out? Like at five?"

Gil felt tears well up in his eyes. He hugged his wife. "You'd better rest up. I'll be home by four-thirty."

***

Sara surprised Gil when he stopped by her house again with a few more questions. She began by saying, "I bet I know why you're here, and I'll cut to the chase. I don't have an alibi for much of last night. I came home after I dropped Lurleen at her house around four. Walked Bug around six and again around nine last night. Someone might have seen me. Talked to Sanders around six this morning. I usually talk to him before he leaves for work. Neither of us are nighthawks so our conversations are better in the morning."

Gil wondered what Sara meant by "our conversations are better." Did they argue less? Or was their conversation more interesting? He always found it odd that she called her boyfriend—he knew that was an archaic term but it seemed appropriate—"Sanders" not "Eric." He decided his curiosity about these details wasn't relevant to the case. However, he wanted to know more about Sara's relationship with Pete Jansen. Mitzi's comment that Pete Jansen and Sara were "good, very good, friends" intrigued him pruriently and from a practical view of the case. He found Sara attractive and assumed most men—well, *mature* men—would. He supposed Pete Jansen as a chemical engineer with lots of international experience would intrigue her, but she'd never mentioned him, or for that matter Lurleen, previously. That didn't suggest closeness, but then he doubted Sara would talk openly about a married man if she was having an affair with him.

He also thought it odd that Sara had admitted at the onset that she didn't have an alibi. Was she defying him to arrest her or take her in for questioning? He doubted it. She recognized she wasn't a good bluffer and was smart enough not to try. She showed no sign of nervousness as he questioned her for ten more minutes. He concluded she hadn't participated in the murder, but she probably knew more information that could help him solve the case. "Sara, I have to give you the standard advice—don't leave town for the next few days."

Sara leaned forward. "That will be a problem, and you know it. Sanders and I are booked to go to India in a couple of days."

Gil groaned. Sara had told him and Ulysses Howe last week as they finished the investigation of drug smuggling in New Mexico and Texas that she and Sanders were going to India on vacation. It had sounded like Sanders was finally going to propose to her. "Shoot—I forgot."

Sara leaned farther toward him. "Despite Mitzi's comments, you know I'm innocent. Looks like you need my help to get this murder solved fast. By the way, you never gave me an estimate of Lurleen's time of death—only that it was last night. Has Ulysses found Pete Jansen yet?"

He realized Sara was back to being her usual self—intuitive, smart, and bossy. "I, I... never said the FBI was involved. And I only said we'd had a long talk with Mitzi."

Sara rolled her eyes. "You wouldn't have visited me twice today if Mitzi hadn't implicated me. It's logical to involve the FBI in this case because Pete is most likely in Aruba. Ulysses as an FBI special agent could find Pete much more easily than you could as a local police chief."

Gil hunched over Sara's kitchen island. "I'm not up to this investigation. My wife Jen has taken a turn for the worse. The cancer has spread to her spine now. Can't concentrate." He didn't add the obvious he had already told Sara too much. That was a mistake he rarely made with suspects.

Sara put her hand on his shoulder. "I bumped into Chuy last week at McDonald's. He's said you might go part time to spend more time with your wife. I'm sorry." She paused. "I can't help Jen, but I think I can help you solve this case quickly. Then you can do what's important, and I can go to India with Sanders."

He snorted and pulled out his phone.

"You didn't tell me much about the crime scene. Probably shouldn't because..." She shook her head. "But I know a lot about Lurleen. The number of suspects can't be many. She never allowed anyone into that house, except her family and occasionally me and a cleaning crew. She made few attempts to get to know her neighbors. Didn't go to any church or social clubs, but she volunteered as an accountant for two churches."

"Are you sure about the cleaning crew?" Gil didn't even lift his head as he texted. One of his officers had already talked to all of Lurleen's neighbors. They'd confirmed Lurleen seldom had visitors, except a woman who drove a blue Subaru. That described Sara's car.

Sara giggled. "Hard to believe but when the pests get bad enough, she calls a cleaning service. Then she complains for months afterwards. Not about the costs, but about her loss of her privacy. Unless the crime scene suggests otherwise…?" Sara peered at Gil.

He shook his head. "You're out of line, but go on."

Sara smiled. "I'm fairly certainly she didn't use drugs, other than prescribed medicines. I've never seen her drink alcohol. Actually, that's how we became friends here at La Bendita. In an adults-only community, over consumption of alcohol is often a problem. Lurleen and I always brought our own diet colas to events, and very few others did." Sara paused. "After she left La Bendita, I think she switched from diet colas to regular cola. She claimed aspartame and saccharine in diet sodas bothered her stomach." Sara winced. "I always wanted to ask her how she came to that conclusion, especially after watching her eat half a cream pie for lunch. Lurleen didn't gamble either."

Gil kept texting on his phone. "What does that prove?"

"Doubtful she was killed because of drugs or gambling debts. You said the scene was bloody. That suggested a drug-crazed killer or killers. Not hired contract killers."

"You're building a case against yourself."

"No, I didn't kill Lurleen. I'm saying that Lurleen was killed by a relative. Both her and Pete's parents are dead. She had no brothers or sisters. That leaves seven people: her husband Pete, her daughter Mitzi, Mitzi's children Kayla and Matt, and Lurleen's son Bill and his family in Omaha."

Gil stopped texting. "Mitzi mentioned her brother and his family to two officers this morning. We've already had Omaha police contact them. The son and his eight-year-old daughter were in Omaha and have air-tight alibis. His wife was in Houston at M.D. Anderson Medical Center undergoing chemotherapy. Problem is we can't find Pete Jansen. He's not in Aruba—at least at home or at work. His secretary said he'd flown into Phoenix on the corporate jet Monday evening. She said he planned to visit several water recycling projects and take a few vacation days."

Sara lost the smile that had indicated how much she'd enjoyed piecing bits of evidence together for him. "That's too bad. I'd hoped Pete had an alibi."

He looked at his watch. "I've got to go. Jen needs me."

CHAPTER 3: Sergeant Chuy Bargas of the Mercado Police

It was four-thirty—too late to update Gil. Besides, Gil didn't need more bad news.

Gil had been a father figure to Chuy ever since Gil had become the Mercado police chief six years ago. He had encouraged Chuy to broaden his horizons two years ago and join the New Mexico Gangs Task Force and then found a place for him back on the Mercado police force after his near fatal accident. Of course, no one had thought his recuperation would take so long. Gil had been shorthanded and overworked for almost a year—a terrible time during which Gil's wife had been diagnosed with stage four breast cancer. Chuy didn't want to do anything that would increase Gil's stress load.

More importantly, Chuy saw this murder case as an opportunity. He needed to take control of it and prove he was ready for a promotion. Chuy knew he wouldn't be considered a serious contender for Gil's job when Gil retired unless Chuy achieved the rank of lieutenant and showed solid administrative skills.

Gil had thought he'd outsmarted Mitzi this morning. He'd sent the two officers who had interviewed Mitzi to talk to Kayla and Matt after Mitzi had refused a ride to her home and stayed with her SUV until technicians had finished searching it for clues. Gil had also arranged for two of the Sandoval County sheriff's deputies to be present while the officers talked to Mitzi's children

The interview was a bust. Chuy suspected Mitzi hadn't been concerned when Gil indicated that officers would stop by her house to talk to her children because she understood them. Kayla was only thirteen, but she knew enough to refuse to talk to the officers. She even claimed her Miranda rights before the officers mentioned them. When Matt started to mumble a bit, she pinched him and screamed, "He can't talk." The officers noted Matt seemed to communicate with Kayla with grunts or unintelligible words.

Ten minutes ago, Mitzi's lawyer called and claimed the Mercado police had traumatized Matt and Kayla. Mitzi and her children were so overcome with grief that they couldn't come in for further questioning until tomorrow morning. The only thing good about the situation was Gil had been smart to have the sheriff's deputies present when the Mercado officers tried to interrogate Kayla and Matt. It was obvious Mitzi and her lawyer wanted to claim police abuse, but couldn't. Chuy knew he wouldn't have thought to have extra witnesses present when the children were interviewed.

The medical examiner's office gave him bad news, too. It had been a busy weekend in the gang and drug scene in Albuquerque. Thus, a staff member from the office had called with several preliminary comments because the full autopsy report would not be ready for a week. "No one here has seen this pattern of stab wounds before." The technician noted that the wounds around Lurleen's mouth were deeper on the right than on the left side. "That could indicate the murderer gained confidence as he or she worked or that were two stabbers. However, the cut across the jugular was done with practiced precision." The technician also noted, "The rope burns on Lurleen's wrist and ankles suggested she'd struggled to escape and was alert during the whole horrible process." The medical examiner planned to check for bits of glass in the wounds and had ordered tests for drugs.

Chuy figured no professional killer would have taken the time to make the wounds around the mouth, even though the killer appeared to know enough anatomy to locate the jugular vein. No one in Lurleen's family had a medical background. There was no evidence that Lurleen had been gagged, and he assumed she had screamed mightily. Surely, someone had heard her screams. However, none of the neighbors had noticed anything unusual at Lurleen's house until police cars arrived.

Chuy had contacted the New Mexico Children, Youth, and Families Department because the adoption process for Mitzi's children had been unusually prolonged. The infamous CYFD had been unhelpful as usual. However, a social worker had admitted—Chuy suspected on purpose—there were "substantial medical records on Kayla, Matt, and Mitzi Jansen in her files." However, no data could be released without a court order. Chuy thanked her and added Mitzi's name to his request for a court order to see all medical or psychological evaluations of the family. He was sure the juvenile court would be sympathetic to his request but it could be a week before CYFD released the records. Their employees were always slow.

He re-read the terse email from Ulysses Howe.

We think Pete Jansen is in the Albuquerque area and has been since last night. Carbonne is on it and will call you when he has more information.

Finally, some good news. Paul Carbonne did not fit the usual stereotypes of FBI agents but was perhaps the best undercover agent in New Mexico. Unfortunately, he soon wouldn't be doing much case work because he was slated to replace Ulysses Howe as interim chief of the FBI group in Albuquerque in six months when Ulysses retired.

His phone rang. "Pete Jansen is digging a hole in the backyard of Lurleen's house." The phone went dead.

***

Chuy turned off the siren three blocks from Lurleen's house. He noted the yellow police tape on Lurleen's front door was intact and no cars were parked in the driveway. A bicycle leaned against the side of the house. He was sure the bicycle wasn't there when he left the crime scene around noon.

Chuy slipped past the house and onto the tree-lined patio, which connected the house with Pete's man cave. He stood under the trees by a picnic bench as he looked at the orchard in the backyard. The property must have been a double—more likely a quadruple—lot of at least two acres. About forty sapling pecan trees were spaced across the yard.

For a moment Chuy forgot the case and thought it would be nice to own a property like this. The trees probably didn't produce many nuts yet. The saplings were only about fifteen feet tall. A mature tree would be twenty to forty feet tall. He remembered as a child visiting his grandparents and helping them harvest pecans each fall from the orchard behind their house in Mesilla in southern New Mexico. His uncle lived there now.

He snapped out of his reverie and focused on something moving at the back of the property. A blond, tall, reed-like man was hunched over a pile of dirt near a trench down the middle of the orchard. The man looked like photos of Pete Jansen, but he was too far away to be sure.

Suddenly Chuy felt a hand on his shoulder. He tensed.

A low voice said, "Let's watch Pete for a couple more minutes."

Chuy turned to see a man of average height with a scraggly dark beard and a big brimmed straw hat. The man's clothes looked like those of indigents who stopped cars at intersections in Albuquerque to beg for money. The man lowered his hand to shake Chuy's hand.

"Carbonne—glad to see that your impending administrative work hasn't crimped your style."

"Unfortunately, it has." Carbonne removed his hat to reveal neatly trimmed short dark hair. "Let's move inside while I update you a bit. Also, gets us away from the stink."

"I noticed the odor this morning. I figured it was a septic system gone bad, but when I inspected the area, I realized that didn't make sense. The lot has a fancy pumice stone water purification system for graywater." He pointed to the trench which seemed to be filled with white sand. "And a septic tank for their blackwater."

"I'm a city boy from New Jersey. Explain your mumbo jumbo."

Chuy smiled. "New Mexico's regulations allow the water from laundries and showers, called 'graywater,' to be recycled and used for certain types of irrigation without processing. However, the water from kitchens and toilets, called 'blackwater,' must go through septic systems or public sewers. Looks like the Jansens use an expensive pumice-stone filtration system to purify their graywater before they use it for irrigation. That's overkill because that water is then clean enough to be drinkable."

"Okay. Why did this fancy system fail?"

Chuy shook his head. "Not sure it did. There's no standing water anywhere like you get when a septic system fails. The toilets in the house flushed normally this morning, but it does stink."

As they entered the building, Chuy noted the door was unlocked. He doubted the technicians had left it unlocked when they finished their work around noon, but he asked anyway. "Did you find the door unlocked when you arrived?"

Carbonne looked at Chuy with disgust and ignored the question. He led Chuy past the large picture window in the workspace facing the backyard to a small window in the kitchenette. "Pete's less apt to notice us as this window."

The man in the backyard had left a stick with a white flag by the last hole and was now digging another hole to the right of the trench in the orchard. Chuy noticed there were three other sticks with tags along the trench.

Carbonne pointed at Pete Jansen. "Our man flew to Phoenix on Monday night on a corporate jet. Met with city and state officials involved in water recycling projects all day Tuesday and then rented a car and returned to his hotel. Odd—he didn't stay in the Westin or Hyatt Regency but in a La Quinta Inn."

"I assume you have a theory why an executive with presumably a generous per diem would stay in a cheap hotel?"

Carbonne shrugged. "Could be because he planned to leave in the middle of the night and didn't want others to know. He settled his hotel bill around six last night. The maid found his key on the bed this morning. But maybe not. He might just be frugal or figured he had a lot to do today. A man trying to hide his movements wouldn't use a credit card, certainly not one issued by his employer, to pay for all his meals and gas. Seems he filled up at a Shell station in Grants around four this morning and ate at the Frontier Restaurant on Central in Albuquerque around seven."

"Odd that he didn't fly to Albuquerque."

"Not really. The company jet had been chartered for other use several weeks ago."

Chuy nodded. "He's pretty close to having an alibi. The medical examiner estimated Lurleen was killed between four and six this morning."

Carbonne shook his head. "Forget it. Doesn't matter what the daughter Mitzi said. This man didn't actually do the killing. I saw the photos of the messy murder scene. Lots of blood. Look at him. He's even neat when he's digging holes. He puts the rug down each time before he kneels on the dirt, and he's leaving tags at each hole."

"Don't be so sure. The bloody smears inside might have been an intentional distraction. The killer or killers wore gloves. The technicians examined the blood smears carefully. There were no fingerprints. Just smears created by a smooth surface like plastic gloves. However, he's got fabric gloves on now."

Carbonne was surprised by Chuy's assertive answer. He'd not worked much with Chuy before, and his boss Ulysses Howe had warned him that Chuy might be a bit shell-shocked and hesitant. Several key witnesses, including Sara, had been killed or almost killed because Chuy had been slow to react when he worked on the New Mexico Gangs Task Force. Even Gil Andrews, his mentor, admitted that these mistakes and his work-related accident had left Chuy "a man constantly second-guessing himself."

Chuy's comment made Carbonne to think that he and Chuy might be a good pair. He appreciated investigators who were careful about details. He decided to throw out a theory he'd been toying with for the last hour. "If Pete Jansen wanted to pay a hired killer or meet up with a druggie who accidentally killed his wife, the Frontier on Central Avenue in Albuquerque is the perfect place. The place is a mix of curious tourists and my kind of people." He pulled at his torn clothing and his ragged beard. "He could have met the killer at the Frontier after the crime. That would fit the medical examiner's time estimate."

Chuy nodded. "Do you know where he went after the Frontier? When did you start tailing him?"

"The FBI got his travel arrangements, including info on his car rental, from his secretary and alerted local police about his rental car—a gray Honda Odyssey—around noon."

"I saw the APB. I was surprised he chose a hatchback. It suggests he planned on moving something or several people. Or he's just being cheap again."

Carbonne pointed to Pete. "He's found something. See the white object in his hand. Oh look, he's being Nelda Neat again."

They watched Pete rub dirt off the white object and then place it in a blue plastic box. Then he again began to slowly probe the hole.

"He acts like he's looking for something fragile. Maybe we should go out and start questioning him."

Carbonne put his hand on Chuy's shoulder. "No. Let him do all the digging, not us. Got more to tell you. Albuquerque police spotted his car at the Home Depot at Cottonwood Shopping Center around one. Ulysses pulled me off an undercover sting I was running on Central Avenue and rushed me to Cottonwood. Got there before Pete Jansen ambled out of the store with a shovel, that blue container, and other supplies. We followed him here. My support team heard your siren and left to relieve the agents who've been sitting near Mitzi's house since ten. Didn't want it to look like a stake out on this street. By the way, Pete's car is parked here in the three-car garage."

Chuy swallowed hard as he tried to tactfully ask the next question. "I wasn't surprised when Gil called Ulysses to notify him that Sara Almquist might be involved in this murder. They've worked together on several cases. But I was surprised when Ulysses made it a high priority case for the FBI so fast. The FBI ignores most murder cases in Albuquerque area."

Carbonne laughed. "You forget how important Sara's testimony will be in several upcoming federal cases against drug lords in the Southwest. The U.S. attorney about had a heart attack when Ulysses called him this morning. He's afraid someone from a drug gang killed Lurleen and framed Sara so she'd lose her aura of integrity. The U.S. attorney thinks even if the press mentions she's a suspect, he might be unable to convict all the drug lords. Her testimony is *that* important. He told Ulysses to get to the bottom of this case fast. Ergo, I'm whisked here with my bike."

Chuy wanted to ask more questions. He hadn't realized the U.S. attorney was nervous about what he thought were solid cases against those whom Carbonne colorfully called drug lords. But Chuy was distracted by what he saw in Pete's hand. "Look—he's found something else."

This white object was bigger than the last one and more oval.

"Oh no." Chuy felt like vomiting.

CHAPTER 4: FBI Agent Paul Carbonne Finds a Partner

"Guess it's time to approach Pete." Carbonne shook his head. "I enjoyed watching him work. He's so neat that it makes me suspicious. At the least, he's anal retentive. Wonder which came first—his wife being a slob and a hoarder or his fussiness? Bet he displayed the original pathology."

Chuy's Adam's apple bobbed in his throat. "I would never have thought of it that way."

"Of course not. You earned a two-year degree in criminal justice and made your family proud when you became a police officer. My parents had sticks up their asses, probably like Pete's. No, not quite. My parents were poor while his were rich, but my parents had high ambitions. They approved of my major in psychology at Fordham University and were as pleased as Punch when I got accepted into its law school, but they threatened to disown me when I became a NYC cop instead. After two years, I decided they were right on one point. Being an FBI agent is safer than being a NYC beat cop."

Chuy reddened and the muscles of his lower face tightened. "Are you... are you saying I'm not...?"

"Didn't insult you. Wish I came from a well-adjusted home. But my background gives me insight into Pete's neuroses. Want you to take the lead with him, so I can just observe. Don't worry. He'll take one look at my clothes and your clean-cut appearance and assume I'm not important."

As they left the building, Carbonne added, "I doubt he'll be violent, but I'll have my gun ready."

Carbonne stayed one step behind Chuy as he walked toward Pete who was on his knees cleaning another oval ivory object.

"Sir, why are you digging holes in this yard?"

The man slipped the ivory object in the box, snapped the lid shut, and then looked up at Chuy who looked official in his navy-blue shirt and pants with a black tie and shiny Mercado police badge. He only glanced at Carbonne. "It's my yard. I can do what I want."

"Didn't you see the yellow crime scene tape across the front door?"

"Yes."

"Weren't you curious?"

"I knew she was dead."

"How?"

Pete ignored the question. "I figured you'd arrest me if I walked into the Mercado police station because Mitzi would have done her usual badmouthing. I wanted to show you these." He pointed toward the box in which he'd been placing the ivory round and oval objects. He opened the lid. "I think these tell a different story."

There were two small skulls probably from cats and larger skulls probably from dogs in the box. The worst part of the collection was the partially decomposed heads of two large dogs.

Carbonne always felt sick when he saw hordes like this for two reasons. The poor animals didn't deserve this, and the bastard who did it was going to be one disgusting, sick puppy.

Carbonne glanced at Chuy who was hyperventilating. He studied Pete. The man was crying. Carbonne thought that was a good sign. "Do you know how these got here?"

Pete stared at Carbonne. "Who are you? I thought you were just a bum who stumbled onto me and called the police."

Chuy stopped breathing hard. "He's with me but working undercover. I'm going to record this conversation. Tell me how these got here."

The man stood. "My daughter Mitzi adopted two children. She's made a lot of mistakes, but adopting those two was her worst. Lurleen used to have a little blue point Siamese cat. The children played with it when they were little. About six years ago, I found it in our backyard at La Bendita with its skull crushed. I told Lurleen it was no accident. She thought one of her neighbors must have been angry at her. Although several of her neighbors were strange, I doubted any were that crazy." He paused. "But I only visited occasionally. So, I talked to her one normal neighbor—Sara Almquist."

Carbonne wished Pete would speed up his story but guessed Chuy's patient, thorough approach was better.

Chuy cleared his throat. "What did Sara say?"

"She was worried about Bug, that's her dog, and admitted she never let him out in her backyard if she couldn't watch him constantly."

Pete cocked his head and smiled. "Smart, normal woman, except when her dog is concerned. Said she'd never seen or heard of pet abuse at La Bendita, but she'd be on the lookout." Pete just looked at the ground for a minute with tears streaming down his face.

"What happened next?" Chuy hesitated. "If this story progresses as I think it will, we need to act before others are hurt."

"I know." Pete sighed. "I began to think. Matt was rough with his toys. He liked to use them as bats to hit other toys or furniture and it drove Lurleen crazy. More important Lurleen found several of his stuffed animals with their heads cut off. When I suggested he was too violent, Lurleen told me I didn't understand children. He was developmentally delayed. Mitzi knew what to do because she was trained in early childhood education. We fought more."

Chuy nodded. "Did Lurleen always take Mitzi's side?"

"Yes. She was convinced that Mitzi and she were being cheated because of my parents' will."

Carbonne was tempted to stop Pete and have his explain the last comment. He decided it would be a mistake to break Pete's momentum.

Pete continued, "Finally, five years ago I knew I was ready for a change but wanted to give Lurleen one more chance. We moved to this house. I built the second building behind the main house for myself, established this orchard, and spent a lot of time with Matt. Almost immediately I began finding dead dogs and cats in the orchard. I told Lurleen our grandson was progressing down a dangerous path. We fought more. I accepted position in Aruba and filed for divorce last year."

Chuy pulled one stick with a tag from the ground. "What about these?"

He shrugged. "I'm an engineer. I wanted to show the progression of Matt's deterioration. You'll note no tissue is left on the small cat skulls. They've been in the ground the longest. I marked the tags by spots where I found those skulls with ones." He paced to the pole with a tag labeled with the number two. "There's still a bit of flesh on the skulls of the small dogs, so I labeled those spots with twos."

Carbonne interrupted, "You figured those skulls had been buried a shorter time? What about these?" He pointed to two large dog skulls with skin and hair still adhering.

"I think he progressed to larger animals fairly recently. They were at sites three and four."

Chuy shook his head. "What made you look?"

"I guess I might as well admit Lurleen called me in Aruba on Monday around six a.m."

Carbonne said, "I wondered when you'd admit that detail. The FBI checked your overseas calls for the last week."

Pete studied Carbonne. "She was scared and begged me to get here by Wednesday."

"Did she say why Wednesday was important?"

"No, but she said the yard smelled and something like, 'He's doing it again.' Probably not quite that."

"What did you think 'doing it again' meant?"

Pete shook his head. "She assumed the smell was from a decaying animal carcasses because she knew our water processing system was working. Two years ago, I found a dead cat buried in a shallow grave after Lurleen complained of odors."

While Chuy arranged for the crime lab and medical examiner to send staff, Carbonne continued to question Pete. "Why didn't she call the police on Monday?"

"Dunno. Probably wanted to protect the boy. I asked her to call the psychiatrist—Dr. Piaget—whom Matt sees.

"Did she?"

"Doubt it. Lurleen never likes—I guess that's now *liked*—my ideas." He shrugged. "We couldn't even agree enough to get a divorce. The marriage really ended when she and Mitzi moved to La Bendita more than fourteen years ago even though she knew I wouldn't retire for at least eight more years."

Carbonne felt sorry for Pete. He was bright man, but not a brave one. He was sure that Mitzi had lied. Sara would have no romantic attraction to this man. She liked smart men who acted on their beliefs and opinions. Pete was smart but not forceful enough to interest her.

It was time for him to talk to Sara—not as a suspect but as an analyst. He'd have to be careful. Technically Sara was a suspect, but he was sure that was nonsense. He was eager to hear Sara's observations on Pete and Lurleen. Sara had been good at analyzing relationships and giving insights into suspects' actions on the last two cases they'd worked together. She was also a good cook, especially if Sanders was about to swoop in, as he usually did when Sara was in danger. Carbonne wouldn't mind a home-cooked meal for a change and maybe even a chance to hear Sanders's thoughts on the case.

He was about to tell Chuy he was leaving when he noticed Pete had pulled a plastic bag from the front pocket of his slacks, taken off his gloves, shoved them into the plastic bag, looked around the yard, and finally walked to the patio. Carbonne's attention became more focused when Pete shoved the bag into the sleeve of a neatly folded jacket on the picnic bench. This might be another example of Pete's obsessive neatness, or Pete was hiding something. Carbonne sauntered over to Chuy and whispered, "I'm leaving. Keep him busy while I extract a suspicious bag he just hid in the sleeve of his jacket."

Chuy nodded. "Saw that, too." He waved to Pete. "Instead of waiting outside for the lab crew, let's take a tour of the house. I particularly want you to show me where Lurleen put important documents or sentimental trinkets."

Pete started to lean toward the bench to pick up his jacket, but Chuy put his hand on Pete's shoulder and guided him toward the back door of the house. "You know your wife was no housekeeper, and we're confused." As he unlocked the back door of the house, Chuy winked at Carbonne.

Carbonne now understood why Gil Andrews had told Ulysses Howe, "Chuy is ready for the challenge of this case."

CHAPTER 5: Sara Tells Secrets

Carbonne seemed in a hurry when he arrived unannounced at Sara's door. He ignored Bug who twirled on his hind legs and the agent didn't bother with any pleasantries. "Sara, I got a FAX from Sanders. He provided proof that he called your landline number at ten minutes to six this morning. It takes about fifteen minutes to get from Lurleen's house to your home. Now, you only need to account for your time from four to five thirty this morning."

Sara was worried. Even Carbonne suspected her of Lurleen's murder.

Carbonne wandered past the sofa in her great room and seemed to scan the piles of paper on her dining table around her computer. "You must be working on another project for USAID." He seemed to sniff the air. "But aren't cooking supper yet."

Sara sighed. "I'm too nervous to be hungry." She noted Carbonne shook his head as he walked back to her sofa to pet Bug without ever looking at her. She thought her comment hadn't been wise because nervousness often suggested guilt. "I'm innocent and had no reason to harm Lurleen. We were friends."

Carbonne continued to pet Bug and avoided eye contact with Sara. Two hours ago, Gil Andrews had acted the same way when she said that she considered Lurleen a friend, granted a needy friend. She knew she should remain silent until she talked to a lawyer, but that action felt like an admission of guilt or an admission of more knowledge than she had. She decided to trust her gut and not her brain.

Someone, probably Mitzi, must have falsely intimated that she was somehow in league with Pete Jansen. There was no other explanation because Gil had said they hadn't talked to Pete or Mitzi's children yet.

She cleared her throat. "Something about Mitzi never rang true with me. She claimed the only thing she wanted in life was to be a mother, but she seldom seemed happy when she was with her children." She paused to study Carbonne. She hadn't piqued his interest yet. "For example, she often couldn't find time to take them to their appointments with doctors, social workers, and teachers. Lurleen took the children to at least two or three appointments or special lessons every week."

Carbonne squinted at her. "Okay, tell me about Mitzi."

At least he was looking at her. "Part of the problem is Mitzi isn't logical when it comes to her children. She transferred Kayla to new schools twice after teachers told her Kayla was a bully and needed psychological counseling. However, she refused to take Kayla to a psychologist, except for a short period after Kayla threatened Lurleen with a shard of glass."

Sara noted Carbonne gulped, but he replied noncommittally. "So, she was overwhelmed by the demands of her special needs kids."

"Perhaps, and her inconsistent style of discipline made everything worse."

"Why do you think so?"

She forced herself not to say "er" or act flustered. "I saw Mitzi at Target last spring. She had a black eye which she said she got while playing ball with Matt. When I mentioned that to Lurleen, she laughed. Seems Mitzi wrote at least two reports for Kayla last spring. They earned Kayla a C in her science class and a B minus in history. Kayla was so angry she socked Mitzi in the eye. Evidently, Mitzi didn't discipline Kayla for the physical assault, but she was constantly correcting Kayla for the use of curse words."

"That's just one case. Lurleen might not have told you the whole story."

Sara felt Carbonne hadn't grasped yet how odd the relationships between Mitzi and her children were. "When they were little—when Lurleen still lived next door to me here—Kayla often pinched Matt until he cried. Mitzi never punished Kayla. Instead, she told Kayla that she was pretty and smart."

"Do you know why?"

Sara noticed Carbonne was uncharacteristically staring at his phone and not looking at her. "Mitzi claimed Kayla pinched Matt because he got so much attention from doctors for his medical conditions and Kayla was jealous."

"Mitzi's response wasn't totally irrational."

"I'm not finished with the story. A couple of months ago, Lurleen stopped by with her grandchildren without Mitzi. I saw Kayla pinch Matt repeatedly and noticed he had bruises on his arms. When Lurleen reprimanded Kayla, she stuck out her tongue at Lurleen and said, 'Mom doesn't care. Why do you?'"

"So, Mitzi isn't the mother of the year. We already guessed that. Chuy has subpoenaed the CYFD records. The extended delays in the adoption process suggest that a social worker was troubled by something in the family dynamics." He frowned. "Could have been induced by the stress of the adoption process. Those records won't have anything on the family after the adoption was finalized. When was that—six or seven years ago? I'll suggest he also get all the school and medical records for both kids."

At least Carbonne was listening to her, even if he was avoiding looking at her. "How about medical records for Mitzi? Lurleen frequently moaned about Mitzi's respiratory distress and depression. At least, that was one of the reasons Mitzi used to get money from Pete's parents' trust fund."

Sara was pleased when Carbonne appeared to make a note on his phone. She'd given him an idea. She hoped it wasn't to evaluate her dislike of Mitzi.

"Pete mentioned that Lurleen often complained about his parents' trust fund. Do you know anything about it?"

Sara was surprised by the last comment. Gil had said they hadn't located Pete yet. Of course, a lot could have happened in the last two hours. "Not much until yesterday. Pete's mother was a member of the DuPont family. His father's family had been part of the management of Royal Dutch Shell for generations."

Carbonne looked at her quizzically.

"I assume his parents were wealthy. All I know is Lurleen complained his parents never liked her and put their estate in a trust fund to spite her. As I understand it, the trust fund was primarily designed to provide money for the education of their grandchildren and great-grandchildren and so on."

"Sweet."

"But that's not all. The funds could also be used to pay a mother a stipend so she could stay home with her children until they went to first grade or if they were sick. I knew Mitzi had gotten this stipend ever since she became a foster parent to Kayla. Yesterday, I learned that Lurleen's son Bill had never claimed these funds because his wife Gail preferred to work as a lawyer." Sara smiled. "I suspect the will and the trust fund are the key to Lurleen's murder. At least, it was all she could talk—no, *rave* is a more accurate word—about yesterday."

Carbonne looked up from his phone. "Don't drag this out. I don't like taking notes. FBI agents already talked to Gail Jansen, Lurleen's daughter-in-law, while she was in Houston getting treatment at M.D. Anderson Medical Center."

"What did she say?"

Carbonne shook his head. "Remember, this time you aren't an analyst, but a suspect. Tell me what *you* know."

"Gail thought Lurleen was a bully and forbid Lurleen to visit her home except for a two-week period each summer and for one week in December."

Sara peered at Carbonne. When he smirked, she figured he already knew the two women didn't get along. "I found out yesterday that Gail convinced her husband Bill that he should apply to the family trust fund for a stipend for her because she wanted to quit work and spend the time she had left with her eight-year-old daughter. Seems her breast cancer has metastasized to the liver and bone."

Carbonne nodded. "Like Gil's wife. Only Gail's cancer has progressed further according to her physicians."

"Interesting. Lurleen said yesterday that she thought Gail was exaggerating her problems. Anyway, Lurleen was furious because Pete, as the sole trustee of his parents' trust, was going to eliminate Mitzi's stipend but give a stipend to Gail and Bill. I couldn't follow all of Lurleen's comments because every other word was a curse. She kept saying, 'My princess deserves more.' I figured Mitzi was too lazy and unskilled to get a decent job. Workers in preschools get minimum wages. I suspect the stipend was more generous." Sara frowned. "That's all I know about the trust, unless you can jog my memory with additional info."

"Mmm. Just a minute." Carbonne texted several messages and then stepped out of the house.

Sara assumed he was talking to Ulysses. She thought a second. Carbonne was always hungry, especially when he worked undercover. His clothes today suggested he'd been working undercover when he was reassigned to this case. She melted butter with several cloves of minced garlic, sliced a loaf of French bread, and slathered the butter on the bread. As the slices browned in the broiler, she pulled jars of olives, a roll of salami, and a container of carrot and celery sticks from her refrigerator.

She noticed in the past he relaxed and talked more freely at meals or snacks.

Carbonne sniffed the air when he returned. "You are desperate. You're bribing me now with food." He grabbed a crisp slice of bread from the platter on her kitchen island. He gulped it down and picked up an olive. "You didn't need to. Ulysses agrees with me. We know—at least in our guts—you didn't kill Lurleen. Officially, we can say I shared information with you to facilitate the investigation."

Sara handed him a plate and napkin. "Why don't you stock up before you tell me what Gail said about Lurleen. I doubt it's nice."

Bug had been eyeing the kitchen island as she put out the spread. As soon as she handed a plate to Sanders, Bug sauntered over. He didn't bark but stared at her with pleading eyes. She gave him two small pieces of salami.

Carbonne returned to the sofa with a full plate. "Gail's comments reflect what you've said but they weren't sugarcoated." He almost inhaled two slices of salami. "Appreciate the spread. Gail said Lurleen was…" He looked at notes on his phone. "…a ruthless control freak who had destroyed the lives of everyone around her. She wasn't surprised Lurleen was murdered, only that it hadn't happened sooner."

Sara bit her lip. "Did she say whom she suspected?"

"Not really. Gail just supported your comments and my observations. She was surprised Pete didn't divorce Lurleen sooner. He certainly hated her. As she gained weight, he ate less. As she hoarded and became more of a slob, he became more fastidious. Gail said she didn't want her daughter exposed to that type of hate and avoided contact with Pete and Lurleen. However, she seemed sad Pete wouldn't be visiting her in Houston during her hospital stay."

"I assume agents talked to Lurleen's son Bill. What did he say?"

"Either the Omaha police aren't as good at interviews as cops in Houston, or Bill is tight-lipped. He gave them details on the trust funds, cried as he said his wife's prognosis was bad, and matter-of-factly said either his father, Mitzi or her children had killed Lurleen."

"You're leaving out a lot. Why wasn't he with his wife in Houston? Wasn't he at least surprised or angry about his mother's murder?"

Carbonne stuffed another piece of toast in his mouth. "He and his wife are committed to raising a normal child. They want their kid's schedule to be unaffected by Gail's illness. So, the daughter continues to go school during Gail's absences." Carbonne stopped eating and stared at the ceiling. "Your second question is harder to answer. Psychologists say the opposite of love isn't hate but apathy. Bill appears to have only apathy for his mother and sister, but pities his father."

"I guess the emotions may have been mutual on Lurleen's part. She seldom spoke of her son and his family. When she did, she was angry, but would say at the end of an outburst, 'Oh well, it doesn't matter.'" Sara wiped tears from her eyes. "In contrast, I always thought Lurleen genuinely cared about Mitzi and the children, until yesterday."

"Figured you were saving the best for last. Spit it out."

"Lurleen seemed frantic about Matt. She's not Catholic. So, going to the Catholic chapel at Chimayó for holy dirt was an act of desperation."

"Did she explain?"

"Not in words that I understood. Here's the gist of the rants I listened to as I drove to Chimayó. She always thought Pete was boring and married him for his money. His parents died just before she moved to La Bendita. She moved here planning to divorce him as soon as his parents' estate was settled. Then he dropped the bombshell of their will and the trust fund. She hired a lawyer and learned the only loophole was for Mitzi to have children and prove she or the children were ill."

"Was she that blunt?"

"You said I sugarcoated my comments about Lurleen. I hadn't until now. At the end of the trip, I felt mainly disgust for her." Sara chomped on two carrot sticks. "It was a really horrendous trip. Back to what I learned. Lurleen bragged that she started looking for a husband for Mitzi immediately after she learned the details of the trust. Said the future bridegroom didn't have to be rich or smart because Mitzi could divorce him after, I'm quoting her now, 'He served his purpose and was a good stud.' As I listened to Lurleen, I realized why Mitzi was depressed."

"Can't believe you ever liked this woman."

Sara sighed. "Guess I never saw Lurleen's dark side until yesterday because she was in control, although it didn't seem like it."

"Be specific. What else did you learn yesterday?"

"Let me think." Sara chewed another carrot stick. "Lurleen admitted she forced Mitzi to become a foster parent after Mitzi divorced her husband after a couple of months of marriage. She evidently told Mitzi it would be a way to make money and not have to work." She crunched a celery stick. "I don't think it took much convincing. Mitzi told me several times that she never wanted to be in a classroom again with a bunch of rug rats."

Carbonne chuckled. "When in this story did you move next door to Lurleen?"

"I moved here nine years ago. At that time, Mitzi was already a foster mom for Kayla and Matt, was receiving a stipend from her grandparents' trust fund, and was fighting with the Children, Youth, and Families Department because they weren't enthusiastic about allowing her to adopt the children.

"You mean CYFD? We hear lots of complaints about that agency."

Sara nodded. "Their reluctance seemed strange then. I doubted anyone else wanted to adopt those two. Matt had already been diagnosed with developmental problems and epilepsy, and Kayla was willful and belligerent. On the other hand, I understood the social workers' concerns. Mitzi seemed overwhelmed by the children and left them with Lurleen most days for four or more hours. I figured Lurleen was a good-hearted woman who was trying to help her daughter. Boy, was I wrong. Everything was a ploy to break a will." Sara shook her head. "Can't believe I read the situation so wrong."

"Not much you could testify to in court, but the records in CYFD will be a treasure trove." He stroked Bug's ear. "How did your little guy react to the kids?"

Sara stared at the ceiling for thirty seconds. "You know he's a pet therapy dog and visits children at University Hospital every week. He's not afraid of children and seemed to like Matt, but he always avoided Kayla."

Carbonne choked. "Do you realize that Pete believes Matt has killed many pets? He thinks the first was Lurleen's cat. It happened while she lived next door to you."

Sara felt a chill.

CHAPTER 6: Sanders in Washington, D.C.

Eric Sanders had left work early to stop by the bank. In the small booth, he pawed through the contents of his safety deposit box. His mother's sapphire and diamond cocktail ring was gorgeous, but not right for Sara. It was too bulky and ostentatious to wear every day. She would describe it as "too frou-frou." He agreed.

His grandmother's ruby and diamond Art Deco ring was more Sara's style. The emerald-cut diamond with two ruby triangles set in platinum was simple but elegant. However, he knew Sara wouldn't wear the ring when she gardened, kneaded bread, or did household tasks because the ring might be damaged. She wore only cheap jewelry when she did pet therapy with Bug in local hospitals or consulted in developing nations because she felt expensive "power" jewelry made it harder to gain the trust of those with limited resources. He suspected her attitude reflected her background. Her father was a sharecropper farmer in the Midwest. She knew what poverty really meant and how hard it was to claw out of it.

Sara would treasure his grandmother's ring but seldom wear it. He returned all the jewelry to his safe deposit box and whistled as he left the bank. He'd made the right choice.

Sara's calls and his conversations with Carbonne and Chuy Bargas this afternoon had alarmed Sanders. He needed to think about Sara's current problem. He couldn't do that on the Metro and the exercise of a long walk would be good for him.

He'd met Lurleen and her daughter Mitzi several months ago. They'd stopped by Sara's home when he was staying there to recover from injuries from the shootout when the drug gang leaders had been trapped and arrested. At first, he thought he'd somehow offended Lurleen, but he soon realized she exuded contempt for everyone. She belittled her husband, daughter, son, daughter-in-law, and neighbors. Lurleen was a prima donna who insisted on calling him "Eric," even though he made it clear that he never used his first name.

Her daughter was harder to categorize. She trilled in a high soprano and tried to act like the perfect lady, but her treatment of her children was erratic. Mitzi would literally stroke them one minute and snarl under her breath at them the next when she thought no one was looking. *Sneaky* was the best word to describe her.

Most surprising at the time had been Sara's behavior. She wasn't offended by Lurleen's comment about Sara's "unkempt hair" or "stupid fawning over a dog." When he questioned her later, Sara had said, "I can't argue with her. The statements are basically true. My hair is usually a mess. Note she was smart enough to say *my behavior* was stupid, not that Bug was stupid. I would have asked her to leave if she insulted Bug. Besides, she's just a lonely woman who is trying to help a daughter who has made one bad decision after another." She shrugged. "One thing I learned in academia was not to be sensitive to barbs from people who aren't important in your life."

He loved Sara's generous spirit but occasionally her do-gooder attitudes made her seem naïve. He suspected Lurleen had been killed by a family member for a good, although not legally valid, reason. The unfortunate part was Sara had foolishly befriended the woman and hence become implicated in her murder. No evidence, except Mitzi's testimony, would be found implicating Sara. However, until she was cleared completely—or someone else was formally charged with the murder—Sara might not be able to leave the local jurisdiction, let alone go to India.

For months, Sanders had tried to convince Sara to vacation with him in India. Although she thrived on challenging consultations in exotic areas, like Bolivia and the Middle East, she'd resisted his efforts to plan a vacation for the two of them in India. She hadn't articulated her reasons except to say, "Life is so cheap there." He hadn't countered with the obvious. The lives of the poor, especially women and children, are undervalued in many places. Instead, he'd emphasized how romantic the Taj Mahal would be.

He'd succeeded last week. Federal and state prosecutors had reluctantly agreed that Sara could travel internationally because they thought all major drug gang members with potential grudges against her were awaiting trial with bail denied. Sara said yes, and he immediately booked airline tickets and hotels, which was not easy because their trip would be during the holiday of Diwali, the Hindu Festival of Lights. He'd even arranged for Bug to stay in a posh dog kennel, euphemistically called a "spa," in the Washington area. Now an obnoxious ex-neighbor and her daughter could ruin his plans.

He was within two blocks of his townhouse in the Capitol Hill neighborhood of Washington and still hadn't addressed his biggest concerns. Would Sara say yes to his marriage proposal? Did he really want to be married?

His boss—an assistant secretary of state—had said, "Sara would make the perfect modern wife for an ambassador." He had worked enough with Gil Andrews when rescuing Sara from gang leaders to know Gil thought Sara deserved better than a part-time boyfriend. Sanders's fling with a beautiful young woman, who unfortunately worked for a drug cartel, only lowered Gil's opinion of him further. Carbonne, who had worked security for Sanders in Cuba and then had helped Sara ensnare several gang leaders in New Mexico, had even called him last week to say, "Don't blow it with Sara."

Sanders was ashamed that his first thoughts were of others' opinions. Now he assessed his own feelings. He admired Sara as a versatile, smart professional and respected her integrity and inner strength. He cherished her as a friend and companion and enjoyed her as a sexual partner. He guessed that was love.

He thought Sara felt the same. Neither of them particularly considered marriage an ideal state. They both had seen more unhappy than happy marriages. They both were self-reliant and didn't need someone to cook their meals or care for them. Of course, Sara turned to him when she was in danger, but he depended on her good judgment, both professionally and in his personal life. He appreciated her understanding, he wasn't sure *forgiveness* was the right word, when he'd recently made the dangerous liaison with the young woman. Sara was also good nurse during his recovery from triple bypass surgery and from wounds gained while capturing the gang members. However, he was glad Bug usually took the brunt of her mothering.

The most important reason was silly: He'd seldom been lonely in the past. Now he was lonely when Sara and Bug weren't around. Thus, he planned to propose in India. To be honest, he doubted she'd say yes to marriage but was sure—well *pretty* sure—she'd say yes to continuing and deepening their committed relationship. Sanders knew she'd not tolerate another dalliance on his part. Ergo, he needed a ring that didn't scream engagement ring. He thought he'd found it.

He unlocked the door to his townhouse and called Sara

CHAPTER 7: Sara Is Scared

Sara turned off her television when the *Nature* episode on PBS ended. "Time for our walk, Bug." The little dog trotted to the front door.

The full moon and the street lamps gave enough light to walk to the grassy knoll on the corner. Even so, Sara turned on her camping lantern. Bug was a brave dog, but he was more skittish in the dark. She was, too. Besides, she'd need the extra light to clean up after Bug.

The homes in the gated community of La Bendita had xeriscape landscaping with lots of gravel and rocks, but the community had splurged and surrounded the clubhouse and entrance with grass and elaborate plantings of bushes. The grassy knoll a block from Sara's house was a favorite spot for dogs and their owners. As Bug wandered from plant to plant sniffing each carefully and then marking them, she looked around. Four rabbits were on the knoll, but no other dogs and owners. Rabbits didn't interest Bug and he never tried to chase them. Sara heard the howls of coyotes from the nearby bosque and then a train whistle from the station several miles away. It was amazing how howls and train whistles could echo for miles in the desert, especially at night.

Bug wandered from the knoll down a macadam side path. There was no grass along this path, but the plants were larger. Sara thought she heard steps behind her and turned. Someone without a dog spun around and walked away. That was odd—people on the paths at night without dogs generally walked with purpose. She didn't recognize the person from the back. The individual was thin, short, in jeans, and with a long, dark green hoodie pulled up over his or her head. The individual was probably not one of the residents, but maybe a visiting grandchild.

Bug wasn't in a hurry and neither was Sara. Early October was a wonderful time in the high desert because the blazing summer heat and monsoon rains were over. This was the perfect night for a walk. They meandered from the macadam path onto a sidewalk along a cross street. After a couple of minutes, Sara thought she heard steps behind her again. She turned to greet the person and saw the same hoodie and jeans on someone loping toward the macadam path.

She began to wonder what was going on. Robberies were rare in the community, but. not because of the walls and gates. Any agile teen could get over the walls in less than a minute. The electronics at the gates could easily be outwitted. There were few robberies in La Bendita because many of the older residents spent much of their time staring out their windows and reporting anything unusual to police. Gil Andrews once complained that he got more calls from La Bendita than any other part of his jurisdiction. To alleviate the "nervousness" of the community, he arranged for squad cars to drive through La Bendita several times every night. One usually circled through the community between nine and ten and stopped anyone—usually teenagers—who looked out of place.

Of course, there was another reason that Gil had his officers circulating through the community every three hours during the last week: There might be a price on Sara's head. Although others would testify against the gang leaders in the upcoming federal racketeering trials, everyone else was either a law enforcement officer, a gang member who had struck a deal, or a homeless person. Accordingly, the U.S. attorney prosecuting the cases against the drug leaders thought Sara was a particularly important witness—one a jury could easily identify with.

Before all the key gang members had been arrested, the U.S marshals had sequestered Sara unsuccessfully for several days. She'd been recognized and attacked. Then she'd found some protection by "camping out" in the FBI building while serving as a consultant. That arrangement was more pleasant for Sara than being sequestered by U.S. marshals, but was not a long-term solution to her need for security. Last week, after the final arrests of the remaining gang members, she'd returned to her home in the gated community.

Sara figured both Gil Andrews and Carbonne would be glad when she left for India with Sanders because it would lessen their workload. She knew the U.S. attorney and the FBI wouldn't have allowed her to travel to India alone, but Sanders was an expert on security in international settings for the State Department. Some might say he was a spy, but technically he was an expert on collecting and analyzing data useful to U.S. international interests.

Now wasn't the time to think about Sanders. Sara increased her pace, pulled Bug along, and headed for the main street past the clubhouse. When he resisted her, she scooped him up. Bug thrashed about a bit but quickly settled under Sara's left arm. She raced home gripping her keys with them spiking out between the fingers in her right fist. Sanders had taught her several self-defense moves like this and a groin kick. As usual, she had on heavy walking shoes. So, her groin kick was apt to be effective. Once inside her home, Sara checked the locks on all her doors and windows. She recognized her behavior as paranoid, but she'd been stalked before and knew details were important.

After she gave Bug his bedtime snack, he didn't settle down but paced back and forth by her back patio door. She turned on the light to her backyard. and saw something move by the corner of the house—a flash of dark green, maybe the sleeve of a jacket or hoodie. Sara was spooked and cursed that she hadn't installed a flood light in her backyard, even though it was against the covenants at La Bendita. She slid a metal bar into the patio door's track.

The good news was the stalker seemed timid and was probably not a professional criminal. When she'd been followed by gang members, they didn't run away three times. They attacked with guns blazing and had shattered her windows and patio door.

Sara speed dialed Carbonne. She was glad he'd given her his private number during the investigation of the case they'd concluded last week. "Saw a short, thin individual with a dark green hoodie following me while Bug and I took our evening walk. Twice. They turned away both times. Could be a boy or a girl. Just saw someone in the same hoodie running from my backyard. Will call 9-1-1 now."

"On it. Will notify Chuy." The phone went dead.

The call with the 9-1-1 operator was slower paced. The operator seemed to dawdle as she checked details. Sara suspected the operator was working as fast as possible, but she seemed slow because of Sara's agitated state.

"You know we get frequent calls about peeping toms. They're seldom dangerous."

Sara cuddled Bug. "Yes, but I'm a witness in several major cases involving gang leaders. My house has been attacked before. Ask Chuy Bargas or Gil Andrews."

There was a long pause. "Oh…" The operator voice became shrill. "You're *that* Sara Almquist? Sorry for the delay. Officers should be at your house in three minutes. Please stay on the line."

There was a thump on her patio door and then another. Sara thought she heard the glass crack. She stifled a scream, tore back the drape over the door, and saw a hooded figure. "Someone just threw rocks at my patio door and cracked it. He's running from my backyard now."

As the operator asked for details, Sara grabbed a handgun from a kitchen drawer with her right hand as she held Bug under her left and whispered, "Mom will protect you." She thought about adding, *or die trying.*

CHAPTER 8: FBI Agent Paul Carbonne an Hour Earlier

Carbonne had a bad feeling when the lights went on almost simultaneously in every room in Mitzi's house around seven. The garage door opened a minute later and Mitzi's SUV shot out. He ordered two agents to follow the SUV while he waited in a darkened, parked car. A bicycle without any lights was wheeled from the backyard within five minutes. The biker was short and slim and wore a dark green hoodie. Carbonne couldn't tell whether it was Kayla or Matt. He decided not to follow. Instead, he walked to the front door and rang the doorbell, waited, and then paced around the outside of house looking in windows. No one appeared to be home but a radio blared rap music. He wanted to search the house, but he could think of no excuse to do it without a search warrant. However, he thought the case against Mitzi's family members for the murder of Lurleen might be good enough to get a warrant from a sympathetic judge.

He called the Mercado police officers who Chuy had circling Lurleen's house every hour. They could account for all the vehicles parked on the street, and they'd not seen Mitzi's SUV. However, a teen on a bicycle had glided by a few minutes ago. Maybe the teen had on a green hoodie; they weren't sure. To please Carbonne, the officers reluctantly agreed to check the backyard and patio. They noted the main house and the back building were secured with new locks.

While Carbonne worked on the paperwork to get a subpoena to search Mitzi's house, the two agents who had followed Mitzi's SUV reported the vehicle was now parked at the Walmart less than a mile from Sara's home. They saw a single person in a dark green hoodie leave the SUV and enter the superstore. A couple of minutes later, another larger figure in a dark green hoodie left the SUV and also entered the store.

The Mercado police officers guarding Lurleen's house apologized when they called back. One of the planters on Lurleen's patio had been overturned. Dirt was strewn everywhere. Carbonne requested back up from the Mercado police to stay at Mitzi's house as he rushed to examine the upturned planter. While there, the agents at Walmart reported that no one in a dark green hoodie had exited the store, at least by either of the two major doors, but that left at least five other unaccounted for exits.

Carbonne had just completed the paperwork and filed a request for a search warrant for Mitzi's property when Sara called.

***

Chuy already had two officers with Sara when Carbonne arrived at La Bendita. He went directly to Chuy's location at the usually closed emergency entrance to the gated community. Now the gate was wide open. The scene was organized chaos, lit by emergency search lights. An EMT was threading an intravenous line into a boy's arm while two officers rolled him on a gurney toward an ambulance. Carbonne noticed the boy's dark green hoodie had been slit from the shoulder to the wrist on one arm to allow the EMT to work.

Two Mercado police officers with flashlights were crawling in the scrub weeds close to the gate looking for evidence. Another officer was idling a squad car, ready to follow the ambulance.

Chuy was on his phone talking rapidly. He handed the phone to an aide and waved to Carbonne. "Two officers found the boy trying to climb over the gate. He resisted…"

The aide interrupted, "Must be a soccer player. The kid could really kick."

Chuy nodded. "When they finally lifted him off the wall, the boy began to sob and moan, 'I was bad. Bad, bad boy.' Wouldn't even tell the officers his name. As they fumbled with recording his moans and calling me, the kid pulled something from his pocket and swallowed it."

The aide lowered his head. "It all happened so fast in the dark. We weren't even sure."

Chuy grimaced. "By the time I arrived and called the ambulance, the boy was moaning less and was unable to stand. The EMTs think he took a powerful sedative, but they can't be sure. I can only guess, but I think the child is Matt Jansen." Chuy wiped his eyes. "He might not make it."

Carbonne thought the meager details he'd accumulated weren't what Chuy and his team needed now, except one piece: "Mitzi Jansen and presumably Kayla are at Walmart now. Or at least, they want us to think they're there. Doubt they'll answer their phones. You complete your search here while I talk to Sara."

***

As expected, Sara didn't want to be placed in witness protection because she didn't think her stalker had been hired by the drug gangs. She was at least partially right. The person stalking her, presumably Matt Jansen, was certainly no threat to her now. On the other hand, a person stalking Sara could have overmedicated Matt to lull Sara and the police into lowering their guards.

Arguing with Sara was difficult, and Carbonne was thankful for an interruption by the two agents parked at Walmart. Mitzi and her daughter Kayla had just strolled from Walmart to their SUV. Neither woman had on a dark green hoodie, but they carried several bulky bags. He suggested the agents tail the women rather than detain them. If they confronted Mitzi and Kayla, the agents would have to admit Matt was on his way to University Hospital. He suspected Matt would be more apt to tell the truth to Chuy if Mitzi wasn't present. Of course, Carbonne didn't even know for sure the boy in the ambulance was Matt.

Carbonne stepped out of Sara's house to call Chuy, who was on his way to University Hospital, just in case the boy made any useful comments. Chuy would notify Mitzi only after he had proof of the boy's identity.

Carbonne's phone pinged. The judge and Ulysses Howe had acted rapidly. They now had a search warrant for "all of Mitzi's property." Crime lab technicians were on their way to Mitzi's house. The problem was what to do with Sara and Bug.

Carbonne fingered an object in the back pocket of his jeans as he entered Sara's house. "Sara, you and Bug are going with me and these Mercado officers..." He pointed to the two officers guarding her. "...to Mitzi's house. Now, let's be clear from the start—you're going to stay in the car."

***

Carbonne was lucky and arrived at Mitzi's house first. Lurleen's daughter and granddaughter had fortunately decided to stop at a Sonic before they returned home. FBI agents and crime lab technicians arrived shortly after Carbonne. Thus, the technicians were busy, and an agent was posted at the front door when Mitzi arrived.

Mitzi started screaming about police harassment as soon as she rolled down her window.

Carbonne tried to suppress a smile as he handed Mitzi the search warrant. "You can call your lawyer, but at least one person in a dark green hoodie tried to physically assault Sara Almquist in her home earlier tonight. Agents followed you to Walmart and know you and your daughter had on dark green hoodies."

"We don't now." Mitzi looked triumphant and didn't resist when a technician began to search through the three bulky bags in the SUV.

Carbonne didn't wait for the bad news. He stepped outside the garage and called Chuy. Mercado police officers would check all the trash cans in Walmart and not allow employees to empty anything into the store's dumpsters until the search for the green hoodies was complete.

When he returned to the garage, Mitzi finished sending a text message, looked up, and sneered. The technicians had found no dark green hoodies in the SUV. Kayla had left the vehicle and seemed oblivious as she danced around the garage to the rap music emitted by the buds in her ears.

Carbonne knew families differed in how they grieved after the murder of a relative, but neither Mitzi nor Kayla showed any signs of grief over Lurleen's death earlier today. Maybe he could scare them. "My agents saw someone in a dark green hoodie bicycle away from this house after your SUV left this evening" He noticed neither Kayla or Lurleen blinked. "The officer guarding the crime scene at your mother's house saw a bicyclist fitting that description at that location." He knew he was finessing a bit, but it was legal. "Afterward they found a planter had been upset and found something odd."

Kayla bit her lip. Mitzi continued to stare at him with a vacant smile.

He pointed at a lone bicycle in the garage. "Strange that you have only one bike here but two children live in the house."

"Matt often leaves his bike in the backyard."

Carbonne shook his head. "Agents already looked. No bike."

Mitzi sighed. "I don't think you realize the severity of Matt's medical problems. He loses things constantly and can't remember where he's been for long stretches of time." She returned to poking at her phone.

Carbonne was surprised Mitzi hadn't seemed concerned about the whereabouts of her son, especially considering his age and disabilities. However, that was to Chuy's advantage now. Before Carbonne could enter the house, one agent whispered to him, "We've found nothing so far, but Sara has ideas."

As he opened a rear door to the waiting Mercado police car, Sara said, "Find the holy dirt."

J. L. Greger

Carbonne knew this was not going to be a brief discussion because he had no idea what she was talking about. He slid into the back seat of the police car next to her. "What's holy dirt?"

Sara patted his hand. "No need to be grouchy. I know you're under stress. Remember Lurleen and I went to Chimayó the day before she was killed?"

He stared at her, waiting for the punch line.

"You're new to the area. You may not realize that the dirt at Chimayó is believed to have curative powers." Sara frowned. "Probably nothing but a placebo effect, but pilgrims evidently carry away more than twenty-five tons of dirt from the site annually. The church workers replenish the pit in the chapel with dirt from the nearby hills."

"Get to the point."

"Lurleen in her usual excessive manner filled two pint-sized container with dirt." Sara must have noticed Carbonne's glassy-eyed stare. "You know—two cottage cheese containers?"

He sighed.

"Lurleen planned to slather it on Matt, but didn't explain his specific ailment. She also muttered someone else also needed the dirt when I asked why she collected *two* containers worth."

Carbonne blinked and sighed, "I don't get it."

"Where are the containers of dirt? I know Chuy checked the garbage at Lurleen's house. He never mentioned finding any containers of dirt."

Carbonne muttered, "It would be easy to miss. What makes you think the dirt might be here? Or that it might be important?"

"Mitzi isn't religious. She never goes to church or sends the children to church. Somehow, I think Mitzi or Kayla would be annoyed if Lurleen tried to daub dirt on them and pray. Maybe one of them would be mad enough to lash out at Lurleen and then take the dirt home."

"Doubt it."

"If the dirt wasn't at Lurleen's, it's most likely here."

"So, we'll look in Matt's room."

"That's what I'm getting at. I don't think Matt would be annoyed if he was daubed with dirt. He's been subjected to many medical treatments, and he always remained... placid. He also was always less annoyed by Lurleen's possessive bossiness than Kayla and Mitzi were."

"Where do you think we'll find the dirt?"

"Either in Kayla's or Mitzi's room. The one who has it is the one who was the most annoyed by Lurleen's actions on the night Lurleen was killed."

"It'll prove nothing."

"Agreed." Sara smiled. "However, if you find it, you may evoke real emotions from Mitzi or Kayla. They might slip and say something useful."

Carbonne's phone rang. He was too tired to step out of the car as he listened to Chuy. Mercado police had found two dark green hoodies stuffed in a trash can by the closed register at the exit to the garden section of Walmart. One was a small size and would fit Kayla. The other was a medium and would fit Mitzi. Chuy planned to send them to the crime lab for DNA analyses to prove they belonged to the Jansens.

Chuy confirmed he'd found no containers of dirt at Lurleen's house or in her garbage. Carbonne couldn't believe his ears when Chuy said, "I like Sara's idea. I'll fill up a cottage cheese container with dirt and see how Matt reacts. Of course, that conversation may need to take place tomorrow. Matt's conscious now, but confused and doesn't seem to know his name."

"Anything else?" Carbonne didn't want to say much in front of Sara. Not because he cared if she knew, but because it would look bad during a court trial if a defense attorney forced her to admit she'd overheard crucial evidence from him.

"It's preliminary, but the lab tech here is sure Matt swallowed a sedative. Check Mitzi's medicine cabinet but work fast. Once Matt tells us his name, you've got to notify Mitzi of his location. Hasn't she asked already?"

"No. Got to go." Carbonne turned to Sara. "Do you know anything about Mitzi's health?"

"Not really. Lurleen often said Mitzi was depressed but was insulted when a doctor suggested Mitzi needed to see a psychologist or a psychiatrist."

"What do you mean insulted?"

"On more than two occasions, Lurleen sat in my house and raved that a physician was 'picking on Mitzi' after he or she suggested Mitzi needed to consult a psychiatrist. I think Mitzi eventually found a doctor who would give her tranquilizers, but I'm not sure."

"Explain."

"On the drive from Chimayó, Lurleen muttered something like, 'Mitzi's fine as long as she gets her pills.'" She frowned and shook her head. "It seemed out of context. Lurleen was complaining at the time about Mitzi arguing more with her lately. I figured Mitzi had finally developed a backbone and wasn't allowing Lurleen to steamroll over her all the time."

Carbonne stretched after he climbed out of the car. "Looks like we have to catalog all the medications here carefully. You and Bug might as well try to sleep in the car since we can't agree on where to stash you tonight." He started to walk away, fingered something in his pocket, motioned to the officer to roll down the car's window, and handed a sheet of paper that had been folded multiple times to Sara. "Think about this."

CHAPTER 9: Sara Explains Details

Sara thought she felt a hand was on her shoulder. She kept her eyes shut and tried not to move even slightly because she didn't want to alert anyone that she was awake. She needed a few seconds to think. She never used to be so nervous but the attacks of the last year had made her wary. She knew she wasn't in her own bed and this one was one was cramped and rough. The blanket over her stunk.

She heard Bug's contented snort and decided he must be okay. Finally, she remembered she'd fallen asleep in the back seat of the police car. She opened her eyes. Carbonne had the back door by her head open and was staring at her. "I admire your ability to sleep anywhere. Time to work."

"Can I get out of the car and stretch my legs first? Bug may also need a bathroom break. Then I'll be able to concentrate. By the way, I recognized the object in the photograph." She sat up and tried to get out through the door next to Carbonne.

"Better if you exited on the other side and wore this hat." He shoved one of the props for his homeless disguises at her. "Put this over your hair."

"Ugh. It stinks."

"I'm dead tired. Been on my feet for fifteen hours. Humor me and wear the hat. I don't have fleas, at least not now."

She sighed, put on the hat, and crawled out of the car after a Mercado officer opened the other door. Bug bounced after her. She wished they could walk a couple of blocks but kept Bug within a few feet of the car. As usual, he seemed to understand and adjusted to the restrictions better than she did.

When she crawled back in, Carbonne was shoving a white container at her. "Recognize it?"

Sara squinted to read the print on the container. "It's a Daisy brand cottage cheese container. It's not labeled low fat. So, you didn't get it from my house."

He removed the lid. The container was filled with reddish brown dirt.

Sara sighed. "I can't say for sure that this is one of the containers of holy dirt that Lurleen collected. It's the right color. The lab could analyze the soil to determine whether it matches the soil in the Chimayó chapel pit. What did Kayla and Mitzi say?"

"Haven't shown it to them yet. Wanted to be sure. Somehow, I don't think this will rattle them. Mitzi's so calm now that ice wouldn't melt in her mouth. Thought I'd confront them separately with both the dirt and this photo." He reached into one of the pockets in his jacket, then another, and finally pulled out a page from a pocket in his jeans. Carbonne unfolded the page and held it in front of Sara.

Sara almost laughed. Carbonne reminded her of the cop played by Peter Falk on the old TV show, *Columbo*. They both disarmed witnesses with their disheveled appearance and apparently random questions.

She studied the page. "Lurleen wasn't much for jewelry. Surprising since she collected everything else. Anyway, she always wore a heavy gold chain bracelet with pendants like this—hearts cut in half. Funny thing is that Lurleen didn't have the pendants soldered onto the chain. She had each attached with a little lobster clamp to the chain so they could be removed. Never figured out why." Sara pointed to a tiny blackened circle at the top of the object in the photo. "You can see the hole at the top of the pendant. At least I think that's a hole. Looks like it's filled with dirt. How did that happen? Lurleen was messy but not dirty."

Carbonne looked disappointed. "Lurleen must have lost it when she was potting a plant on her patio."

Sara snorted. "Never saw Lurleen garden in all the time I knew her. Any plants on the patio were potted by Pete."

He smiled. "I finally have something to make Kayla nervous."

"Care to tell me what you're thinking?"

"No."

Sara tried not to smirk. "I know you don't want to hear one of my long explanations, but it might be worth your time. Lurleen had her bracelet custom made."

Carbonne pulled out his phone.

"Sorry, you're going to be disappointed. I don't know the jeweler." She sighed. "Let me think. She had the three heart pendants engraved with the names of either Mitzi, Matt, or Kayla. Then she had the jeweler cut the pendants in half with a zigzag and put a hole and a ring in each half. So, the names were cut in half, too. Three pieces were attached to her bracelet. The other halves of each pendant on her bracelet were attached to separate gold chains for Mitzi, Matt, and Kayla. She gave them as Christmas gifts a couple of years ago." Sara felt tears forming in her eyes. "Really sentimental. The side of Lurleen I liked."

Carbonne stopped poking at his phone. "Now, I've got to find four bracelets?"

"I don't think so. As I remember, she attached the pendants to longer chains for Kayla and Matt. We discussed it. I didn't think the children would wear bracelets; Lurleen agreed. But I don't know what she did for Mitzi."

Sara could tell Carbonne was tired as he hoarsely talked into his phone. Sara listened intently.

She placed her hand on the phone. "No, you're wrong. The necklaces aren't apt to be in the back of a drawer. Every time I saw Kayla or Matt, they had the necklaces on underneath their shirts. But I never saw Mitzi's."

Carbonne looked askance at her. "How did you see the necklaces under their shirts?"

"Okay you caught me in an overstatement. I can't say the children always wore the necklaces, but they always had them on when they went swimming at La Bendita."

He rubbed his eyes. "Remember I'm tired and a little slow on the uptake."

"When Lurleen came to visit, she usually took the children to either the indoor or outdoor swimming pools at La Bendita." Sara paused. "I know they wore the pendants because no guest can use a pool at La Bendita unless a resident is with them." She sighed. "One of La Bendita's many rules. I hate public swimming pools. Think they're a breeding place for germs and never go there, except with Lurleen and her grandchildren."

Carbonne snickered. "Doesn't sound like the whole reason. You're not a germaphobe. You visit the hospital weekly with Bug and never blink as you clean up after him."

Sara knew she was turning red but doubted he would noticed in the dim light of the car. "You caught me again. Actually, I hate how I look in a swim suit."

"Doubt that bad."

"I look horrible with my hair wet and slicked to my head."

"And?"

"I can't take Bug to the pool." She paused. "We've worked on too many cases together. You know me too well."

He reached in his pocket, pulled out a device, and pushed a button. "And that's why I never considered you a suspect and want to keep you safe." He smiled. "Sara, I've recorded all our previous conversations because I'm afraid the defense will claim you were given special treatment and get the case thrown out. Gil and Chuy have the same fear. And whoever killed Lurleen will kill again." He pushed a button and slid the device back in his pocket. "Let's keep to the details of this case."

Sara grabbed the page from her purse. She pointed at the photo of the pendant on that page. "See. There's no engraving visible on the photo you gave me. I assumed it was the back side of the pendant. Let me see the photo you just showed me. It was different, I think."

He shoved the page toward her. "See? This one is engraved with *MIT* and must be half of Mitzi's pendant—the part on Lurleen's bracelet." She hoped she wasn't overstepping the boundaries again as she added, "Why don't you ask to see Kayla's pendant and have Chuy check whether Matt is wearing his pendant? By the way, was the bracelet found on Lurleen's body?"

Carbonne got out of the car and made several calls. Before he departed, he leaned back into the car toward Sara. "Think I'm now ready to confront Mitzi. If I'm successful, these officers can take you home."

"Wait— I remembered another detail. I'm surprised I forgot it since it's really odd—Lurleen marked one lid with a red permanent marker as soon as we got back to the car in Chimayó."

"You mean the lid on one of the cottage cheese containers with holy dirt?"

Sara nodded.

"Why?"

"Don't know, but the marking will be red and small. I asked her why she marked one container and not the other. She spooked me when she said, 'One is a blessing. The other is…'"

"Hurry up. Our beds are waiting."

"I think she said, 'a prayer for forgiveness.' It didn't make sense at the time and I didn't ask for an explanation because her monologue during the drive to Chimayó had been so unpleasant. I was determined to keep the conversation focused on silly gossip and the weather over lunch and on the way home."

CHAPTER 10: Sergeant Chuy Bargas Thinks about Children with Special Needs

The last hour had been a roller coaster ride. Chuy thought a bit. The ride had been more of a hair-raising descent with only small lifts.

The EMT from the ambulance took one look at the boy at the back emergency gate to La Bendita and dosed him with the opioid depressant Naloxone because it wasn't supposed to produce side effects in those who hadn't taken opioids but prevented respiratory failure in those who had overdosed. The boy's blood pressure remained abnormally low. His breathing remained labored as the crew rapidly prepared to transport the boy to University Hospital in Albuquerque.

Then Chuy remembered an important detail. Pete Jansen had told him that Matt suffered from multiple medical conditions, including epilepsy. He even mentioned a Dr. Piaget. Chuy checked his notes. The social worker from CYFD had mentioned a child psychiatrist and several physicians were familiar with Matt's problems. This was a medical emergency—federal regulations concerning privacy of patients no longer applied. Chuy spoke to officials at University Hospital. They agreed, confirmed Matt Jansen saw several physicians associated with the medical school, and ordered the EMT to draw a blood sample.

By the time Chuy reached the pediatric intensive care unit of University Hospital, the lab had found high levels of the anti-anxiety drug diazepam and the anti-convulsion medicine carbamazepine in the boy's blood. Chuy wished doctors didn't use so many complicated terms, but a woman physician had been nice and explained them. She also noted the boy appeared to be Matt Jansen—looked like the file photo and fit the medical profile.

Then her comments got interesting. Matt had been hospitalized several times for overdosing on his medications. Each time Dr. Piaget, his psychiatrist, had determined the boy was not suicidal but nervous about preventing seizures. The psychiatrist had speculated in his notes that the problem was complex. The boy was intellectually disabled and didn't understand his medication regime. His extremely erratic mother either ignored the boy's symptoms or overreacted to them. He thought the latter was the bigger problem. The woman physician concluded her comments with, "This time I think Dr. Piaget will have to call the overdose intentional. The drug levels in the boy's blood are so high."

***

Now Chuy sat in a room with floor-to-ceiling glass sliding doors in the pediatric intensive care unit. Monitors attached to the patient were clicking and flashing numbers. One screen monitored the boy's heart rhythm. The pattern was generally rhythmic, but occasional lapses in the spikes caused a nurse to fly into the room. The child was moaning constantly now and talking nonsense although occasional words were recognizable. Chuy recorded the moans because he hoped someone else, hopefully in the FBI, could listen and interpret them. He was sure he'd heard the boy say, "Bad boy" and "Mommy" many times.

A man in loose khaki slacks and a faded blue shirt entered the cubicle. He pushed the long light brown hair from the boy's forehead. The man stroked his salt and pepper beard. "This is Matt Jansen."

"Who are you?"

"I'm sorry. I should have introduced myself, but the nurses told me you'd been waiting for me for almost an hour. I'm Rene Piaget, Matt Jansen's psychiatrist." He proffered his hand to Chuy. "It's not often a police sergeant waits by the bedside of an overdose patient, but then you're from the small town of Mercado. Charming village."

Chuy shrugged his shoulders. "I didn't want to call the mother until I was sure of the boy's identity. She's already been stressed today by the murder of her mother."

Piaget sighed. "And she suspects—and so do you—that her son Matt is the killer." He walked into the hallway and pulled a chair in. "First off, it's fortuitous you couldn't identify the boy definitively and delayed contacting her. Did she even ask about his whereabouts?"

Chuy gulped. "Not that I've been told."

Piaget sat. "That's par for the course." He rubbed the boy's hands. "Where should I begin?"

"I've recorded the boy's moans and mutterings. They're mainly gibberish, but perhaps they contain several important hints?"

Piaget frowned. "I can listen to them and try to interpret." He continued to stroke the boy's hand. "Matt is never articulate because of his intellectual disabilities and his overpowering household environment. To be honest, I don't understand Matt. He's a quiet, gentle boy when I

Dirty Holy Water   53 see him, but his mother routinely finds animal carcasses in her mother's yard. She's convinced he's killed the animals. When I ask, he admits it, but that doesn't make sense. He remembers almost no details and takes no delight in his kills. In fact, the boy shrinks when he sees pictures of his victims, which he calls 'poor doggies and kitties.' I've hypnotized him and looked for multiple personalities but found none."

Chuy stopped taking notes on his phone. "His grandmother went to Chimayó on the day before her death. She evidently thought the holy dirt would help him. Could her act of daubing or somehow slathering him with dirt upset him?"

Piaget coughed. "Nothing, except his mother and sister, seem to upset the boy. He is genuinely fond of his grandfather and thought his grandmother, who he called 'Grandma Lu,' was funny. I'll listen to the tapes, and suspect I'll eventually have to testify in court. Killing animals is occasionally a juvenile, not an adult, manifestation of extreme narcissism and indicates a complete lack of empathy. In theory, the boy as a recorded serial killer of animals could have progressed to murdering his grandmother, but I doubt it because the boy does display empathy for others." He paused. "Too bad, you can't get a psychological profile of his sister. However, the mother always flares when I suggest she get help for the girl."

"Doctor, what makes you think Kayla Jansen should be evaluated psychologically?"

"Teachers have repeatedly reported Kayla is a bully. Several claimed she had tripped them and stolen small items from other children, but the school couldn't prove the claims. Kayla always was sullen when Mitzi brought her along to Matt's appointments with me. Of course, sullen behavior by a sibling of a sick child reflects jealousy and isn't unusual."

Chuy shook his head. "Why did our Children, Youth, and Families Department allow the adoption?"

"CYFD staff are overworked. As I remember the file, one social worker had doubted Mitzi's ability to raise two children, especially when one was hyperactive and the other was an epileptic with intellectual disabilities. Another social worker noted Mitzi's erratic mood swings." He hesitated. "But Mitzi, or more correctly her mother Lurleen, hired the best lawyers. Nothing specific against Mitzi could be proven and the biological parents were drug addicts. I believe one or both may be dead now."

J. L. Greger

The boy had begun to move, finally opened his eyes, and smiled. "Hi Doc. Bad again?"

"Well, Matt, only you know the answer. Before we talk, let's have this man leave."

Chuy stood. "I'd better contact Mitzi now."

Piaget followed him out of the cubicle and slid the door shut. "When did this murder occur? Was a gun used? I don't want details but I want my questions to be as effective as possible before the mother arrives."

"Early this morning, around four to six. Let's just say, the victim was stabbed."

Piaget nodded. "Please note I'm not accusing Mitzi of being a bad mother. Only one overwhelmed by circumstances." He winced. "Sad, very sad. Most people have no idea how difficult it is to provide adequate medication to a growing child, especially as they approach their teenage years. Their requirements vary with their activity level, rate of growth, appetite, and other medications. The list is so long. It's a full time job even for a well-organized parent. And her other child is wild. Always disappearing and belligerent when disciplined. And it's getting worse, as one would expect in a thirteen-year-old."

***

Chuy called Carbonne, who agreed to have FBI agents escort Mitzi to the hospital. Then he sat in the hallway outside Matt's room too tired to do much but wait.

This case had made him think about parenthood. He and Elsa, his wife of less than a year, wanted a family. They were both in their mid-thirties. Elsa had been his partner when he was on the New Mexico Gangs Task Force. She had recently been promoted in the Albuquerque Police Department. Chuy had thought when he returned to being Gil Andrew's right hand man in the Mercado Police Department that his life would be routine because Gil handled most of the sticky situations or provided strong back up for those who did. Jen Andrew's illness had changed Gil. He needed more personal time now. Chuy's position had become a lot more demanding. Several friends had already warned Elsa and him about the difficulty of balancing a family with two demanding careers. They'd talked about the potential challenges.

Now, for the first time, he realized how these responsibilities would be impossible if their child had severe health problems and both he and Elsa worked full time. He decided that he'd break their rule of not talking about their cases at home. The thought of having children like Kayla and Matt was mind boggling. Of course, Elsa wouldn't drink or take drugs during her pregnancy like Kayla and Matt's birth mother had. The more he thought about it, the more he felt sympathy for Mitzi. She'd bitten off more than she could chew when she adopted Kayla and Matt.

He saw a woman screaming at the nursing aide at the front desk of the pediatric intensive care unit. It was Mitzi. He recognized one of the two FBI agents in her wake. He swallowed hard. The roller coaster ride was going to get a lot bumpier. At least Kayla wasn't lurking by her side. He hated to admit it, but Kayla scared him more than Matt. She either scowled or smirked at him and had a swagger when she walked. The swagger was a combination of come-hither sexuality and anger at the world. Her language alternated from a sweet sing song to a snarl interspersed with curse words.

CHAPTER 11: Pete Jansen Worries

Pete Jansen sat in his hotel room because he couldn't stay at Lurleen's house or even his garden house retreat. It was all considered a crime scene. He hated sitting in a hotel room clicking through channels on the TV, waiting for Mitzi to call, and doubting she would.

He'd spent his life trying to be useful. That's what engineers did. He'd succeeded at work and had been rewarded. Home had been different. He hadn't pleased his wife or daughter in a long time. If he was honest, he knew the core reason. He'd been too wrapped up in his work and taken too many overseas assignments. Lurleen had evolved from being a highly motivated accounting whiz at DuPont who balanced work and family into a dissatisfied stay-at-home mom. As the tension at home had increased, so had his willingness to take on challenging assignments, especially if they were abroad.

His son Bill was six years older than Mitzi and had been less affected by the tension. Maybe because Bill had been exposed to the tension for less time. He had graduated from high school at sixteen and never returned home for more than two weeks after he went to MIT to major in chemical engineering. During the summers, Pete had taken Bill along on his work assignments. In graduate school, Bill married Gail. Lurleen and Gail had taken an instant dislike to each other. The net result was Pete was welcome in his son's apparently happy home; Lurleen was not. The most unfortunate part of this arrangement was it isolated Mitzi further from everyone but her mother.

Back to Mitzi's problems. Pete figured in a day or two the police would come to the obvious conclusion that Matt as a serial killer of animals had murdered Lurleen. He couldn't believe that gentle, slow Matt was a murderer, but Pete knew Matt would need a good criminal attorney. He also knew now was the time to find the right lawyer, but he needed to make Mitzi think it was her idea. That wouldn't be easy.

Mitzi had never trusted his advice. When she graduated from college, he offered to get her a position anywhere in the world with DuPont. She wasn't interested in his offer and instead took Lurleen's advice to immediately marry the first man who showed any interest in her. He wasn't surprised when she sought a divorce within weeks after her lavish wedding. He thought Mitzi had been more enthralled with the wedding process than with the man. Pete tried to divert her from isolating herself with Lurleen and a foster child or two and offered to set her up in business with a preschool of her own. Mitzi wanted no part of his idea. Once the adoption became official, he'd offered to hire a nanny so she could return to work because he thought she needed to get out and see someone beside Lurleen, Kayla, Matt, and her children's doctors. Lurleen had convinced Mitzi that Pete's offers were ploys to deprive her of money from his parents' trust fund.

Mitzi had stopped speaking to him a year ago because she thought he was rejecting her when he requested a divorce from Lurleen. He thought that was a childlike response, but it only reinforced his belief that he'd never understood his daughter. Now he feared Mitzi's work skills were so rusty she probably couldn't find employment. With Lurleen's death, she was totally isolated.

Then there was Kayla. He'd told Lurleen more than a year ago that Kayla's precocious sexuality was alarming and he suspected she'd become pregnant soon. Lurleen's solution—to get a birth control pills prescription for Kayla without consulting with Mitzi—had infuriated Mitzi.

Finally, there was Matt—dear sweet Matt. The boy of twelve still slept with stuffed animals. Of course, they were occasionally replaced after they were mutilated. Lurleen and Pete had talked about the boy. Matt's occasional bouts of anger didn't made sense. He was the least angry individual in Mitzi's household.

The increased turmoil of the last six months had begun when Lurleen had talked to a priest about "exorcizing the demons in Matt." He found Lurleen's actions odd because she wasn't even Catholic. However, Mitzi response had been typical. She had gone into a rage because Lurleen hadn't asked for Mitzi's permission beforehand.

Usually Lurleen was contrite after she over-meddled in Mitzi's affairs, but she wasn't this time. Her message on Monday was ominous. She'd hinted they may have made false assumptions about Mitzi and her children when she said, "Our princess needs you in ways we never suspected."

It was time to stop wallowing in should-have-beens and be useful. Besides Pete wanted to stay one step ahead of the police. That might be

J. L. Greger

easy with the local officers but the FBI, especially the unkempt agent, worried him. He called Mitzi's home number to volunteer to take care of Matt for the next few days. It might be his last chance to be with the boy.

A male voice answered the phone. He soon learned FBI agents had a search warrant and were completing a search of Mitzi's home. They connected him to Mitzi so quickly that he suspected they were tired of listening to her scream. When she answered the phone, he knew he was right. She was hysterical and muttered something about being betrayed. She also casually mentioned that she'd just learned Matt was in the hospital again because of "confusion over his medications."

He knew better than pry into her comment on betrayal and volunteered to go to the hospital. She emphatically said, "No, I will talk to Dr. Piaget." He thought that was too bad because he'd like to meet Dr. Piaget. Lurleen had liked the psychiatrist's common-sense approach.

Pete countered, "Well, then why don't I pick up Kayla. She probably would be happier in a hotel with me than in her home as FBI agents rifle through it." Mitzi did not rush to answer. He thought he must have annoyed her more.

He was surprised when she said, "Maybe that's wise. I don't want agents bothering her when I'm not present. How soon can you get here?"

CHAPTER 12: Sara at the End of a Long Day

Sara wanted to stretch her legs but that would disturb Bug curled in the police cruiser floor well by her feet. As she yearned for her soft bed, she remembered the poem "Self-Pity" by D. H. Lawrence. The poet was right. At least Bug and she were safe with two police in the front seat, even if they were snoring. She heard a thump on the window.

Sara didn't sit up, but slid down into the other back seat well. She didn't want to be a target framed in the window for a shooter. She slapped herself mentally. This stalker probably wouldn't use a gun.

The officers in the front seat spluttered in surprise. She heard Carbonne's voice. The officer in the driver's seat lowered a window. "Sorry—we must have dozed off."

Carbonne didn't seem annoyed. "Just as well. Mitzi didn't notice you when she left with two FBI agents because all your lights were off. Neither did Pete Jansen. He's inside with Kayla and the lab crew who are finishing up their investigation of this house." He flashed a light on the back seat. "Sara, good to see you haven't lost your protective reflexes. Mind if I join you in the back seat?"

Sara laughed. "You might have to pull me out of this well. It was easy to slide into it but may be hard to crawl out. Don't step on…" Bug jumped onto the seat before she could finish her sentence. Sara contorted her body to get her rear back onto the seat. She was glad it was dark so she couldn't see Carbonne's face. She knew she looked ridiculous.

Carbonne slid onto the rear seat. "This is off the record. Would you and Bug be willing to spend the night in a hotel room next to Pete Jansen and Kayla? I'm short of agents…."

"No. I doubt Matt killed all those animals and Lurleen, but I can imagine Kayla doing it. I'd be terrified for Bug. I'd rather be in my home without a guard. Besides, Sanders will probably arrive at Kirtland Air Force Base in Albuquerque sometime between five and six in the morning. He was going to try to hop a military cargo transport from Joint Base Andrews in Washington.

"Figured he was on his way." Carbonne paused. "Agree with your assessment. I suspect Pete does, too. Otherwise, he wouldn't have welcomed agents accompanying him to the hotel." Carbonne paused again. "I need your help to concoct a couple questions for Kayla because I doubt I'll have access to her again without lawyers and Mitzi."

Sara thought for a second. "How did Mitzi and Kayla react when you asked them about the holy dirt?"

Carbonne sighed. "Sorry to disappoint you. Mitzi remained relatively calm when we showed her the dirt. Claimed 'Matt was always digging holes and collecting dirt.' When I told her it had been found in her bedroom closet among her shoes, she shrugged and said, 'Ask Matt.' Kayla refused to answer my questions. By the way, one container had a red mark on the inside of the lid, as you predicted."

Sara sighed. "I really thought you'd get something useful from Mitzi or Kayla. What about the pendant?"

"Think it did the trick. Mitzi turned red when she saw the photo. 'Looks like one of the pendants on Mother's bracelet. Was it in this house?'"

"Did you lie?"

"Agents don't lie. I just smiled. She got redder. Decided it was time to tell her about Matt being in the hospital. She had only one question—'Is he coherent?'" The agents taking her to the hospital had to run to keep up with her. Luckily, Pete called."

"Why is that lucky?"

"Mitzi wanted to take Kayla with her to the hospital. Pete convinced her to leave Kayla with him. She left before he arrived after she had a tête á tête with Kayla. First time I ever saw Kayla lose her attitude."

"Doesn't sound like you riled either of them enough to slip and tell the truth."

"Maybe not. The agents said Mitzi muttered a lot in the car. They had recorders in the back seat that amplified the sound. It sounded like Mitzi said, 'Kayla knew I didn't....' Then it becomes slurred. The lab may be able to enhance it.

"Is Chuy ready to follow up on your so-called leads?"

"Actually, the agents with Mitzi will ask the questions. Chuy's gone home. Fresh agents went with Pete and Kayla to his hotel room. These officers will take you home. With Kayla and Mitzi under the supervision of rested agents, you should be safe until Sanders arrives. I'm going to bed, too. But first, we've got to devise one or two key questions? I shouldn't ask for your help, but I'm fried."

"Why not start with a bluff and surprise Kayla?"

"Like?"

"Your mother was really angry that you hid the pendant. Why did you do it?" Sara frowned. "Or what else will agents find hidden in the flower pots on your grandmother's patio?"

CHAPTER 13: Sara on Day 2 of the Investigation

Sara settled into her bed next to Bug. He licked her hands when she stopped massaging his back, a ritual she'd done every night since she first gotten him as a three-month-old pup. She was weary but afraid to sleep.

How had she gotten so involved in the warped dynamics of Lurleen's family? Matt's and Kayla's problems had seemed distant until yesterday. The murder scene must have been horrific. Carbonne had even refused to show her the pictures, and he knew she'd seen some pretty bloody crime scenes. What would cause a child to mutilate his grandmother's face? This wasn't a murder resulting from a sudden burst of temper. This murder required planning—premeditation. It took time to tie up someone and ritually stab their face before cutting their throat. What horrors or fears lurked in the murderer's mind?

Sara shivered, squeezed Bug, and got up to check the locks on all the windows and doors again. She stood and looked out her front window. The streetlights and the lights by the front doors of several homes were on, otherwise the street and the homes along the street were dark. She saw no movement of cars, people, or pets. This proper "over-fifty" community was locked up tighter than the proverbial drum.

Sara wondered if she should give up on La Bendita and move. She'd always felt like an outsider—not attuned to the retirement lifestyle of card games, dominoes, potlucks, drinking, and gossip at the pool. Her testimony at federal racketeering trials over the next six months would rile her neighbors. Several felt she brought the attention of "undesirable elements" to La Bendita. However, Lurleen had fit in perfectly here as she tended her grandchildren playing at one of the pools several times a week. If Lurleen's family was an example of typical residents, those undesirable elements were already in the community.

That brought her back to several nagging questions. Did the violent behavior by Matt and/or Kayla reflect their early exposure to drugs and alcohol while with their birth parents or their exposure to the stress of living with Mitzi and Lurleen? Sara guessed the effects of the multiple factors were cumulative.

Sanders would be here in a few hours. She sat down on the sofa to think.

***

Someone was tinkering with the lock on Sara's front door. She felt Bug nuzzle her foot. Her living room was no longer dark. Light was beginning to filter through the shade of the window that faced east. She dropped to the floor on her knees because she didn't want to be profiled in the window. She looked around and saw a pair of sewing shears on the end table by the sofa. She grabbed the shears. They weren't going to dissuade an armed intruder, but might buy Bug and her a little time. She grabbed Bug with her other hand and crawled to her phone. She'd begun to dial 9-1-1 when Sanders entered.

"I rang the bell and knocked. You must have been sleeping very soundly. So, I used my key." He stared at her. "Why don't you loosen that stranglehold around Bug's middle?" He dropped his bags and helped her rise from the floor. Then he squeezed her shoulders and gave her a gentle kiss. "I think Lurleen and her family have spooked you more than all the gang members in the past."

"Yeah. This time it's like Pogo said, 'We have met the enemy, and he is us.' I knew Lurleen and her family were odd at times, but she was my friend."

Sanders pushed her toward the sofa to sit. "I think *friend* might be too kind a term. Although you never admitted it, I think you viewed Lurleen and her family as a moral responsibility. It's like I always said...."

Sara interrupted, "I'm a nosy do-gooder." She sniffed. "I had more in common with Lurleen than many of my neighbors. She didn't drink to excess, smoke, gamble...."

"And she could carry on an intelligent conversation. I've heard this before." He kissed her again this time on the lips, slowly. "However, I could add she was usually sarcastic, particularly toward men. Poor Matt—as the lone male under Lurleen's total control, he may have suffered more mental abuse than you realized."

Sanders walked to the kitchen and opened cabinets and the refrigerator. "How about I make breakfast for you and Bug"

Sara suddenly realized she'd not eaten since she'd been scared by the stalker. She'd walked over to Bug's bowl. At least she hadn't forgotten to feed and water him. All the treats were gone but about one-half of his kibbles were still in the bowl.

Bug was a picky eater. He refused to even taste canned dog food. And the nonsense about dogs preferring high quality dog food was just that—nonsense. She'd bought every dog food sold, well almost every one, and Bug generally ate only about half the five-pound bag before he refused to eat more. She figured the dog food was stale, but she tried to keep it fresh by storing it in sealed plastic containers. "Tell you what, I'll try to please Bug while you please me. You've got the easier task since I'm starved. While you're cooking tell me about your week."

***

Bug trotted along the trail in the bosque, only occasionally pulling on his lead as he sniffed a bush. They eventually came to a barricade. The nearby Rio Grande River was higher than Sara had seen it during the last few years. The net result was two massive cottonwoods had fallen into the river because the saturated bank had collapsed nearby.

Sanders had never spent much time in the Southwest and was amazed. "I don't see how the so-called monsoons—those spotty rains you get in the afternoons and evenings of hot August days—could produce enough water to raise the level of the Rio Grande so much."

Sara watched the brown water swirl past the fallen trees. "Well, we also had a lot more snow in the mountains this year. And the sandy soil here doesn't have the ability to soak up moisture like the rich soils you're used to." She sighed. "It's nice to see the Rio Grande deserve its name for a change. During the last couple of years, you could almost walk across the river bed. Then I called it the Rio Patéico."

"Does anyone else call it that?"

Sara felt her good mood disappear. "Pete Jansen always laughed when I called the Rio Grande the Rio Patéico. You know he's a real expert on water. He spent his life building plants and systems for desalinizing and purifying water."

"I thought he worked for DuPont and now Dow."

"Right, but an important part of quality control in manufacturing chemicals is being able to have pure enough water to process the chemicals and then cleaning up the effluent cheaply. You should see the fancy water processing system he installed at his house. He uses the graywater from the showers and laundry to irrigate an orchard behind the house."

"Doesn't it stink?"

"No. He used a really cool pumice stone system to purify the water. More than what was needed to make the graywater usable for irrigation. The water from his system could pass standards for drinking water. Neat. Pete also installed a septic system to handle the water from the toilets and kitchen, which wasn't recycled. That's why Lurleen knew something was buried in the yard when it began to smell."

He put his hand on her shoulder. "You like Pete Jansen."

"He's had an interesting career. Water management is so important but is usually ignored by the general public and politicians. We've had good discussions." She turned and studied Sanders's face. "But I didn't like him in a way that should make you jealous." She brushed her lips across his right ear lobe and cheek and then nuzzled his lips. They parted and the kiss deepened as he held her tightly.

Bug pulled on his lead and brought her back to reality. Sanders sighed. " I swear Bug is the most rigid chaperone I've ever seen."

They took an alternative trail that led back to La Bendita. "Do you think Pete is hiding something?" Sanders's voice deepened. "He must suspect which of his family members killed Lurleen and why."

"I suppose so, but he'll be prejudiced. He loves Matt and spends most of his time in New Mexico with him. He's more distant with Mitzi and Kayla. However, I know he volunteered to care for Kayla so Mitzi could be with Matt in the hospital last night. I was surprised because Lurleen always claimed Pete disliked being alone with Kayla."

"What do you mean?"

"Her wild, precocious sexiness lately would make any decent man nervous. Mitzi thought it was cute, but it troubled Lurleen. She told me on our drive to Chimayó that she'd gotten Kayla a prescription for birth control pills about a year ago."

Sanders fingered her free hand. "Carbonne hates working cases with children."

"Because he hates to show his soft side."

"I bet he might find useful a list of details about Matt, Pete, and Kayla from you. This will be a hard case to solve because no one will tell the truth—or even know the truth—though they think they do. It will be difficult to distinguish the victims and the villains in this dysfunctional family."

CHAPTER 14: FBI Agent Carbonne Searches for Clues

Carbonne's short conversation with Kayla the previous evening had yielded little of interest except Kayla burst into tears when he said, "You sure made your mother angry when you hid that pendant. It's all she talked about on the way to the hospital. Do you know why?" Kayla's tears had convinced him that the pendant was important. It wasn't easy to make a tough cookie like Kayla lose her cool. Unfortunately, his comments had annoyed Pete. He'd asked Carbonne to leave immediately, but he had agreed to be at the FBI building in Albuquerque with Kayla at one today.

In preparation for his meeting with Pete and Kayla, Carbonne started his day on Lurleen's patio with three FBI technicians. Four pots on the patio contained pampas grass. The tall, elegant stalks of now largely ivory foliage waved in the breeze. The fig trees in two other large pots on wheels were less graceful. He almost tipped one over when he dug a bit in the dirt. It was easy to see how someone might have tipped the one planter over last night as he or she rode a bike too close or fiddled with dirt in a pot.

Although Mitzi and Kayla had tried to create the impression they were together last night at Walmart while Matt rode his bicycle to La Bendita to stalk Sara, Carbonne doubted the scenario. Another possibility was equally likely. Technicians had found multiple fingerprints on a bicycle in a culvert just outside the emergency gate at La Bendita. The prints were from Matt and another child, probably Kayla. The police watching Lurleen's house had thought the bicyclist was short and thin. Mitzi was of average height and build. Thus, Carbonne guessed Kayla had ridden the bicycle from her house, stopped at Lurleen's house, unbeknownst to Mitzi, and then continued to La Bendita. It was Matt in the SUV and at Walmart last night with Mitzi, at least at first.

That was too many assumptions. The reason for such a complex subterfuge also wasn't clear, but it suggested Matt wasn't the only one with psychological problems—or at least secrets—in the Jansen family. His reverie over, Carbonne assigned two technicians to dig into the dirt of each pot looking for buried items. He led the other technician into the main house.

Yesterday, the techs had marked all the locations where they'd found smeared blood. The lab had confirmed all the smears were of Lurleen's blood. Carbonne and the technician tried to guess the most likely places where the gloves used to smear the blood could be hidden. If the gloves were found and contained Mitzi's DNA inside, he thought it would guarantee Mitzi could be charged with abetting murder or at least tampering with evidence. The threat of jail time over those charges might make her more cooperative.

The problem was there were hundreds of boxes in the kitchen, living room, and dining room. Carbonne guessed Mitzi most likely would not have put the bloody gloves in boxes, which were stacked beneath other boxes. That left the boxes on top of the more than forty stacks. He suggested the technician start with piles that were only three or four boxes high. Mitzi would probably have had to climb on a chair to open boxes at the top of stacks of five boxes. However, his hypothesis could be wrong. Several of the boxes not atop a pile had smears. Any box with smears needed to be checked regardless of its location.

Carbonne left the unhappy technician at work and went out to the patio. Each pot now stood on a big square of white paper. Dirt surrounded two of the potted figs. A technician pointed to items laid neatly on a white paper on the picnic bench. She had found in one pot a gold half-heart pendant engraved with *TT* and a gold necklace with a half-heart pendant, engraved with *LA*. He assumed these were Matt's pendant and Kayla's necklace and pendant.

The other technician was burrowing in a pot of pampas grass. The large ivory spikes surrounded her head and shoulders. The plant almost looked like it had sprouted legs. He doubted either technician would laugh at his observation so he only said, "Keep up the good work."

Carbonne heard a squeal. The technician in the pampas grass leaned back on her knees holding a gold bracelet. As she cataloged it, he noted two charms were attached. One half-heart pendant was engraved with *MA*, the other with *KAY*. He assumed this was Lurleen's bracelet. The pendant found last night engraved with *MIT* must had been ripped from this bracelet. There appeared to be blood on the bracelet, but it was hard be sure with all the dirt.

J. L. Greger

The technician dove into the pampas grass again and more dirt fell onto the white paper. When she reemerged from the vegetation, she held a pair of bloody cotton gloves.

Carbonne's phone rang. Chuy was almost screaming into the phone. "You aren't going to believe what happened! Mitzi sat at Matt's bedside all night. The agents monitoring her said she whispered to him almost the whole time. Literally talking into his ear. The recorders I planted in the room caught nothing. The agents said around five this morning Matt seemed calmer and stopped moaning. No more irregular heart rhythms. Around six as the sun rose, Matt talked a bit. The recorders caught him saying, 'Played cowboys and Indians. Grandma Lu... cowboy.' Mitzi whispered some more. Matt groaned, 'Grandma lost.'"

"That's it?"

"No, here's the weird part. The agents said Mitzi smiled, slid open the glass door to the central area of the pediatric intensive care unit, and motioned for the agents to enter. "Matt has something to say. You'd better record it because he may not say it again. His memory is best in the morning."

"Did they read Mitzi her and Matt's Miranda rights before they took the deposition? I guess that's what this recording could be considered."

"Yes. They were careful and recorded themselves reading the Miranda rights and Mitzi agreeing to them and the tape recording. They even made her state the date and the time. One agent apologized to me for proceeding with the deposition before I could get to the hospital, but he feared Mitzi's cooperative attitude might not last."

Carbonne looked around the mess on the patio and sighed. He was grateful that Chuy had agreed to be the lead investigator at the hospital. He found extracting information from a frightened child, as he had to do in a recent case, to be excruciating. He'd much rather be digging in the dirt. "Sounds good. What did Matt say?"

"Listen to the tape yourself." A halting, childlike voice said, "Played cowboys and Indians. Grandma Lu... cowboy. Grandma lost... screamed... stopped."

"Is that supposed to be a confession?" Carbonne heard Chuy say something to someone else apparently with him.

"The agents thought the same thing and asked Matt questions. He kept repeating those phrases. They called Dr. Piaget back to the hospital. I got to the hospital about the same time as he did. He listened to the tape and asked Matt questions. Dr. Piaget and Mitzi allowed me to record his interview with Matt."

"Sound like you have everything under control."

"There's more. Matt just blinked and said 'game' or 'bad' in response to questions, such as 'How was Grandma tied up?' and 'Why did Grandma stop screaming?' I assume forensic psychologists at the FBI will listen to the tapes, but Dr. Piaget said these were typical responses for Matt."

"Piaget say anything else?"

"He said, 'As his physician, I couldn't legally alert the police that Matt might be a developing killer because of patient-client privacy.' Besides, it seems for a variety of reasons Dr. Piaget didn't believe Matt killed any animals, and thus doubted he was Lurleen's murderer."

Carbonne wanted to change the subject slightly. Matt was spooky. Come to think of it, the whole family was. "I'm making progress here. We found Lurleen's bracelet and Kayla' necklace and charm. Can you check to see whether Matt has a gold chain around his neck? And more important, we found a pair of bloody cotton gloves."

"I'll check, but I think you'd better listen to the rest of my story first. Mitzi just asked, 'Can you charge Matt with Mom's murder and close this case?' I was stunned and said nothing more could be done until you and I talked to the U.S. attorney and the district attorney for Sandoval County."

Carbonne nodded. "The U.S. attorney will say the case is up to the DA to prosecute. When he does, I'll be pulled off the case."

"And the DA will accept Matt's plea. In family cases, he always says it's not worth figuring out the puzzling details of family dynamics." Chuy paused. "That would make my life easier."

Carbonne ignored Chuy's last comment. "Don't see why Mitzi's in a rush. Did she give any logical reasons?"

"She said, 'Matt needs help and I'm afraid he'll attack Kayla and me next.' Tears ran down her face as she spoke. I think she meant it."

Carbonne wondered whether Mitzi was acting. Last night, she hadn't even seemed to notice her son was missing. Perhaps the pendant had scared her into action.

***

Carbonne met Chuy at the FBI building at noon. Chuy had suggested they meet at the hospital but Carbonne had wanted to avoid an encounter with Mitzi. He thought he might vomit if he had to watch her sudden motherliness toward Matt. He also wanted to stop by the lab. The technicians liked his attentions and gave more detailed clues when he talked to them personally, not just read their reports. At the last minute, Ulysses Howe decided to attend the briefing and hold it in his spacious office. Carbonne had been pleased. He didn't have to clear a chair for Chuy in his own small, cluttered office.

The meeting started as a data swap. Ulysses Howe began. "The district attorney for Sandoval County will handle this case in state courts because given the available evidence there is no reason to suspect federal laws have been broken." Then Ulysses surprised Carbonne who expected to be pulled off the case immediately. "This decision won't be formalized until tomorrow. Gil Andrews called me this morning. The understaffed Mercado Police Department needs our help because Gil's taking a leave of absence for a few months. He didn't say it, but I owed him a favor."

Chuy trembled a bit. "I knew it was a possibility, but I hadn't heard anything. I missed our usual morning meeting because I was at the hospital."

Ulysses nodded. "I know. That's why he called me and asked me to break the news to you. He expects the mayor will appoint you acting chief after he talks to you at four."

Carbonne noticed Chuy smiled slightly for a couple of seconds. He figured although Chuy was proud of his wife's success in the Albuquerque Police Department, he was also slightly jealous of her success. Chuy wanted this promotion even if it was only temporary. He thumped Chuy's back and said, "I'm not sure whether congratulations or condolences are in order."

Ulysses drummed his desk with his fingers, the way he always did when he was eager to move forward with his agenda. "Accordingly, we need to get this case closed. I've spoken to the DA's office. An assistant DA has already said she would accept a plea agreement from Mitzi's— technically Matt's—lawyer. After a state-appointed psychologist interviews Matt and the agreement is approved by a juvenile court, the boy will be sent to an appropriate juvenile psych facility until he is twenty-one. The assistant DA is aware of Pete Jansen's wealth and noted that the juvenile psych facility could be a private one if the facility could show proof of adequate security."

Carbonne was appalled. "So, the DA doesn't care whether Matt is the murderer, only that his office can mark this case as solved?" He noted Chuy looked like a deer in headlights. Carbonne couldn't guess his thoughts. "Think we ought to at least follow up on several key pieces of info for the next two or three days." He stared at Ulysses. "We have a good case against Mitzi for abetting Lurleen's murder or at least tampering with evidence. She's definitely hiding something and has a lot of animosity for Sara." He turned to Chuy. "Don't you agree?"

Chuy blinked. "I think she's a distraught daughter and a worried mother who made mistakes."

Carbonne shook his head. "I think she snowed you with her act at the hospital and could be a threat to Sara. Bet the U.S. attorney will agree with me." He smiled at Ulysses. "Besides, if the DA delays charging Matt and gives us a couple more days, we might find the evidence to force Mitzi to get psych help for Kayla. That kid may have not killed Lurleen but she will kill *someone* in the next ten years. She has so much anger."

Ulysses spoke slowly. "Sara can't leave the country if she's a suspect for Lurleen's murder. Once Matt is charged, Sara can travel."

Carbonne groaned. "You know Mitzi's claim against Sara is just an example of jealousy. However, not having to guard Sara during the next week would give me us more time to investigate this crazy murder case."

Ulysses frowned. "All family murders are crazy because you can't separate the victims from the villains. However, you were right on one point. The agents watching Kayla last night and this morning reported she exceeded their expectation of a bratty teenager. Evidently, she managed to almost knock one of them out as the agent tried to follow Kayla leaving the hotel. Kayla must have taken a running jump at an ajar door and smashed it into the agent."

Carbonne snickered. "Told them she had a lot of pent up anger."

Ulysses opened his under-the-counter refrigerator and handed a diet cola to Carbonne. "Chuy, your preference?" Chuy chose a bottle of water. "Okay. Tell me what you've got."

Carbonne didn't give Chuy a chance to speak. "First, the update from the lab. They found traces of human blood in the crushed glass by the broken vase on the work bench in Pete's retreat. Rapid DNA analyses indicate that the blood on the glass and the blood smeared throughout the house is Lurleen's. Means we can claim the murder weapon was a large shard of glass, later reduced to crushed pieces. It will be several weeks before thorough DNA analyses are completed. Remember the victim and one suspect—Mitzi—would have similar DNA, at a fifty percent match. So, I think the extra tests are warranted."

Ulysses smiled. "Good work. I…"

Carbonne rushed on. "It's inconceivable that Matt with his limited intellectual abilities had the sense to destroy the murder weapon. That's proof he had an accomplice or someone trying to protect him. It also explains why Mitzi was so slow to call 9-1-1. We'll have more evidence soon. The lab found a pair of bloodied cotton gloves in a flowerpot on the patio this morning. The blood was Lurleen's. They haven't identified the source of the DNA on the interior of the gloves yet."

Chuy stopped playing with his phone. "I just found something interesting in Gil's interview with Sara. I hadn't read all of it until now. Lurleen claimed that Kayla once broke a vase and threatened to use the pieces to cut Lurleen's throat." He eyed his phone. "That was in response to Lurleen disciplining Kayla for using the vase as a basketball hoop." He studied the note. "Oh my—Sara thought Kayla was only around six at the time. Of course, this is hearsay evidence."

Carbonne interrupted, "I'm interviewing Pete and Kayla at one and I'll try to get confirmation of that story." He turned to Chuy. "You might check to see whether one of the CYFD social workers heard about that incident. Bet they were slow in processing the adoptions for a reason."

Ulysses sighed. "I think they, like you, suspected but couldn't prove Kayla was not thriving, at least in a good way, under Mitzi's foster care. Circumstantial evidence won't work in a murder case."

Chuy nodded in agreement.

"Humph. We've got more." Carbonne held up three fingers, thought for an additional second, and held up a fourth finger. "Technicians found a gold bracelet with two pendants, a loose pendant engraved with *TT*, and a matching necklace of Kayla's—gold chain with half-heart pendant engraved with *LA*." He peered at Chuy. "You said Matt had a gold chain around his neck." Carbonne paused and frowned. "I hadn't thought about this but the jewelry wasn't all in one spot. Kayla's and Matt's jewelry was in a pot with a fig tree on Lurleen's patio. Lurleen's bracelet was found in a pot of pampas grass."

"The one you found tipped over last night?"

"Yeah. I found the pendant engraved with MIT in the dirt by that pot." Carbonne beamed. "And now for the best part. The technicians also found a pair of bloody cotton gloves in that pot. If the blood is Lurleen's and the DNA inside the glove is Mitzi's we've got her conclusively for tampering with evidence at a crime scene or more."

Ulysses sighed. "You really want to lock Mitzi up?"

Carbonne shook his head. "I want to force her to tell the truth, and I want to separate her from Kayla and Matt. They'd be better off in a psych ward than with her."

Ulysses drummed her fingers on his desk. "You don't know that. What will be gained?"

"You didn't see Lurleen. She had six bloody gashes around her mouth. Blood was everywhere. She had rope burns on her ankles and wrists. Whoever did this murder liked blood... and inflicting pain. I can't believe they won't kill again." Carbonne seemed to stare blankly ahead for several seconds. "I understand trying to protect your kid or kids, but Mitzi had to know when she saw her mother that Matt and/or Kayla were menaces to society. Trying to hide the evidence is just plain stupid."

Ulysses stopped drumming his fingers on the desk. "Maybe that's why she spent the night at Matt's bedside and encouraged him to confess. Of course, that doesn't absolve her of tampering with evidence, but a jury will be sympathetic and probably won't convict her."

Carbonne shook his head. "Another thing—there's no way Matt weighing only seventy pounds could have bound a strapping woman like Lurleen to a chair. She weighed almost three hundred pounds."

Chuy stood and paced. "I don't buy Matt's explanation that he was playing cowboys and Indians with Lurleen either." He stopped. "Well, he might have thought he was playing cowboys and Indians but he didn't tie Lurleen to the chair alone. Kayla might have helped him, but she weighs less than a hundred pounds, too."

Carbonne rubbed his wrists. "Kayla's smart enough to have tricked Lurleen. But who tied those knots? They held while Lurleen struggled mightily."

Ulysses frowned. "Are you sure Matt and Kayla couldn't tie strong knots? Sara called me just before this meeting and said she remembered something that might be useful. She thinks she watched Pete teaching Matt and Kayla to tie knots. Evidently it was years ago when Lurleen was her neighbor. Pete evidently liked being a scout leader for the two children—he took them camping and taught them lots of odd outdoor skills."

CHAPTER 15: Pete Jansen Tells His Story

Mitzi called Pete Jansen mid-morning and calmly told him that Matt had admitted to killing Lurleen. Pete figured she was in shock. Why else would his daughter, who became emotional over minor disappointments, be calm as she recounted how her son had murdered his grandmother? However, Mitzi became more emotional as she lectured him. Police were not to question Kayla without a lawyer being present. Mitzi didn't want the police to fingerprint or take a sample for DNA analyses from Kayla either. She was hysterical as she warned him to not allow Kayla out of his sight today because the police might try to intimidate her. However, Mitzi admitted upon his persistent questioning that she'd allowed police to fingerprint and take a cheek swab for DNA from Matt.

Obviously, Mitzi had given up on protecting Matt but was prepared to act like a mother bear protecting her cub in regard to Kayla. She certainly was as grouchy as an old bear. He suspected Mitzi's decisions were not based on facts but on her preference for Kayla. He just wasn't sure.

Pete was nervous about his upcoming interview with the police because anything he said, especially his suspicions about Kayla, could be misinterpreted. He'd always found her to be an unpleasant child. She was vain but generally obsequious around Mitzi and Lurleen with only occasional temper tantrums. However, Kayla ruthlessly bullied Matt when she thought no one was watching. She had always regarded Pete with contempt even when he tried to teach her scouting skills. At first, he thought her aloof behavior reflected Mitzi's and Lurleen's opinion of men, but he noticed that she was equally snippy with female teachers, clerks in stores, and Sara, even when they'd done nothing to provoke her.

Thus, as he drove to the FBI building for the interview, Pete tried to sort his feelings from his experience. He thought Kayla knew who had killed Lurleen. He guessed it was because she was the murderer. She'd made several comments about the police being too dumb to ask the right questions or look in the right places. He also knew both children desperately needed intense psychological counseling, but Mitzi would never allow psychologists to work with Kayla. He decided many things could happen today that wouldn't please Mitzi but in the long run might be best for Matt and himself.

***

Pete quickly agreed to talk to Carbonne and Chuy Bargas without a lawyer present and allowed them to fingerprint him and take a DNA swab. He saw no reason to object because FBI agents had admitted last night that his travel timeline made it doubtful he could have murdered Lurleen. They thankfully hadn't realized how fast he drove from Gallup to Albuquerque. Besides, the FBI agents were more apt to believe him if he controlled his nerves and acted confident.

He also agreed to another of their requests. Kayla would wait in another room, which Pete could watch through a video monitor, during his interview. Per Mitzi's instruction, he didn't grant Chuy permission to fingerprint Kayla or take a sample for DNA analysis. However, he didn't object when agents offered Kayla a can of soda even though he guessed police could lift the needed samples from the can. He told himself that he'd not directly defied Mitzi's wishes. Besides, if Kayla was involved in Lurleen's murder, she needed psychological help.

Chuy started the questions by asking Pete about Lurleen. Pete described her as she was when he first met her at work—an energetic young certified public accountant. Then he described her as a young wife and mother who balanced work and her two children well, until his many overseas assignments had forced Lurleen to give up her career.

Carbonne, the more impatient of the two officers, interrupted his reminiscences. "Okay, you may have been getting a divorce, but you once loved your wife. Give her the respect she deserves and help us find her murderer or murderers."

Then the officers barraged him with questions about how he interacted with Kayla and Matt. Carbonne and Chuy finally stopped those questions when Pete said, "Look I'm no expert on children. Lurleen and Mitzi were, but I was a scout leader for my son. I played that role with Kayla and Matt because Mitzi didn't otherwise allow her children to participate in after-school activities. The boy seemed to like doing things with his hands, and Kayla didn't complain much."

Carbonne's next comments broke his false sense of security. "I drive to Gallup a fair amount and I make real time at night. Thus, I don't think you went to the Frontier as soon as you arrived in the Albuquerque area. Let's start with the easiest question. We know you didn't eat alone at the Frontier because your credit card bill for the meal is too large. Who ate with you at the Frontier?"

Pete knew lying would be counterproductive. "I ate with Matt and Kayla."

Carbonne smiled. "How did you set up that meeting?"

Pete decided it was best to be cooperative but not offer anything extra unless it was requested. "I called them from my car."

"Okay, before you continue with your game of hide and seek, let me tell you something. We know your call around six was transmitted through a cell tower near Mercado."

Pete blinked.

"That's a tower not far from your house. That means you were near your house or maybe in it at the time your wife was murdered." Carbonne winked at Chuy who was gulping nervously. "But I don't think you killed your wife. Others aren't so sure because divorces drive lots of people crazy. Me, I've never been married, so I don't know if that's true. I think you're trying to protect someone. Stop being a fool—what did you do at your house? What did you see, hear, and smell? Tell us everything. Doesn't have to be in order."

Pete hesitated, not because he didn't want to cooperate, but because he didn't know where to begin. Pete wanted to hang his head but thought it was important to watch Carbonne and Chuy. "I drove by the house. Lights were on at the front of the house in the living room. Thus, I doubted Lurleen was alone. She never wasted money by leaving on lights in unoccupied rooms. I also knew she seldom got out of bed before ten. But there was no car in the driveway. I parked on a nearby side street and tramped through backyards on the way to my orchard."

Chuy nodded encouragingly at him. Carbonne's eyes never blinked. Pete glanced at the screen. Kayla was playing a game on her phone.

"The orchard smelled but the ground wasn't soggy. I knew Lurleen was right." He frowned. "She called me on Monday morning. She was worried about Matt, but more about Mitzi." He shook his head. "She was always protective of Mitzi, but this time was different. She said I had to get to her house by Wednesday."

"Why?"

"She didn't say." Pete shrugged. "Except to say Mitzi needed me, and *she* needed me."

"What did you do when you got to your house?"

"I guess you'd say I cased out the situation. Lights were on in the living room, kitchen, and dining room, but not the bedrooms. All the shades were down. One light was even on in my retreat."

"Couldn't you see shadows through the shades? I noticed the shades weren't that heavy."

Pete realized Carbonne knew a lot more than he'd mentioned. He'd better give all the details. "I saw shadows in the dining room. Someone—probably an adult—was seated. I saw... I saw two figures moving."

Chuy smiled. Carbonne only stared harder at him. "What else?"

Pete debated about what to say next. "I heard a scream and then silence. I knew it was Lurleen, and I knew I was too late." He felt tears dribble down his face. It was the first time he'd cried about Lurleen's death.

Carbonne handed him a box of tissues. "I figured you loved your wife even though you couldn't stand to live with her. What did you do?"

Pete wiped his face. He felt better in an odd way. "I thought a bit and called Kayla's cell phone. She's proud of it and always keeps it by her side. I... I thought I'd die when I heard the phone ringing in the house... in the kitchen." He frowned. "Oh, I forgot to tell you that rap music was playing in the house. It was pretty loud, and I couldn't hear anything else inside the house. Except I did hear Kayla's phone ringing and she answered eventually. She was excited and yelling. I panicked and blurted out that I wanted to take her and Matt to breakfast. Said I'd pick them up at their house in ten minutes."

"What did you do next?"

"I ran to the front of the house and hid in the bushes by the garage, expecting to see Matt and Kayla emerge from the front door to run home. Instead, the garage door creaked open and Mitzi's SUV barreled out."

"Who was in the car?"

"Mitzi's SUV has darkened glass. I saw nothing." He paused. "Kayla doesn't have a driver's license, but Lurleen said Kayla drove all the time. She has for a long time. One of the many things that Lurleen, Mitzi, and Kayla argued about."

"What else?"

"That's it." Pete gulped. "Well, I rushed to my car and picked up Matt and Kayla. I never saw Mitzi, but I didn't expect to." He paused. "I don't think I've ever seen Mitzi out of bed before eight in the morning.

She's like her mother and sleeps late. So, I asked whether Kayla and Matt had left a note for Mitzi." He paused to think. "Matt started to sing a ditty, and Kayla ignored me. Then I told Kayla she looked pretty. Actually, she looked like a whore with her dark eye makeup and her sports bra and tight pants." He smiled. "That got her talking." He stared at her on the screen. "Look at her now. It took her almost a half-hour to get ready to come to this building. I wish she cared about anything but her appearance."

Carbonne interrupted Pete's musings. "What did the children say during the drive from their house to the Frontier?"

"Not much." He paused. "No—I'd forgotten. Kayla told me a funny story. Not humorous but odd. I guess Lurleen had wrangled Sara into driving her to Chimayó on the day she was killed."

Carbonne shook his head. "No, the day *before* she was killed. Because she was killed early in the morning—yesterday."

Pete winced and wondered whether he could have saved Lurleen if he hadn't taken a nap before he left Phoenix. He realized Carbonne and Chuy were staring at him. "I'm sorry. This is hard. Evidently Lurleen asked Mitzi to bring the children and come for supper. Kayla mentioned they had pizza as usual."

Carbonne typed rapidly on his phone.

Pete continued. "Sorry. Don't know the details. Kayla said she wanted dessert and was pleased when Lurleen pulled out two plastic tubs from the cabinet. Evidently, Mitzi was annoyed because she was on a diet and stormed to the back bedroom." He paused. "I don't know what Mitzi did but she wasn't with Lurleen and the kids. Nothing unusual. She frequently disappears when she doesn't feel like arguing with Lurleen. This is where Kayla's story began. I figured out the setting later."

Carbonne spoke softly, "Let's hear Kayla's story."

Pete smiled as he watched Kayla on the screen. She looked normal, if you ignored the black smudges around her eyes. "Lurleen made both children move their chairs close to hers. She told them, 'This treat is for your souls.' She stuck her finger into what Kayla thought was chocolate pudding and traced a cross on Matt's forehead. Matt must have thought she was being funny and dipped his finger in the tub too and tasted it. Kayla said he screamed, 'Yuck.' I think she was telling the truth because Matt stopped singing his ditty and began to chant 'yuck, yuck' in the car. Kayla said Matt looked so funny that she asked for a cross too. Then Mitzi came back into the room." He felt tears streaming down his face again.

"Do you know why Mitzi came back into the room?"

Pete sniffled. "Don't know. Maybe she heard the children giggling. Kayla said Mitzi's face was red. Her anger must have been obvious because Matt stopped chanting 'yuck' in my car and instead wailed 'Mommy mad.' Then Lurleen opened the other container and said something, which made Mitzi even angrier. Kayla slurred the words." He paused. "I don't think she wanted me to know, and the rest of the story was confused."

"So?"

"Evidently Matt thought Lurleen's suggestion was funny. He stuck both his hands in the mud and ran toward Mitzi. All Kayla would say in response to my questions was that Mitzi was angry when Matt spread mud on her face. I think she was telling the truth because Matt sitting in my back seat stopped chanting, 'Grandma Lu laughed.' and instead wailed, 'Mommy mad.' Then he began to cry, and Kayla began to giggle as she said, 'You're so stupid,' over and over."

Pete studied Kayla on the monitor. He'd probably sealed her fate. After a moment of silence, Chuy touched his sleeve. "We know this was hard. Mitzi has made it clear to us that she doesn't want a psychologist to talk to Kayla. But if Kayla was involved in Lurleen's murder, she needs psychological help. You've just begun the necessary process."

Pete hoped Carbonne had also bought his story but couldn't tell from his facial expressions.

CHAPTER 16: Sara En Route to India on Day 3

Sara's phone rang around one in the morning. She awoke with a start, ready to grab the phone on her bedside table. Then she realized she was in bed with Sanders in his home in Washington. She, Sanders, and Bug had gotten the last flight from Albuquerque into Washington, D.C., around eight last night.

She finally realized the ringing was from her cell phone tucked in her purse. She thought she'd left her purse in his living room but wasn't sure. One of the things she did regularly, which she knew drove Sanders wild, was having to search for her purse at his home. She always tried to leave it hanging on the coat rack by his front door but… she'd been unable to establish a consistent habit in his home. Thus, she ignored Sanders's questions and clambered from bed being careful not to step on Bug. She found her purse and answered the phone assuming either Carbonne or Chuy had an important update on the case because she'd given the number to only a handful of people.

There was a crackling noise indicative of a poor connection. "You won't return from India." It was a man's voice. She was too stunned to reply. The phone clicked. Maybe she hadn't heard right?

Sanders and Bug were now standing by her side. They both looked worried. Sanders said, "You screamed."

Sara gasped. "I did?" She organized her thoughts. "A man just told me that I wouldn't return from India."

Sanders gave her a quick hug. "Sounds like a gang threat, not one from Lurleen's family. While you call Carbonne, I'll make some calls."

Carbonne was slow to answer his phone. She must have awakened him from a deep sleep or interrupted his time with his new girlfriend. Sara had introduced them during the last case she'd worked with Carbonne, but she knew better than to mention the girlfriend. Carbonne kept his private life very private. He listened to her short explanation.

"Damn—didn't expect this. Will get the call traced to at least determine the cell tower nearest the caller. Can I assume Sanders is contacting Ulysses Howe or the U.S. attorney to ask that the FBI investigate this call?"

She repeated the question to Sanders. He held up two fingers. "Yes, to both. And Carbonne, one more thing—I haven't given my cell phone number out much."

"Yeah, you use it more as a one-way signal. You call out but turn the phone off the rest of the time. Drives us all crazy. Why did you have it on?"

"Because Sanders gave me a lecture. He said you and Chuy had enough problems without having to go through his phones to reach me. My cell phone will work in India, too, because Sanders made me buy an international calling plan for it, even though his phones will work anywhere."

Carbonne chuckled. "Wow. Got new admiration for the man. Back to business. Did you ever give your cell number to Lurleen?"

"Don't think so, but I'm not sure. I doubt it."

"Okay, so you don't know. And I assume you plan to leave later today for India, despite the call?"

"Yes—should I wear a disguise? I've done that before to avoid recognition by gang members when I returned from Bolivia."

"Not a bad idea. Hell, Sanders is the expert. Put him on the phone."

***

Sara loved to sit in airports, especially international terminals, and watch people. It was easy to imagine all sorts of scenarios. For example, twelve women had seemed to float into the waiting area a few minutes ago. Instead of scrounging for available chairs, they seated themselves with crossed legs on the floor, interrupting the flow of passengers through the terminal. Sara doubted it was a protest. Their posture was too perfect, and they carried no signs.

Sara nudged Sanders. "I think those women are proof we're in the right waiting area. You don't see a group of women assume the lotus position often, except in yoga classes. I bet they're going to some sort of ashram in India."

He smiled, but seemed a thousand miles away and not in India. She was worried about him. The last year was not a good one for him. His unblemished State Department record had been marred by his own mistakes and factors beyond his control. During the last year, he'd labored to clean up the security issues at the U.S. embassy in Havana including an outbreak of neurological damage among the embassy staff. Scientists had hypothesized two potential causes: bombardment with "direction auditory and sensory phenomena" and exposure to a fumigant used against the Zika virus. The latter seemed more likely to Sara, except similar neurological damage had been reported in staff in a Chinese embassy. Now Sanders was leading a team seeking ways to define and block any new technology used by America's adversaries. That had meant many long flights but had gotten him out of Havana. She thought that was best for their relationship and for him.

Sara hated the way several of Sanders's colleagues in Havana snickered about how he had foolishly allowed himself to be outsmarted by a young embassy employee, whose first loyalty was to a drug cartel. Sara was willing to forget his fling because he was contrite. Of course, many serial philanderers are contrite after each fling, but she believed he wouldn't stray again because it would effectively end his career, which Sanders valued more than anything. That was probably a sad statement on their relationship. The good part of this mess was he was slightly more patient with her now.

Sanders grabbed her hand. "I'm sorry for being distracted. This trip is my way of apologizing to you for my bad behavior in Cuba. Looks like I'm not off to a good start. I was thinking about an email from my boss."

Sara stroked his cheek with her other hand. "She sent me an email too. Said I shouldn't let you spoil our time in India by working. But I'm guilty, too. I was reading an email from a former student. He's studying a strange epidemiology problem in India. Seems almost one-fifth of agricultural workers living along the southeast coast of India in the state of Andhra Pradesh suffer from a chronic kidney disease of unknown etiology. Physicians in India have hypothesized this often-fatal condition could be due to chronic dehydration and exposure to toxins, such as heavy metals, in the air and water."

"Wait—how did he know you were going to India? I thought we agreed not to discuss it with anyone who didn't need to know. The threats from the gangs are real."

Sara noticed a bit of annoyance in his voice. She didn't like his tone but figured she should be thankful he was concerned. "He doesn't know I'm going to India. He wrote me because renal failure is also common among agricultural workers in the sugarcane fields of Nicaragua and Honduras. He thought I might know something about it because of my work on science issues in Latin America, especially in Cuba. You know they burn sugarcane fields to remove the outer leaves around the stalks before harvesting in Cuba, just as they do elsewhere? The smoke is horrendous. However, the lead and cadmium contamination of drinking water is probably less in Cuba and Central America than in India."

"You epidemiologists do love your medical mysteries."

She noted his eyes glazed over as they often did when she went into scientific details on issues not of interest to him. "Don't tune me out. This may have relevance to our trip."

"How? We'll only drink bottled water."

"Indian farmers are notorious for burning crop residues on fields so they can quickly plant the next crop. That's how they get three crop cycles a year off most fields. This burning of the rice fields in northern India is one of several reasons for the smog alerts in Delhi. During the last few years, the smog in Delhi has surpassed that in Beijing by ten-fold in November."

"Why didn't you mention this earlier? We should have brought masks."

Sara shrugged. "Didn't think of it until I read my colleague's email. Besides, the rice crop harvest occurs in October and November, and the farmers usually burn the fields at the end of the harvest. We should luck out because it's only early October now.

Sanders nodded and then peered around the waiting area as if he was searching for someone.

Sara thought this was this a bad omen for their trip, but he was often nervous before flights, although he'd never admit it. He had talked to Carbonne so long this morning that she alone had taken Bug to the pet spa where he would spend the next ten days. She hadn't complained because she didn't want Sanders to see her cry as she left Bug, who had done his best to convince her not to leave. He had whined and tried to bolt to the door when the attendant took his leash.

***

The lines for the immigration check at the Delhi airport were long, especially for those holding tourist visas. After an hour, Sanders became restless and wandered away to determine the problem. When he returned he said, "India has the biggest biometric ID system in the world because it has no equivalent to Social Security numbers for its citizens. Anyway, the officials are scanning the fingerprints of all incoming passengers. Their fancy scanning system, which has recorded the fingerprints of over a billion Indians, is having trouble screening the fingertips of Americans."

Sara, who had only half-listened to his explanation, straightened. "Then I'll *definitely* have a problem. Before I could visit patients at University Hospital with Bug, I had to be fingerprinted. The police lab couldn't get usable prints from me and the volunteer office had to vouch for me. They said a lot of the older volunteers, especially women, had no usable fingerprints." She held up her hands. "I wasn't surprised because my fingertips are almost shiny."

"I know potters and chemists sometimes lose the distinct ridges on their fingertips. You're neither, but you do garden a lot and never wear gloves when you use cleaning supplies."

"Thanks for not saying the obvious: I'm an old woman."

He hugged her. "You're not old—just *mature*. I guess I made the right decision this morning. Carbonne almost convinced me you'd be safer if you wore a wig and other disguises. I agreed but thought a fake nose might pose a problem with the Indian biometric identification system, and more importantly you'd resist or complain during the whole flight."

Around midnight, the line speeded up. The officials just waved incoming tourists through without scanning their fingertips.

CHAPTER 17: FBI Agent Carbonne on Day 4

Ulysses Howe was lecturing him again. Carbonne's relationship with Ulysses had been great until Ulysses had announced his impending retirement. Then Carbonne had foolishly agreed to serve as the associate director of the FBI office in New Mexico—and potentially Ulysses's replacement—at least on a temporary basis. Now he started many days reviewing budgets and minutiae with Ulysses. Today's topic was "unnecessary lab costs."

He knew this subject could turn ugly quickly because the search for clues in Lurleen's hoard had been a bust. Three FBI technicians had spent the last two days looking for clues, especially a bloody pair of plastic gloves, and still had not examined even one-half of the boxes in Lurleen's kitchen, living room, and dining room.

Ulysses's hands shook as he picked up a sheet from his back table. "This lab report is an example of wastage. The lab reports that three…"

Carbonne tried to keep his face blank.

"Three technicians spent most of yesterday cataloging the contents of boxes at the Jansen house. They reported they found no blood smears inside the more than sixty boxes they inventoried." He glanced at Carbonne. "They say they found gold fractured heart pendants and blood-stained cotton gloves the previous day. Is that right?"

Carbonne nodded. He thought the less he said, the better, because Ulysses appeared to be in a prickly mood this morning. Carbonne suspected Ulysses was eager to get onto the next phase of his life because he was finding excuses to leave work early several days a week now. In the past, he'd been one of the last to leave the building most days.

Ulysses stared at the paper. "Yesterday they found mainly papers with no apparent significance to the case and—am I reading this correctly?—*baptismal fonts.*" He stared at Carbonne.

"It took us a while to figure out what the giant stone, wood, and marble goblets were. Some without pedestals were only a foot high and wide, but many were three or four feet high. Most were padded carefully inside boxes. So, the lab crew had to dig through a lot of paper in most of the boxes. We noticed they all had crosses painted or carved on them. That got us thinking."

"Enough. The leader of the crew brought me this report late yesterday because she doubted it was worthwhile to examine more boxes today, especially since murders on the Jemez and Zuni pueblos yesterday were stretching the lab's capabilities thin. She says they could manage it, if the pueblos weren't at the far ends of the state." He shook his head. "That woman is quite capable of telling other agents 'no,' but she said you were a special case." He shook his head. "Seems you are the lab's favorite agent because you work *with* them to uncover evidence."

Carbonne saw a chance to make a point—the real reason he'd accepted the position of associate director the Albuquerque office. "I'll say it again." He wanted to say, "the majority," but instead said, "*Several* of our agents here are egotistical pricks."

Ulysses cleared his throat. "They recognize their talents lie elsewhere. And not in sweating the details."

"Yeah. They're Wyatt Earp knock-offs, who value guns and fancy martial arts, but little else. They belittle...."

"I know they gave you a hard time at first."

Carbonne forced himself not to raise his voice. "Enough for me to notice how they treated women, people on the street, and minorities, especially Native Americans. They meet the letter of the law and are polite. But they're always distant and give less weight to the comments and problems of those they don't respect. They also don't want to get their suits dirty digging for evidence. I worked in enough FBI offices to know the best agents do *not* have the Wild West hang-up." He wanted to say "many" but decided to be polite. "Several have that mentality here in Albuquerque."

"Few have your knack for disguises or ability to sift through clues. That's why the head technician came to me. She believes you and Sara are right. There are clues somewhere in that house but she doubts they can be found in the next day or two. I know you want to solve the Jansen case before Sara returns from India. But why the rush? Sara will be gone for a week. Furthermore, those clues will be there a week from now. Meanwhile, evidence will be lost at the pueblos if her crews don't act quickly."

Carbonne was sure his face was redder than usual. "I wish the technician had come to me directly."

Ulysses smiled. "She planned to, but you weren't available late yesterday afternoon because you had gone undercover on another case, as a favor to another agent." He sighed. "Which is the real point of this discussion. You're an administrator now, or will be soon. You can't do everything. I also think the lab costs for this crime—Lurleen Jansen's murder—will be reduced if we don't rush. One of the family members will crack and provide the needed clues if you keep constant pressure on them." Ulysses winked. "Let *them* do the sweating instead of *us*."

Carbonne pretended to study his pile of papers. "Of course, those murders at the pueblos take precedence today. However, you don't understand: The Jansen family is a powder keg. The murderer—or murderers—will kill again… soon. Their probable target will be Sara when she returns from India."

Ulysses drummed his fingers on his desk. "I know you put great store in Sara's hunches. I do, too, but we're all wrong sometimes. She thinks Matt is incapable of murdering his grandmother even though he's confessed and everyone but you are ready to close the case. Anyway, Matt's not a threat to Sara while he's in a psych unit."

Carbonne couldn't remain quiet. "Matt's psychiatrist Dr. Piaget agrees with Sara and me. Matt's confession is almost unbelievable and full of holes. We know his sister Kayla was present at the murder with a still unidentified person."

"Yes, I saw the summary of your notes from interviews with the victim's husband Pete. You know for once there could be a simple explanation to one of your cases. The two children did it together. Focus on interviewing the girl and forget about looking through more boxes."

"The mother Mitzi Jansen is litigious and has slowed the process."

Ulysses drummed his fingers on the table again. "I thought she was cooperative and gave us access to the son and helped us gain his confession."

"Another funny part of this case. She's a different person when it comes to access to the daughter. After Pete identified Kayla at the murder site yesterday, I obtained a court order. A court-appointed psychologist will interview Kayla today. Chuy Bargas is also a problem." When Ulysses's face remained blank, Carbonne added, "Mitzi has snowed Chuy Bargas with her mother act around Matt."

Ulysses winced. "You're used to working with Gil. It's unreasonable to expect Chuy to have Gil's skills and insight." He scribbled on the page from the lab. "We're agreed no more examination of boxes at the Jansen house until we have better leads."

Carbonne tried to keep his face blank as Ulysses put the page in his "out" basket and then picked up a stack of papers from his back table. "Now for our big problem."

They began to discuss again the continuing problems of murders on the Indian pueblos. It was unbelievable but they were averaging at least three murders a month. This month, four people had already been killed. Most were simple cases to solve, but the bigger problem was how to prevent these often alcohol-fueled crimes of passion. Carbonne suggested a video conference on prevention measure with pueblo tribal police, FBI agents, county sheriffs, physicians from Indian Health Services, and pueblo leaders participating.

The front desk buzzed Carbonne. They had been instructed not to bother either Ulysses or Carbonne during their meeting, unless it was an emergency. The woman at the front desk said Pete Jansen looked distraught and had announced he wouldn't leave until he talked to Carbonne.

Carbonne quickly decided Pete's arrival was a blessing. Ulysses's initial response to his suggestion was "a conference on public health measures might be a hard sell with rank and file law enforcement officers." Carbonne figured if Ulysses had time to think, he'd be supportive, especially after he talked to the tribal leaders at the Laguna and Acoma pueblos. "Why don't you call a couple of the numbers on my list while I talk to Pete Jansen?"

Pete had been detained in a tiny observation room near the entrance. He remained hunched over the table when Carbonne rushed in. "I… I've been thinking." Pete looked terrible when he lifted his head. He hadn't shaven and the areas under his eyes were swollen and red. "I took control of Lurleen's funeral. Mitzi doesn't like my decisions, but they're necessary. I've told the funeral director to prepare Lurleen for an open casket funeral."

Carbonne gasped. "Is that wise? Makeup can hide a lot, but there will be traces of the stab wounds around her mouth."

"I know. I… I want… I want my family and neighbors to see her. What she went through. Then maybe they'll talk. As far as I know, there are no more tests to run. The autopsy is done." He studied Carbonne.

Carbonne took a seat at the table. "Won't the viewing traumatize Matt and Kayla? Sara won't return from India for almost a week."

Pete lowered his eyes. "I'll start with the easy response first. Sara is the one person who I'm sure is not playing games. She doesn't need to be present. In contrast, Kayla and Mitzi are hiding something. I've watched them the last two days. Lots of whispered secrets. They titter when I make comments about Lurleen or Matt. They both know who killed Lurleen. I've talked to my son several times in the last two days. He's hiding something, too."

"What about your daughter-in-law? Isn't she at M.D. Anderson getting treatment?"

"Gail? She's not hiding anything. She's the one who suggested I have a funeral for Lurleen. She thought Bill needed to say goodbye to his mother and resolve issues with his sister which Gail doesn't understand. She also said she'd be flying home today and could take care of their daughter while Bill attended Lurleen's funeral."

Carbonne wished Pete had been less long-winded but guessed Pete trusted him more than his own family at this point. Poor guy. He knew Ulysses wanted him to dispatch Pete quickly and return to their discussion of preventing murders on the pueblos, but Pete had been struggling with a lot of unanswered questions that might be important in solving this case. "Why do you want the neighbors present?"

"I can't believe several of Lurleen's neighbors didn't hear or see something on the night she was murdered. Maybe even at other times."

Carbonne interjected, "Sergeant Chuy Bargas and other Mercado police officers canvased the neighborhood. All the neighbors said they'd seen nothing."

"Yes, but the shock of seeing Lurleen might get someone to talk. I want you to arrange for hidden cameras and microphones…" He looked up with tears in his eyes. "…or however you do secret monitoring at the casket."

"The neighbors won't attend. I don't think your wife socialized much in the neighborhood."

"But *I* did, and I'm going to personally ask them to attend."

Family members were often intent on finding the murderer of their loved one. Carbonne didn't think he'd seen many who were as focused as Pete, but then Pete was a successful engineer. They tended to be focused individuals. "What about Matt?"

"He's the only one I'm not sure about. Dr. Piaget says a shock might cause Matt to recant his confession or might turn him catatonic. He thinks if he and Matt could view Lurleen alone without interference from others, Matt might be able to enunciate real memories. I want to know whether the court-appointed psychologist who's supposed to talk to Kayla today agrees. I'd like the funeral to occur soon. My son is flying in tomorrow."

CHAPTER 18: Sara in Delhi on Days 4 and 5

Delhi was an assault on the senses. Although Sanders wanted to hire a driver and travel in India without a guide, Sara had convinced him that neither of them had time to plot a trip to India beforehand and a small group tour with an experienced guide would be more relaxing. As she looked out the windows of the bus at the clothing market, she was glad she was safely enveloped in a large vehicle.

It was early morning but a dense crowd surged around a heap of clothing nine feet tall and almost thirty feet long. From the bus, the clothing looked like discards, but men were crawling up the sides of the pile and selecting pants, shoes, and shirts. Occasionally, the men squabbled over a piece of clothing. Women in brightly colored saris stood several yards from the pile holding clothes retrieved by the men.

Sara had been told that India lived in several different centuries all at once. She thought the clothes market was an example of this. All the young men wore modern Western wear—slacks and short sleeved shirts, usually ill matched. They looked a part of the twenty-first century. All the women wore saris. Sara imagined their saris didn't look much different than those worn by Indian women in the nineteenth century or earlier. A few older men wore only a long white cloth wrapped around their loins, which she guessed had been traditional wear for rural men for thousands of years.

In a nearby food market women were the predominant shoppers. Sara was glad the bus didn't stop. The aroma emanating from the market wasn't pleasant, but the noise level wasn't as painful as it had been in the clothing market. She had noted similar odors in open markets of many tropical countries. The smell was an intermingled mix of rancid fats, the pungent aroma of spices, the sickening sweet scent of overripe fruit, and the odor of human sweat and urine.

The stench wasn't actually as bad as she had expected. One friend, an experienced nutritionist, had warned her years ago not to go to Mumbai and Kolkata, cities the British Raj had called Bombay and Calcutta, because the "miasma of death and decay in the back streets is so bad that you can never completely forget it, even years later." Sara respected the woman as a tough professional and had never accepted a public health assignment in India. Granted that was an extreme response on Sara's part.

Now Sara felt ashamed as she sat on the bus. She prided herself on seldom letting "unpleasantries" stop her from doing what needed to be done and thought most Americans missed many great opportunities because of their squeamish behavior. Yet, here she was behaving like a nervous, pampered tourist. This trip would not be relaxing—and certainly not romantic—if she couldn't overcome her negative attitudes about India. Any location, foreign or local, was as interesting as you allowed it to be. At the very least, Sara needed to be honest with Sanders.

Sanders nudged her. "Are you okay? You look pale."

Sara didn't think this was the time to start being more honest. "I'm tired from the flight. I'm sure if I was wandering through the stalls I'd be fascinated by the exotic items, but at this distance the blur is just an argument for birth control."

"It's obvious why spices were so important before refrigeration was common."

Sara squeezed his hand. He was really trying to be pleasant even though she was being grouchy.

The guide announced the bus would next transport them to Chandni Chowk in Old Delhi. This market dated back to the seventeenth century, when the Emperor Shah Jehan had switched the Mughal capital from Agra to Delhi. Sara wondered why this famous emperor had chosen Delhi as his capital but built the Taj Mahal, the mausoleum for his favorite wife, in Agra.

As they approached this shopping district, the traffic slowed, the streets narrowed, and the buildings became older. When they alit from the bus, Sara was amazed by the narrow sliver of sky above the streets. Second and third-floor screened balconies leaned somewhat precariously over the streets with a thick web of dark cables connecting the buildings. Sara didn't think she'd ever seen so many power lines intertwined with clothes lines and supports for signs. At the street level, hundreds of small shops displayed merchandise that ranged from cheap tourist items to expensive brilliantly colored silk saris and jewelry, which had the ostentatious look of 22-carat gold. Food vendors and Hindu shrines were interspersed among the shops.

The guide flagged down seven pedal rickshaws, not the motorized ones powered by propane, to carry the fourteen passengers on the bus. A scrawny, dark haired young man wearing a white, or at least what once was white, shirt and shorts shoved another driver aside and propelled Sara onto his rickshaw, even though she wasn't the first in line. She thought of the telephone threat and resisted long enough for Sanders to hop in. Then she gaped as the offended driver jabbed at her rickshaw driver. The other rickshaw drivers started to yell as they watched the two drivers spar. Finally, an older driver separated the two young men, and the rest of the passengers on the bus were loaded onto rickshaws.

Sara heard the rickshaw driver cursing as he pedaled down the street. She wondered what had triggered his aggressive behavior but decided it was unwise to ask. The driver made no attempt to talk to Sara or Sanders, but that wasn't surprising because navigating through the crowd looked like hard work. He was sweating profusely and appeared to be straining to pedal the vehicle. She felt guilty to be riding in a vehicle propelled by another human being. Thus, she paid little attention to details in the shops and was happy when she recognized they were returning to their starting point after looping around several blocks. Sanders must have felt the same way as he grasped her arm and guided her rapidly back on the bus.

The guide smiled weakly at them as they entered the bus. "Sometimes the rickshaw drivers are overly eager." He turned away quickly.

Sanders whispered, "For a moment. I thought you had been targeted and might be kidnapped but decided after watching the young man that he had no interest in you, other than you were lighter than the other women. He was probably high on methamphetamine."

Sara nodded. "I was so concerned about what he might do next that I really saw little of the shops. That's a shame. If he had ever stopped or even slowed, I would have suggested we walk back. We would have seen more."

He nuzzled her ear. "I was thinking the same thing."

The bus lurched forward as soon as the last passenger was seated. Sara watched the guide. His face was animated as he whispered into his phone and repeatedly shook his head. When the bus turned onto a broader street, the guide audibly sighed and announced, "Now we'll see one of the most important sites on the Yamuna River—Raj Ghat." It was obvious the guide was much prouder of this site than of the Chandni Chowk. He proceeded to explain how a memorial to Mahatma Gandhi had been created here at the site of his cremation.

J. L. Greger

One of the woman on the bus in the middle of the guide's summary of Gandhi's accomplishments asked whether she would see bodies being cremated today. The guide winced and said, "No, this is a memorial park."

Sara wanted to say, "This site deserves the respect we would accord to the Lincoln Memorial," but decided silence was best.

A man said, "I assume the Yamuna doesn't stink like the Ganges. Is the water safe to drink?"

The guide nodded at first but looked alarmed when the male tourist mentioned drinking the water. "The water of the Yamuna is of reasonably good quality here, but you should only drink bottled water in India. We keep a supply on the bus at all times."

Sara felt sorry for the guide. He obviously was trying to show the best side of India and didn't want to admit the truth. She'd read one Indian official had recently called the Yamuna River as it left Delhi a "sewage drain." Instead of embarrassing the guide, she whispered to Sanders, "Remember Gandhi's famous quotation—'Sanitation is more important than political independence.' Too bad the guide doesn't discuss real problems honestly."

Before Sanders could respond, another man raised his hand. "Will this be a quick stop before lunch?"

Sanders snickered, "I thought this group was supposed to be experienced travelers."

***

The quiet simplicity of the black marble platform and orderly crowds at Raj Ghat were a fitting memorial to Gandhi. Only the bright colored saris of the women reminded Sara that she was in India.

The next stop was Lazeez Affaire, a restaurant tucked in a quiet spot in the embassy area of New Delhi. It would be at home in any major U.S. city with its modern décor and buffet. Sara enjoyed its cool, quiet interior and bland Indian food.

Sanders sniffed as they left. "It's dumb to travel thousands of miles to eat Americanized Indian food."

Sara pretended to sleep as the bus returned them to their modern hotel far from the bustle of central Delhi. She and Sanders were out of sync, and she was too tired to pretend to be enthusiastic about India.

***

The next day was better. She'd only dreamed of Matt and Kayla once during the night. At least she only remembered one short dream of the two children walking with her and Bug in the bosque. They had been only around eight or nine in her dream. Kayla was chattering about nothing important and Matt was mainly talking about "doggies."

Thus, she was alert and listened as the guide spouted data on the British rule in India as the bus drove on the wide boulevards in New Delhi around palatial marble government buildings. His dialogue was carefully scripted to hide his emotions. He didn't seem offended that the government buildings built by the British in the 1920s looked as if they'd been transplanted from Britain with only a few Indian flourishes.

She looked at Sanders. He had a smile pasted on his face but his eyes were blank. Maybe she'd been wrong to encourage him to book this tour. She nudged him. "I hadn't realized how completely the British Raj tried to obliterate or at least ignore Indian culture. But our guide seems proud of these buildings."

"Mmm."

"Look at it this way. We're lucky air pollution is low today. We probably couldn't see much in another month."

"Mmm."

"And our next two stops this morning are designated as UNESCO World Heritage Sites. They're bound to be interesting." She rubbed her finger against his cheek. "I should have read more about India before our trip. I guess Paul Scott's novels in *The Raj Quartet* helped me understand only the last hundred years of Indian history. According to the guide's handout, the Qutb complex, which we're visiting, dates back a thousand years."

Sanders smiled. "But you're a fast learner. By the way, Carbonne's emailed me news. The threatening call you received was from a burner phone and originated in Colorado."

Sara gulped. "So, not from Lurleen's family and probably from someone associated with the drug gangs."

"Who doesn't want you to testify at the upcoming trials." He squeezed her hands. "We need to be on guard. Anything could happen in India. I guess I should have canceled this trip."

"Don't be silly. I'm a sitting duck no matter where I am until after the trials. Although I'd feel better if Carbonne checked on Jack Daniels. I know you and Ulysses Howe think I'm paranoid when it comes to Jack, but he'd make a threatening call to me just for fun. And the marshals have never been able to clip his wings, even though he's in their witness protection program."

"Mmm. Carbonne shares your paranoia. He noted that he already asked the U.S. marshals to check on Jack. I hope you two are right., but I think Jack's just a former dirty cop craving for attention and not a threat to anyone... but himself."

"I try not be vengeful but Jack is a blight on everyone around him, particularly women. He's a real bastard."

Sanders laughed. "That's your most animated comment since we arrived. Carbonne also had news about Lurleen's murder. Seems Pete Jansen was probably a witness—an unwitting one—to the killing."

"What?"

"He probably heard her final scream when he was lurking outside her house. It's a long story. You can read Carbonne's email, but the important point is that Pete knows at least two people were in the room with Lurleen."

"So, Matt didn't act alone. Makes sense. He's a follower and could be convinced to sit quietly while someone else acted."

"Pete knows Kayla was in the room. Cell tower transmissions support his story."

Sara felt tears drip down her face. "I always knew Mitzi shouldn't have adopted Kayla. So did Pete." She paused to think. "That's the one point that limits his testimony. He never liked Kayla. No, that's not exactly right, Pere knew Kayla was a problem, but he *adored* Matt."

He nodded. "I'll email Carbonne about your reservations, but I think he's guessed the family dynamics. He wants you to think about Kayla. Are there any questions he could ask her or stories about her past that might trigger honest responses? It's a long shot, but he and Pete think she's hiding something."

"Poor dear. She's hard to like—well for anyone except Mitzi—but Kayla's a child. She's street smart but confused. That's understandable considering the long rough adoption process and her abusive birth parents." More tears rolled down Sara's face. "Maybe that's what Carbonne needs to know. Kayla fights constantly with Mitzi, but Mitzi is the one constant in Kayla's life. Mmm. Although Mitzi's mood swings make her a pretty shaky constant." She wiped the tears away. "Maybe I should respond to Carbonne?"

"I'm sure he'd welcome your thoughts. He only sent the message to me because he knows I check emails and phone message every couple of hours. As he says at the start of the email, 'Sara never responds to phone messages and checks emails only once a day.' You know it's true."

Sara shrugged. "I'm a retired academic, not a spymaster."

Sanders groaned and handed his smartphone to her.

After several minutes of typing, she handed the phone back to him and looked out the window as the bus pulled to a stop. Clumps of children were everywhere. They were in groups of fifty to two hundred. Each clump was clothed identically. The boys' black hair was uniformly cut short, and they wore dark slacks and light colored shirts. The girls' hair was uniformly long; most wore their hair in braids or ponytails. Many of the girls' uniforms reflected Western styles with a pleated plaid skirt, knee socks, and matching blouse. However, the uniforms for several groups reflected Indian styles. One group of several hundred girls wore leggings with long jumpers almost to their knees in shades of green. Another large group of girls wore baggy gray slacks with blue tunics. The cutest uniforms were an attempt to duplicate saris but with no draping. The tunic had a V-shaped, long, pink scarf around the girls' necks.

The guide announced, "Schools arrange field trips for the children during the week of Diwali. They may slow our tour of the Qutb complex." He then mumbled a brief explanation of the site, told them to be back at the bus in an hour, and shepherded the fourteen tourists off the bus.

Sanders was one of the first outside and began to hike rapidly toward the complex. Sara couldn't decide whether his eagerness reflected his enthusiasm to see Qutb after the guide's confusing explanation of it, his chance to get away from her, or a way to beat the children to the site.

Sara rushed to catch up with him. As she passed one group of girls dressed in pink tunics and black pants, several of the girls shyly said "hi" or "hello." Sara, without considering the potential consequences, smiled and replied, "Hello." Almost immediately, the girls surrounded her. Many of them extended their hands toward her. Others took pictures with their phones.

The guide rushed toward Sara shooing the children away. He muttered something about her blonde hair and pushed Sara toward Sanders who was shaking his head. "I should have realized you would attract the children's attention." He motioned toward the other travelers from the bus. "You'll note none of them smiled at or spoke to the children."

Sara shrugged. "They're so cute in their uniforms. The only danger they present is I could have been trampled, but they're much more orderly than American kids would be."

Sanders clamped his hand on her elbow and rapidly led her forward. "Hundreds of Indians are killed annually when crowds panic and trample others as they flee areas with limited exits." He chuckled. "But your friendliness is what makes you a delightful travel partner. I see a different aspect of the people than when I'm alone."

They passed through an arched entrance and moved off the main path to view the site. A tall minaret in varying shades of red sandstone and either yellow sandstone or yellowed marble stood in the middle of a courtyard surrounded by yellow sandstone, flat-roofed structures with occasional domes and arches.

Sara walked closer to the columns on the façade of one structure while Sanders snapped photos. "I understand the guide's comments now. This was the site of several Hindu temples when the Mughals swept in from what is now Afghanistan and conquered the area almost a thousand years ago. The Mughals used the carved columns and lintels from Hindu and Jain temples to create a mosque. Sort of like how the Moslems in Spain converted many churches to mosques. Only in Spain, Christians converted the mosques back to churches when the Moslems were expelled in the early 1500s. Here the site remained a mosque and contained several tombs of Mughal leaders."

Sanders pointed to one section of carving between two pillars. "Most of the old carvings are garlands of lotus and bells, but that section is a depiction of a sex scene in the *Kama Sutra*. The Mughals, as proper Moslems, applied plaster over this particular scene, but the plaster has chipped away."

"Oh, that was what the guide meant when he said, 'Look for the infamous sex scene.' Interesting."

"The guide is good if you can hear him and already know a bit about the topic before he begins."

Sara laughed and grabbed Sanders's hand as she climbed up several stone steps. "That means you're the only one on the bus who is benefiting much from his talks. Although I heard enough to know this pillar is called Qutb Minar and marked the Mughals conquest of the last Hindu ruler in the Delhi area." Sara studied the ribbed minar. "Can't say I'd describe it as pretty. It obviously was built in stages. The red and yellow stone blocks vary with the different stories and not in a planned manner. Besides the color variation, some of the blocks have Arabic calligraphy and others have vines with leaves and flowers that look more like Hindu carvings. Since it's a minaret, I assume there are stairs inside so that someone can get to the top to announce prayers five times a day."

"The someone is a muezzin."

Sara lowered her voice. "With its domed top, the minar looks like a giant phallic symbol that has seen a lot of wear and tear."

"Shhh. The mosque is an active place of worship. And you wouldn't look so great either if your first story was completed in 1199 A.D." Sanders put his arm over her shoulder and they walked in tandem around the site.

***

The next bus stop was at Humayun's tomb. At least thirty groups of noisy school children dressed in colorful uniforms mobbed the parking lot. Sara noticed when groups—each with more than a hundred children—reached the gateways in the rubble enclosure to the garden, they were organized with the youngest children in front. Sara smiled but didn't speak to any of the children as she and Saunders negotiated a path around the crowd. He stopped and stepped off the path when they had a good view of the red sandstone tomb topped with a marble double arch dome.

Sara spoke first, "It doesn't take a degree in art history to realize this structure was a prototype for the Taj Mahal. The dome looks the same, to me. Only here the building is red sandstone and not white marble."

Sanders squeezed her arm. "In some ways this structure is more amazing because it was a new concept in India when it was built in the mid 1500s. The Taj Mahal was built eighty years later and refined the concept." He stepped away from her. "I want to get a shot of you here. Because this is when you finally got into the swing of India."

Sara winced as she recognized the truth of Sander's observation. This was the first time she felt the joy of seeing something unique… important… beautiful in India. "You were right. The guide is worth listening to despite his singsong English. It's interesting that the Emperor Humayun's favorite wife commissioned this monument and hired a Persian architect to design her dead husband's tomb. Guess that means the Mughals allowed women, at least wives of emperors, to be independently wealthy and not dependent on male family members."

They sauntered through the gardens and looked at smaller adjacent tombs, including the so-called "the Barber's tomb." Sanders noted that he'd read it was debatable whether the popular lore for this structure was correct. He also noted this complex had not been kept up and had deteriorated badly under the British Raj. The gardens had been used to cultivate tobacco and cabbages. Serious restoration had occurred after the tomb and its surroundings were named a UNESCO World Heritage Site in 1993.

Sara always appreciated Sanders's knowledge of history and art, but then he majored in history while a student at Princeton. But his knowledge of this site suggested he had prepped intensely for this trip. Then again, he was interested in—and knowledgeable—about so many topics. Suddenly, she remembered something important. "I think I have several pieces of info about Kayla that will help Carbonne and Chuy. Funny how I always think of details like these when I relax.

CHAPTER 19: FBI Agent Carbonne on Day 5

Carbonne smiled as he read Sara's most recent email sprinkled with potentially useful clues. She must be finally enjoying India and had relaxed. Sanders had written their first two days in India were "dreadful."

Carbonne had learned while working other cases with Sara that she was slow in remembering details if she was rattled, and Lurleen and her family had agitated Sara more than the threats of major drug lords. He guessed the problem was more than simple nervousness. Sara felt guilty because she'd ignored Lurleen's problems for years.

Sara's email was long. First off, Sara noted that Kayla had boyfriends—or at least Lurleen thought so—because she had gotten birth control pills for Kayla:

> On the trip to Chimayó, Lurleen complained that one of Kayla's boyfriends was a college student and lived near Lurleen. That boyfriend could have helped Kayla kill Lurleen. It would take more strength than I suspect Kayla has to tie up an almost three hundred-pound woman like Lurleen.

Sara's second point was about Matt's alleged serial killing of pets. She reiterated that Matt liked "doggies" and treated Bug gently. He groaned internally. Anyone, even Matt, would have realized Sara would be an avenging demon if anyone hurt Bug.

Then Sara had added more interesting comments—ones she hadn't mentioned previously. Nothing odd about that and typical of Sara. This trait was not a problem for a consultant but made her look suspicious as a suspect if Carbonne hadn't been sure she was innocent of killing Lurleen.

Sara noted Kayla had seemed ambivalent about dogs, including Bug. She'd assumed this reflected Kayla's limited exposure to pets. However, a comment by Lurleen made her suspicious:

> Lurleen asked an odd question on the trip to Chimayó, "Can you outgrow allergies to dogs and cats?" Mitzi had always claimed she got a rash when around cats and dogs after only a few minutes of exposure, but Lurleen said, "Mitzi didn't get a rash after she slept for several hours in my guest bedroom, even

though I housed a neighbor's golden retriever in the room for two days while the neighbor was in the hospital."

Sara noted recent studies have suggested children may outgrow food allergies, but she doubted that adults outgrew allergies to pets. Accordingly, she postulated that Mitzi might not be allergic to pets and only said it because she disliked them—or knew Kayla did.

Sara's fourth point bothered Carbonne, especially after he found the article in *Science* that she mentioned:

I brought along a lot of old issues of the journal Science *to read on the plane and then pitch. That way I have room for souvenirs. I know that's old fashioned, but the system works for me.*

In any case, one of the recent feature articles was intriguing. Researchers have found witnesses will sometimes falsely admit to crimes if they are pressured with accusatory questioning or if the interrogator lowers the emotional barrier to confessing. I suspect Matt as an insecure young boy might be more susceptible to suggestions than most. Perhaps Kayla, Mitzi, and/or Lurleen accused him of killing animals so often that he believed their accusations. Those animals could have been killed by another neighborhood child or teen. Remember that one of Kayla's alleged boyfriends was a neighbor.

Sara's fourth point morphed into her fifth point:

Chuy said Mitzi spent hours whispering into Matt's ear in the intensive care unit. Is it possible that Mitzi was trying to protect Kayla by getting Matt to confess to Lurleen's murder?

Sara's sixth point was the most interesting:

During our trip to Chimayó, Lurleen mentioned writing a note about her family's situation and putting it in her secret hiding spot. She talked about such a spot at least once before she moved to her current house, so it's likely part of a movable piece of furniture.

Sara's seventh point was succinct:

Did Jack Daniels admit to making the prank call to me?

Carbonne didn't want to answer that question. Jack had denied making any calls to Sara. That didn't mean much to Carbonne because Jack was an expert liar. However, the call had originated near a tower in Florence, Colorado, the site of the high security federal prison housing gang leaders awaiting trial. Jack was in Texas.

***

Carbonne reached Chuy as he was driving to meet the social worker at the CYFD who had delayed Mitzi's adoption of the children. "She was evasive when I interviewed her on the phone but hinted she might leave the file on her desk while she went out for coffee." After a few seconds, Chuy added, "Bet the file has an important clue, and I want it before the court-appointed psychologist talks to Kayla this afternoon."

"No problem. I'll fill you in on details as you drive."

As Chuy pulled into the CYFD parking lot after a long conversation with Carbonne, they agreed on two major points. Mercado police officers needed to interview any men—between the ages of sixteen and twenty-four—living in Lurleen's and Mitzi's neighborhoods. Carbonne would try to find Lurleen's secret hiding spot.

Chuy snickered. "You're not starting from scratch. Didn't you say the FBI technicians had searched and inventoried the contents of sixty boxes? Perhaps Pete can guess Lurleen's secret hiding place?"

Carbonne groaned. "Pete stopped knowing Lurleen's secrets more than twenty years ago, but I guess I have to talk to him again. I hate to. He's an argument for never marrying. As stupid as it sounds, he loved Lurleen."

Chuy groaned. "Know what you mean, but Gil told me to do nothing to dissuade Pete of his illusion. He said the poor guy was going to lose most of his family before this was over. He deserved a few good memories, even if they were false ones."

"Looks like he'll lose the two adopted grandchildren, but he'll have his daughter. Granted, she's not very pleasant company from what I've seen."

"That's what I thought, but Gil said 'don't bet on it.' He thought Mitzi might talk to a grief counselor if they weren't a psychologist. We don't have one on the Mercado payroll. Can you help?"

"Sure, but I doubt Mitzi is grieving. Anger and relief are the only emotions that I've seen her express."

"You didn't see her with the boy in the intensive care unit. She was earnest in her desire to help him."

Carbonne added, "Or to help Kayla."

CHAPTER 20: Sara in Jaipur on Day 7

Sara explored the hotel and grounds for more than an hour before breakfast because both she and Sanders needed private time. Her stroll was fun because the hotel was a beehive of activity. The buzz of electric clippers and mowers filled the air as staff manicured the grounds one more time for the Diwali celebrations. In the lobby, artists squatted on the marble floor and composed a large "painting" using dyed rice, sand, flower petals, and leaves to create a colorful mat of medallions and paisley patterns. She broke her personal rule never to take photos and snapped several of the artists at work. She had long ago learned her shots of standard tourist sites were a waste of time. Better pictures were available in tourist books and on the Web.

When she entered the dining room, the aromas of the large buffet were less than appetizing. She thought several foods smelled of rancid fats. Then again it could be the normal odor of water buffalo milk. The Indians proudly substituted water buffalo milk for cow's milk in custards, ice cream, yogurt, and cheese. She thought the products had an "off-taste" and dabbed only tablespoon-servings of various dishes on her plate. However, the naan, the traditional Indian bread, smelled good, and she thought it would soothe her stomach. She selected two large pieces of naan and joined Sanders at a secluded table for two.

He frowned as he looked at her near empty plate. "The food this morning was better than what they served for breakfast in New Delhi." When Sara didn't respond, he said, "You finished your correspondence this morning before I'd gotten through my first email. Anything interesting?"

"The pet spa said Bug was fine. Pete Jansen is miserable. His daughter and son have threatened to not attend Lurleen's funeral." She looked at Sanders's almost empty plate. "You said you needed an hour to get through your essential correspondence. You must have gotten through your mail faster than you expected, or I'm late."

He smiled. "I decided most of my emails didn't need answers."

As he talked about the latest problems in his office, Sara swallowed two pink tablets from a pillbox in her purse. She hoped they'd soothe the rumblings and gassy feeling in her gut. Now she realized that Sanders was staring at her. He expected an answer, but she didn't know to what. She didn't want to be a typical tourist and complain about her gut health. "I'm sorry I'm in a daze this morning. I was thinking about the City Palace we saw yesterday in Jaipur. The rooms in the City Palace were a psychedelic dream with intricate patterns on everything—ceilings, columns, walls, floors, and cushions. All the complexity was increased by the tiny mirrors embedded in most surfaces."

"The combination of Rajasthani and Mughal art was more flamboyant than what we saw in Delhi, but the City Palace was also built in the 1730s. That's almost two hundred years later than the construction of Humayun's tomb in Delhi. I think the most interesting architecture in Jaipur was the honeycombed, five-story back wall of the Hawa Mahal palace with its almost one thousand windows."

"Hmm." Unlike Sanders, Sara had made no attempt to remember the proper names of the structures, just the anglicized name. "I thought the Palace of the Winds was sort of sad. The windows were the only way the women in the harem could view street scenes. Actually, I would imagine everyone in the court felt like birds in a gilded cage. Wonder whether the current maharaja and his family, who live in sections of the palace, feel that way, too?"

"No more than the British royalty living in Buckingham Palace or the president's family in the White House. Fame and vast wealth are overrated."

Sara leaned over and hugged him. Comments like that reminded her why she enjoyed his company. He was an intellectual snob but he was basically a sensible, good man. "I guess I thought the most interesting garish items on display were the two huge sterling silver water vessels."

Sanders blinked. "Why? I didn't think you were into Guinness World Records. Granted they each could hold four thousand liters of water. What is that? More than four tons each?"

Sara laughed. "Remember, I'm a scientist. I was fascinated that the maharaja would only drink water from the Ganges. Thus, he had those containers made so he could transport all the water he needed when he traveled to England for the British coronation in 1901."

"So, while I assumed he was acting on his Hindu beliefs..."

"I thought he was wise. He knew that typhoid fever, tuberculosis, cholera and other diarrheal diseases were rampant in London then. Remember London at the beginning of the twentieth century had horrible public sanitation systems and horses were still used for transportation. But I can't imagine the Ganges was clean even then. Of course, he, just like modern tourists, had probably noticed tourists and recent immigrants often get diarrhea from eating and drinking foods and beverages that have no adverse effects on local residents."

"Do you know why?"

"No, many scientists think people who are repeatedly exposed to low or moderate levels of certain pathogens develop immunity to them. I don't know of any definitive studies."

"Speaking of upset guts. How's yours?"

Sara flushed. "Why?"

He winked. "When you turn green at the sight of food and eat only bread at a buffet, I know you don't feel well."

"All's quiet but tense on that front. Sorta like how I feel about Carbonne's unwillingness to comment on who made the threatening call before we left. If it was Jack Daniels, he would have told me. The threat was real."

"That worried me, too, but Carbonne's email to me indicated he expected to get answers at Lurleen's funeral." Sanders shook his head. "Hard to believe." He thumbed through the *Hindustan Times*. "Since you're through eating, I can show you this."

Sara winced at the photos. "Ugh. Yes—I saw them in yesterday's paper and thought they were unflattering police mug shots. Then I realized the they were instead photographs of the faces of unidentified dead people that the police found on the streets of Delhi. Evidently, it's a daily feature in the paper."

Sanders continued to thumb through another section of the paper. "Creative, but I don't think Americans would accept photos like those in their daily newspapers next to colorful ads." He handed her a special magazine section. "Look at this. It would fit into any American Sunday paper with profiles of movie stars, makeup tips, recipes, and feature articles on the Diwali holiday."

"Yeah, but it's hard for me to see the appeal of some of these items in a country with so much poverty. The ads for jewelry are over the top. Many of the earrings and necklaces make the heavy Navajo squash blossom necklaces in silver and turquoise look dainty. There's something distasteful about 22-karat gold jewelry with dozens of gems in three or more colors. Who could afford them? And where could you wear them?"

"And that's the charm of India—the flamboyant contrasts."

Sara stroked Sanders's hand. "Speaking of flamboyant displays, I bet Lurleen's funeral will have a couple of them."

CHAPTER 21: Sergeant Chuy Bargas Works a Puzzle

Chuy liked being a police officer because he found working cases to be like solving puzzles. In fewer than three days, however, he'd discovered he didn't enjoy much about being an acting police chief. The details were overwhelming and mundane. He figured with time he'd learn to sort through them rapidly. However, he didn't think he'd ever learn how to deal with all the squabbles among the staff and the jurisdictional battles with other agencies. Today the petty arguments between police and fire crews in Mercado had intensified. He suspected the fire chief wouldn't have argued with Gil but thought a newbie like Chuy would be an easy target. *But*, acting as police chief did raise his salary.

Chuy had accepted the acting chief title three days ago when Gil Andrews decided his wife Jen needed more attention. She'd begun her second round of chemotherapy and had tolerated the first dose relatively well. After two days of bed rest, she'd been able to go grocery shopping with Gil. On the phone yesterday, Gil had admitted he'd forgotten how much fun it was to play rummy with his wife and not have to go to work. He hinted if she survived he might retire after his leave of absence. Chuy guessed Gil would return to work if Jen didn't survive, and that would end any chance for Chuy to advance during the foreseeable future.

Despite his leave of absence, Gill called every day. Yesterday he hadn't asked about the investigation of Lurleen Jansen's murder, but he *had* asked about Sara. Actually, Gil hadn't asked a question. He said, "I was thinking about the warning—the one Sara received on the phone. I think the threat was an attempt to lure Sara back to her home where local drug gangs could attack her." Carbonne had thought the same and had been relieved when Sara departed.

Gil had then offered advice. "You could set a trap for any potential attackers with Carbonne's help. I assume Sara put her lights on timers, but they won't fool any professional hit man. If you change the timers and find excuses to have officers and agents enter the house a couple of times a day, you might convince a hit man that Sara is in the house. Let Ulysses Howe and Carbonne do the rest. I suspect the federal attorneys will be game to cover the bill because they don't want Sara killed before the big trial of drug cartel members."

Chuy had almost choked, but he quickly thought of a logical response. "I... I think neither Carbonne nor I can handle more work. The investigation of Lurleen Jansen's murder is harder than we expected. We've probably got enough with Pete Jansen's testimony to convict Kayla of first-degree murder. Since she's a child, that's enough to put her in a juvenile facility until she's twenty-one. But even the court-appointed psychologist could not pry the identity of her co-conspirator from Kayla during an interview that lasted hours. Although she did claim that older boys in her neighborhood had forced her to have sex with them. The psychologist is not apt to talk to Kayla again because Mitzi has tied up him, Dr. Piaget, and me with legal challenges on procedural details."

"I thought Mitzi had no source of funds but the family trust. If Pete threatened to cut her off, she might not be able to afford all the legal challenges." He laughed and hung up.

Chuy knew he should have asked for Gil's advice on how to handle Kayla's rape claims, but he needed to establish his authority. *His* staff—gee, that sounded good—had identified two students at the University of New Mexico who lived with their parents near Lurleen and Mitzi. Chuy had interviewed them, while his staff had re-interviewed Lurleen's closest neighbors yesterday. No one admitted seeing anything odd in Lurleen's backyard over the last few months or hearing anything on the night she was killed. Both young men had alibis for the night of the murder.

However, the alibi of Josh Ahrens, a nineteen-year-old who lived three houses down from Lurleen, was weak. He denied knowing Kayla or any member of the Jansen family until Chuy pointed out his mother had already said Josh knew both of Lurleen's grandchildren. Josh replied, "Oh yeah, I take those two kids occasionally to the local Dairy Queen. They spend a lot of time with their grandmother, especially in the evening, and they get bored."

When Chuy had asked him if he was home the night Lurleen had been killed, Josh quickly responded that from eight to midnight he'd been at a study section for a physics test at the University of New Mexico. Then he slept in a dorm on campus because the test was at eight that morning. Two of Josh's friends confirmed he had come back to their dorm with them around midnight. Josh had bedded down in the floor lounge while his friends slept in their own rooms.

J. L. Greger

Chuy had thought that Josh could have slipped out of the dorm, helped Kayla kill Lurleen, and then driven back to campus to take the physics test. Thus, he asked Josh to come to the Mercado police station for a second interview.

***

Josh, his parents, and a lawyer showed up early at Chuy's office. During the interview, Josh claimed one reason he'd chosen to major in engineering rather than medicine was he'd almost vomited in a biology class when he was required to dissect a frog. Josh seemed embarrassed enough that Chuy believed the story to be true. Chuy couldn't imagine Josh stabbing Lurleen in the face repeatedly or even watching the scene.

At the end of the interview, Chuy said, "Josh, you and your parents may not know anything about the murder, but the funeral—I guess really a viewing—this afternoon may help the three of you to remember something useful about Kayla and Matt. We don't want a killer to remain free and be a threat to neighbors."

Mrs. Ahrens had quickly said, "We'll be there," but Josh, his father, and their attorney had seemed hesitant. Chuy hoped Josh was not worried that Kayla would identify him as a sexual partner. Neither he nor the Sandoval County district attorney wanted to spend time on a statutory rape case. They were "time sinks" and seldom yielded convictions.

CHAPTER 22: Sara Sheds her Indifference to India Like a Snake

Sara choked as she looked at the remaining two bags. One was maroon; one was purple. The other women had rushed to the front of the bus to select a sari when the guide announced at the end of their trip to the Amber Fort near Jaipur that the women would be given saris to wear to tonight's Diwali party. Sara hated costume parties, and she considered the sari to be a costume. Besides she looked better in pastels, but other women had snatched up the pink and yellow saris. She wanted to wear her black palazzo pants with a pink silk top to the Diwali party, but even Sanders seemed enthusiastic about the saris.

The "fun" continued two hours later when the eight women in the tour group met in one woman's hotel room to don their saris. It almost seemed like the assemblage of bridesmaids before a wedding. There was a lot of flutter and false compliments. Sara thought that bargain-basement, taffeta bridesmaid dresses on young women were much prettier than cheap saris on middle-aged Caucasian women.

There were printed instructions on how to wear a sari along with a matching slip, blouse, and a six-yard strip of fabric printed with gold embellishments in each bag. Sara followed the instructions and gathered a yard of fabric about her waist and tucked the pleated fabric into the elastic at the waist of the slip. However, when she tried to bring the rest of the fabric around her back and over her shoulder, the pleats loosened and the fabric drooped. She repeated the process several times. Finally, the other women helped her, but the sari looked sloppy and felt precarious even after it was pinned firmly to her slip. She'd placed a maroon bindi on her forehead. The so-called "Hindu third eye" didn't look exotic. It looked like an acne outbreak. Sara removed the bindi immediately.

Sanders gasped as she stumbled into the lobby.

"Don't say it—I know I look terrible in a sari."

Sanders was slow to respond. "Let's just say it doesn't fit your athletic style. You move too quickly." After a quick glance at the other women, he whispered, "The sari does show off your slender midriff."

Sara grabbed his arm. "You get an A for effort."

The Diwali party reminded Sara of a number of university receptions she'd attended over the years. Those events were always pretentious and boring. The guide had told them they were going to a Diwali celebration at the home of a Rajasthani family from the soldier caste. Sanders and Sara quickly decided that the home, if it ever was a home, was now a small boutique hotel. The courtyard for the party was surrounded by a modern-looking brick building.

The host certainly had the perfect posture of a soldier and wore a navy Nehru jacket with lots of braid and a turban. A pink scarf wafted down from the top of his turban. Sara guessed the scarf was a holiday addition. Sara noticed immediately that the hostess wasn't wearing a sari. She wore a long, flared pink skirt with a matching pink scarf draped over her black hair. That ensemble was definitely more attractive than a sari. Sara whispered to Sanders, "Now I really do feel like a bridesmaid. The hostess selected a beautiful dress for herself, and we got these ill-fitting saris."

He pushed her away from the others. "Don't be silly. She didn't select your sari. If you act confident, everyone will assume you chose to wear your sari in a sexy manner."

Sara knew Sanders was partially right, but no one would think she looked sexy in this sari.

They moved toward a crowd in one corner. One of the women at the back of the group explained it was a Hindu prayer ceremony. A guru, Sara guessed that was an appropriate name, was burning sugarcane, crushing it, and putting a smudge of the paste on people's foreheads. The smudge was supposed to bring good luck.

Sanders and Sara decided to skip the blessing and wandered to the food table, which had only cold samosas and salads. Sara thought they looked like a tasty way to get food poisoning. Sanders tasted several dishes, but Sara only sipped bottled seltzer water as fireworks exploded over their heads.

Sara suddenly realized why she always went to university receptions alone. She was ready to leave but couldn't because Sanders was looking around the courtyard, expecting the party to improve. Parties at embassies must have been better than parties at universities, which always presented their best food and entertainment in the first hour.

Sanders pushed her toward a far corner of the courtyard where a man in a turban was playing what looked like the Indian equivalent of an accordion, but it sounded like a bagpipe. Another man moaned a song. It was interesting but not terribly pleasant.

Then two tiny girls danced onto the stage. It was hard to believe they were more than twelve. They were several inches shorter than five feet, thin as reeds, and properly covered with long navy and white jackets, red flared skirts, navy veils, and red leggings. Their dance, which included lots of spins, was sedate until the lead dancer strode on stage. She was not a little girl, not prim and proper, and not scrawny. A maroon chiffon scarf cascaded with her long, black hair over her shoulders. It emphasized her low, scooped neckline outlined in gold. Her leggings and flared skirt were bright bands of color interspersed with maroon and black. She looked like a gypsy dancer in a movie but most of her skin was covered.

Then she began her dance. It was a captivating blend of undulating arm movements and graceful slides and spins. As the tempo of the drums increased, the two girls began to spin faster and faster. Their skirts flared out. The lead dancer began to pulsate with the music. Women in the crowd tried to dance with the music too. Their movements quickly degenerated into bump and grind routines. The lead dancer dropped to the floor and slithered with her outspread arms pulsating. Then she rose again. Her movements were mesmerizing and never deteriorated into the burlesque routine of the guests.

Sanders put his right arm over Sara's shoulders. It felt good. When the dance ended, he swallowed hard and said, "I think this snake dance was more erotic than the one Debra Paget tried to create in the movie *The Indian Tomb*."

Sara had not seen the movie nor ever heard of the snake dance. "What is this dance supposed to evoke… besides the obvious?"

"Believe it or not. The snake in Indian folklore is a protective deity. It represents rebirth due to its casting of its skin and being symbolically reborn."

She snickered. "I suspect it makes most people think about slithering between the sheets."

He tightened his grip on her shoulder. "Time to go home for our own action."

Sara agreed. Evidently so did the guide, as he herded the small tour group to the bus.

While Sara and Sanders held hands on the bus, a series of questions flashed through her mind. Maybe the threatening phone message was an attempt to get her to remain in her home and be an assessible target before the trial? Maybe this trip was saving her life. Maybe she thought of this new view point because she was enjoying this trip to India? She had finally shed her skin of indifference to India and Sanders.

Then a memory flashed in front of her almost like a snake emerging from its old skin. Once Lurleen had said something like, "My secret hiding spot is sometimes wet." No, she said, "I can't let my old hiding spot be used to wash Bug." No, that wasn't quite right either. Sara concentrated and remembered the scene. One time before Mitzi had completed the adoption process, Matt had wanted to baptize Bug in one of the many baptismal fonts that Lurleen kept around her house. When he chose one, Lurleen had muttered under her breath. "I can't let my secret spot get wet." She had pushed him to another font. The scene of Matt baptizing Bug had been hilarious. Lurleen had even snapped a photo and given Sara a copy. Where was that photo? And which font had Lurleen not wanted used?

She snuggled close to Sanders. She bet she'd remember more details soon. Funny how often she solved professional and personal problems easily once she really relaxed.

CHAPTER 23: FBI Agent Carbonne Gets a New View

Everything was ready. Lurleen lay in a walnut casket with a large spray of red roses from Pete on the lower closed part of the casket. A large bouquet of yellow and white gladiolas and chrysanthemums from her son Bill and his family had been placed near her head. Two smaller bouquets stood at the foot of the casket. One was of these was nondescript purple and lavender flowers from Sara. The other was white chrysanthemums with spikes of dyed blue daisies sent by a group of the neighbors. Lurleen wore a red blouse and beige slacks because Pete had been unable to find any dresses in Lurleen's overstuffed closets.

Carbonne didn't consider himself an expert, but he thought the red blouse was a poor choice. It seemed to emphasize all the scars on her face, but perhaps that was Pete's intent. He studied the scene carefully to be sure none of the cameras or microphones hidden among the flowers or in the beige folds of fabric lining the casket were easily visible.

Carbonne left the room when Pete arrived early for the viewing. Pete seemed to want some time alone with Lurleen. Besides, it gave Carbonne a chance to review the feed from the cameras and microphones in the salon. As he sat in a side room with all the monitors, he checked for messages. Sara had sent an email.

He was about to open it when he heard Pete. "Honey, I know I disappointed you a lot, but I loved you. We couldn't go on." Pete dragged on confessing his mistakes.

Carbonne was tempted to erase the footage of Pete with Lurleen because it seemed so intimate. However, Carbonne was bothered by Pete's comment—"We couldn't go on." Carbonne wondered if that was an excuse for more than Pete's request for a divorce, but decided he was being silly and scanned the multiple camera shots of the viewing room.

Chuy had posted a uniformed Mercado police officer at the door of the room. She and the mortuary owner were prepared to prevent anyone from entering the viewing room until Pete and Carbonne were ready. Chuy had chosen the officer well. Her uncle had been an employee in a mortuary and the woman sat comfortably at the door to the viewing salon. On the other hand, the mortuary owner fit the stereotype of a mortician. He was a nervous, immaculately groomed man. He kept complaining. "This is highly irregular. I don't think this program fits national mortuary standards. I wish I could have selected the lady's clothes."

The woman police officer stoically responded to the mortician's complaints with "umms" and occasionally interjected, "It's what her husband wanted."

Finally, Pete finished his confession to Lurleen and nodded to the mortician to admit Bill. Pete had insisted Bill be admitted alone first because he believed Bill knew details that might be useful in eliciting comments from others.

Carbonne monitored the cameras as Pete led Bill to the casket. To say the son was horrified by his mother's wounds was an understatement. He turned white and muttered something. Pete guided Bill to the chairs in the back of room. Carbonne could hear Pete's comments through a microphone hidden there.

"Son, I think you're trying to protect someone. Don't, or he or she may later come after you, your wife, and daughter. Anyone you suspect—Mitzi, Kayla, Matt, or a neighbor—needs help now."

Bill's comments like those at the casket were muffled, but Carbonne thought technicians could amplify them enough later to be useful. He doubted Bill had named anyone because Pete had only responded by hugging his son and then shaking his head.

Pete nodded for the mortician to admit all his neighbors together with Chuy. They were Josh Ahrens and his parents, two other couples, and two older women. Pete was standing in front of the casket and announced, "Please, help me. Did you hear any noises from my house on the night of my wife was murdered? Did you see anyone enter the house or in the yard? Think hard. Did you ever see anyone ever in my backyard at night with a shovel?" Then he stepped aside so they could see Lurleen.

There was silence followed by coughs, sighs, and groans. Carbonne could see most of the neighbors looked shocked. Only two came closer to the coffin. The rest looked around the room, everywhere but at the casket, and sank in chairs at the back of the room near Bill. No one spoke to Bill or seemed to recognize him.

Pete said, "Lurleen is at peace now, but you won't be if you don't help the police identify her murderers. The police officers at the back of the room would be glad to listen to any of your observations. If you want more privacy, here's how to contact Sergeant Chuy Bargas of the Mercado police." He handed out Chuy's card and shook each of his neighbors' hands.

Carbonne thought the operation was a bust. The neighbors sat only a couple of minutes before they charged for the door with their heads down. Most looked like they were race horses approaching the finish line. The only positive thing about the viewing was Pete demonstrated he had guts. His steely determination to do "one last thing" for Lurleen was impressive, but Carbonne doubted Pete could maintain his stoic appearance much longer.

As was prearranged, two police officers and Dr. Piaget led Matt into the room. Matt waved shyly at Pete who stood in front of the casket. Pete stepped aside and helped Matt climb two steps so he could better view Lurleen.

Matt touched her face. "Owies." He studied her. "Grandma Lu not screaming anymore." He put his hands on his ears.

Dr. Piaget sighed. Pete shook, bit his lip, and hugged Matt. Carbonne realized the two men had come to the same conclusion he had. Matt had been present when Lurleen was tortured and killed. He'd heard her screams. Of course, he could have been present but not participating in the torture. Carbonne guessed a juvenile court judge would find this evidence less than convincing, but it probably ensured years of psychological counseling, perhaps in a facility, for Matt.

The police whisked Matt away.

Dr. Piaget asked Pete if he was sure he was ready for the next scene. Pete nodded yes.

Kayla was led in by two police officers. Kayla took only one quick look at Lurleen, said nothing, and chose a spot in the front row of chairs before the casket. When Pete sat down by Kayla and kissed her, she didn't cry, but he did.

Pete wiped his tears away, "Kayla, I know you weren't alone with Lurleen when she died. Who else was there? I don't think you were responsible."

Carbonne thought Pete knew Kayla was capable of almost anything. Carbonne certainly did. But Dr. Piaget had cautioned Pete to be non-judgmental, and Pete lied well. His tone was even, and he spoke at a measured pace showing empathy and no annoyance.

Carbonne could see why Pete had been a successful executive in the petrochemical industry. He took advice well and knew how to control his emotions. An unpleasant thought flashed through his mind. Had Pete outsmarted him? Could he have killed Lurleen and made up a story, knowing his daughter and her family were the perfect patsies? Carbonne couldn't think about that now. He needed to concentrate on the scene in the mortuary salon.

Kayla bit her lip. "It's too late."

Pete put his arms around Kayla. "It's never too late."

Kayla hiccupped repeatedly. Carbonne thought Pete might have cracked her shell, and she was ready to talk.

The mortuary owner's high tenor voice could be heard. "Please wait, ma'am." The door to the room slammed open. Mitzi rushed up to Kayla and jerked her out of her chair. She turned to Pete. "You had no right."

Pete stood. "I asked you to come to your mother's funeral and you refused. Kayla and Matt both agreed to come because they wanted to say goodbye to their grandmother. Although they have not been charged with your mother's murder, as you well know, a juvenile court decided they should be held for psychological evaluation and not returned to your custody. Dr. Piaget and a court-appointed psychologist approved this visit."

Mitzi must have loosened her hold on Kayla because Kayla ran up to the casket. First, she rubbed two of the wounds around Lurleen's mouth. Carbonne noted they were the two shallowest wounds. Then she pulled two roses from the spray Pete had placed on the casket. The camera showed tears in her eyes as she lingered staring at Lurleen's face.

Dr. Piaget moved toward Kayla to comfort her, but he was knocked aside by Mitzi. "She's *my* daughter. She wants *my* comfort." She placed her arms about Kayla and glanced at Lurleen in the process, Mitzi. mumbled something.

Carbonne wasn't sure what she said but hoped technicians could amplify the audio.

Kayla squirmed in Mitzi's arms as Mitzi mumbled something else. Again, Carbonne wasn't sure what was said.

When Mitzi started to pull Kayla toward the door, Kayla planted her feet and said, "No."

CHAPTER 24: Sergeant Chuy Bargas Considers His Situation

Chuy thought Lurleen's viewing had been a nightmare. Pete's little rehearsed dialogs reminded him of Rod Serling's comments at the start of each episode of *The Twilight Zone*. The attendees were frightened, but except for Matt and Kayla, had shown no sign of mourning Lurleen's death. All this drama unfolded because Carbonne and Pete couldn't accept that the two children had killed their grandmother.

Worse still, the viewing had created more work for Chuy. The same neighbors who had told officers only a few days before that they knew little about the Jansens because they "kept to themselves," suddenly had a lot to say. But all waited to make their comments until they were out of the range of cameras and microphones. Several didn't even speak to Chuy but thrust unsigned notes at the mortician and the woman officer before they scurried away. Now he and his staff would have to follow up on all of these observations.

The comments fell into two categories. First, the Jansens were not a happy family. Lurleen, Kayla, and Mitzi often yelled at each other. Two of the men admitted having backyard conversations with Pete, who they described as "henpecked and angry."

Second, most thought Kayla was "odd." Two claimed Kayla often sat in the orchard at night and hummed songs. Two others commented on Kayla's sexual activity in the orchard at night.

Chuy feared these comments might convince the DA to file statutory rape charges against one or both of the young men in the neighborhood. Preparing those cases would create a lot of work for Chuy, and would please almost no one. Furthermore, the comment by Josh Ahrens's father—"I avoid talking to Lurleen and Mitzi because they are litigious"—made him nervous.

Chuy remembered seeing letters from lawyers representing Mitzi in the adoption files for Matt and Kayla. Mitzi had sued the social worker and CYFD but had settled out of court. All parties had signed non-disparagement clauses. Mercado police had also found documents on a lawsuit filed by Lurleen against a local building contractor in the Mercado municipal court records. The contractor had settled out of court for an undisclosed amount. Mitzi's lawyers were already harassing Chuy daily. The Mercado mayor would never appoint him as the permanent chief of police if Mitzi filed legal charges against him for mishandling the case, or the Ahrens's family sued the department for harassment. Mr. Ahrens was a well-known businessman in Mercado.

Chuy felt a twinge of guilt. A father fearing statutory rape charges against his son might try to discredit the rape victim—Kayla—and her family as a preemptive move. Mr. Ahrens's comments might have been designed to frighten him. If so, Mr. Ahrens had succeeded. Chuy felt like he was in a no-win situation.

Maybe in a weird way Carbonne was right about pursuing charges against the young men. If Lurleen had known of Kayla's activities in her backyard, she probably made threats to Kayla's sexual partners or their parents. Those threats could have scared one or even two young men enough to murder Lurleen. At least his hypothesis made more sense than Carbonne's fixation on Mitzi. Carbonne thought charging her with abetting Lurleen's murder—or at least tampering with evidence—would loosen her lips, but Carbonne hadn't seen Mitzi's vigil with Matt in the pediatric intensive care unit. She had seemed so distraught, vulnerable, and concerned for her son. Mitzi didn't deserve any more misery.

CHAPTER 25: Sara at the Taj Mahal on Day 8

The guide shook his head as the bus pulled into the parking lot. "We expect the crowd to be ten times normal today because of Diwali." He proceeded to give detailed instructions and noted he wouldn't try to lead the group through the Taj Mahal. An audible sigh could be heard on the bus. A number of her fellow tourists had told Sara that seeing the Taj Mahal was one of the prime items on their bucket list.

Sara studied Sanders. He'd been up much of the night with gastrointestinal distress and looked pale. "Are you sure you can walk around here?" She motioned to the crowd outside the bus window. "This looks like a Big Ten campus after the football game ends. There have to be tens of thousands in the crowd."

Sanders put his hands on hers. "Nothing..." He gagged slightly. "Well, *almost* nothing, would stop me from seeing the Taj Mahal with you."

Sara felt his forehead. He felt warm but not alarming so. "Please tell me when you want to rest. It's okay." She didn't want to add that she found the story behind the Taj Mahal less romantic than most, including Sanders. Shah Jahan, who built the walled city of Old Delhi, commissioned the Taj Mahal to be built in memory of *one of his wives* after she died giving birth to their *fourteenth* child in the early 1630s.

The guide added a few more comments before he let the group depart the bus. He noted the sides of the Taj Mahal were so symmetrical that tourists sometimes lost their sense of direction. Today that would not be a problem because one minaret was being cleaned and would be surrounded by scaffolding. Evidently workmen had applied a special mud over all its marble surfaces and let it bake for a day. When they removed the mud, the marble would be whiter and brighter. Sara thought an entrepreneur could make a fortune selling "Taj Marble and Stone Cleaner" to tourists with the slogan "It's worked for four hundred years on the Taj Mahal." When she told her idea to Sanders and the other tourists on the bus, no one thought it was clever or funny.

Despite Sara's cynicism, she joined the collective gasp as the crowd passed through the gate that allowed the first full view of the Taj

Mahal. Then she and Sanders found a spot where they were jostled less by the crowd near the beginning of the garden in front of the building.

Sara was reminded of the famous photo of Princess Diana sitting in front of the Taj Mahal and thought of a sarcastic comment as she looked at the crowds clogging pathways and covering the terrace in front of the dreamlike white marble structure. Sara wondered if Diana wasn't missing Prince Charles in the famous photo, but instead was thinking she was lucky to see the Taj Mahal with no crowds. She decided that observation was not appropriate and said instead, "Look a photographer is taking photos of tourists sitting on that bench. Everyone wants a photo reminiscent of the photo of Princes Diana at the Taj Mahal. There's as many women in saris as women in Western garb waiting in the line for the photographer. Maybe we can get a photo of us together on the bench?"

"I'd like that," said Sanders. As they joined the crowd, he talked about how Shah Jahan was removed from his throne not long after the completion of the tomb by warring factions of his family.

Sara thought about her unusual response to the Taj Mahal. She guessed it reflected her mixed feelings about Sanders. She had forgiven him, at least she thought she had, for his affair with a woman young enough to be his daughter. The dalliance had undermined Sara's trust of him because they were in a supposedly committed relationship. But Sanders was contrite. Sara slapped her self mentally. The history wasn't important and Sanders wouldn't have been tempted if their relationship had been totally satisfactory.

Sara knew they were well matched in terms of intellect, interests, and temperament. So did Sanders. Well, maybe she was more irreverent, probably because she was no longer interested in building her career. Sanders still hoped to become an ambassador in a major embassy. Sara loved to travel but had consulted enough as an epidemiologist to know she liked visiting exotic spots but not living in them. Besides, Bug was too old to endure relocation to a foreign country. She enjoyed working from her home or in Washington, D.C., on science-based problems for the USAID and the State Department. These were opportunities to be useful, work with Sanders, apply her scientific knowledge to challenging problems, and travel occasionally. She could endure formal receptions in Washington, but knew she didn't want to become a social butterfly at dozens of only mildly interesting events each month as the wife of an ambassador.

Sanders snapped her out her reverie when he pointed out the exquisite lapidary around a delicate marble screen with cut outs of vines and flowers on an interior wall of the Taj. Semiprecious stones, such as lapis lazuli, red and brown agate, turquoise, coral, and jade, had been cut into flowers and leaves and inlaid in the marble. Again, the combination of Hindu and Mughal art was evident. The intricacy of the designs over large surfaces was astounding and every wall was decorated.

The crowd inside the Taj Mahal was respectful and the perforated marble screens allowed for air flow, but after a while the noise and heat in the building were stifling. Sara was thankful when Sanders had seen enough, and they could stroll outside in the garden.

When Sanders spotted their guide standing on a bench at the far corner of the garden, he said, "Our guide is an expert at finding the high ground where he can keep an eye on everyone."

Sara laughed. "You always recognize traits that would make a person a good spy. I guess I should say 'collector of data.'"

"And you always are good at analyzing what motivates people, probably why you were a good advisor for graduate students."

Sara hesitated. "I... I have tried to figure our guide out. He doesn't have the personality to be a tour guide. He's too introspective. I sense he's a Hindu, even though he's never admitted it to us. As one, I think it would be annoying to see tourists *ooh* and *aah* over the Mughal—really the Moslem—influence in India but ignore the Hindu base."

"Interesting comment, but I think *apathetic* would be a better word to describe him."

"You may be right. That's why I think my theory might be close to the truth." She waved her hand back at the Taj Mahal. This structure and all the forts and palaces are beautiful, but the whole court retinues, even Shah Jahan after his sons overthrew him, were trapped inside beautiful buildings and gardens. I suspect most would have preferred less beauty and more freedom. I bet our guide feels trapped, too. A number of Indian graduate students over the years told me they were proud of India, but they hated taking their children back to see their grandparents every year because they found the poverty, the filth, and the crowds depressing."

Sanders winked at her. "Let's see."

During the next fifteen minutes, they asked their guide not about India but about "what he would do and where he would go if he had no restraints." They slowly overcame his reluctance to chat.

124   J. L. Greger

"My brother was interested in physics and computer science. He got scholarships, went to graduate school in Germany, and now works in Hamburg. But neither I nor my wife is a technical person." The guide added that he'd like to move to Europe and lead a variety of international tours but first he had to develop a knowledge of other countries. Unfortunately, there were few tours that included several countries with India and he couldn't afford to travel internationally to gain more knowledge. He was trapped in a dead-end job.

Sara thought that described a number of the people she knew. Chuy was ashamed of being a cop in a small town but probably didn't have the skills to move into more authoritative roles. Carbonne knew his days as an undercover agent in Albuquerque were over. He needed to seek assignments elsewhere or move up the ranks in the FBI. Perhaps the person most trapped was Mitzi. She had no employable skills anymore and was dependent on her parents' aegis.

A strange thought flashed through Sara's mind: Mitzi might not be trapped by her grandparent's will anymore if Lurleen had provided for Mitzi in *her* will. Of course, the fact that her parents' divorce hadn't been finalized might prevent Mitzi from inheriting Lurleen's whole estate, but it still was apt to be a tidy sum.

***

The next stop on the tour was at several artisan studios. The descendants of the workmen who had done the inlays of semiprecious stones in the Taj Mahal ran shops which sold a profusion of tables, boxes, chairs, wall hangings, jewelry, and knickknacks of inlaid marble. The merchandise was beautiful, but Sara didn't want to accumulate more items in her home.

Sanders intently studied one elegant console table. Sara thought it would fit into his eclectic collection of mid-century modern furniture and Persian rugs. "The table would make a nice side table by your ivory leather day bed."

He nodded. "Perhaps, but I thought it might be a start to my daughter's collection of good furniture."

His daughter had another year and a half of law school. She had hinted to Sara before the trip to India that she hoped her father wouldn't bring back anything exotic from India for her. "It's true that she doesn't have any nice furniture in her current apartment. Maybe that's good. She won't have to lug a lot of stuff around as she completes one or two clerkships during the next few years. I bet she's more concerned about having the appropriate clothes for interviews than furniture."

He looked disappointed. "Did she tell you to keep me from buying items like this for her?"

Sara tried to keep her face blank. "You could get her a cashmere or silk shawl. The paisley prints are lovely, but she might like a more modern look. Or give her the money to buy a suit—one she could wear on interviews next spring."

He shook his head. "You're so obvious. She talked to you."

Before he could complain about being henpecked, Sara gave him a quick kiss on his cheek. "Look at it this way: You want her to have plans for her future and not to be just accumulating a trousseau. Why not buy the table for yourself? If she likes it, you can give it to her once she's settled in a home a few years from now. It will mean more to her because the table will by then be a part of you and your home."

He coughed.

While Sanders negotiated the price and shipping for the table, Sara wandered around the store watching tourists, mainly Americans, buying beautiful items they didn't need. That reminded her of Lurleen's collection of baptismal fonts. She guessed the fonts had been impressive when displayed in the large atrium around the indoor swimming pool in her Michigan home. Now, mainly encased in boxes, they were an eyesore. She wondered whether many of these beautiful items wouldn't be in the same situation in a few years.

Sara's thoughts turned from Lurleen's collection of fonts to Lurleen's grandchildren as Sanders and she sauntered out of the busy shop and sat on a nearby bench in the shade of a large tree. "I was thinking about how both Lurleen and Mitzi were pretty poor mothers, and I wondered what type of mother I would have been. I held my grad students to high standards and I am bossy and do nag."

He poked her and in mock surprise said, "Really? I hadn't noticed." Then he turned serious. "You would have treated your children like you treat Bug and I suspect your grad students—kindly but with rules, which you frequently choose not to enforce."

"Oh, dear."

"Nothing to be sorry about. Your children would have been smart and bratty but would have matured to responsible, reasonably happy adults. I guess a lot like my daughter." He paused. "I guess I was a lot like

Pete—gone too much. But unlike Lurleen, my ex-wife did a good job of providing my daughter with a stable home."

"So, you think Kayla and Matt will mature into reasonably happy adults?"

He cleared his throat. "Not really. Lurleen was a control freak, and I suspect Mitzi is too when she's not under Lurleen's thumb. We don't know how Lurleen treated Mitzi as a child, but Mitzi treats her children like yo-yos—cuddly when she wants something, but distant most of the time."

Sara sighed. "Psychologists theorize that children treated, as you say, like yo-yos are more prone to develop narcissistic personalities with little empathy for others. Matt with his intellectual limitations should have noticed Mitzi's inconsistencies less than Kayla, but he's the one who is exhibiting the worse pathology. He's the one killing animals and admitting to killing Lurleen."

"Humph" Sanders stood. "Time to go to the bus." He paused. "Don't be too sure that Matt is displaying the most pathological behavior. He's just less secretive than the other Jansens."

CHAPTER 26: FBI Agent Carbonne Reevaluates Previous Decisions

After Lurleen's viewing, Carbonne did something he seldom did in the middle of a case—he took the rest of the day off. He needed time to think before he plunged ahead with the murder investigation. He had an overwhelming feeling that he'd made a questionable assumption at the start, and it had tainted the whole case. He'd assumed Pete had passively submitted to the whims of his wife and daughter. The man he'd watched today was capable of adroitly manipulating others. Carbonne wondered if Pete could have killed Lurleen and set up his daughter and grandchildren as patsies.

Most of his FBI colleagues when they faced such a dilemma tried to blast away their uncertainties at a gun range or sweat out their doubts in an exercise room. He knew Ulysses Howe usually found an excuse to wander around the sculpture garden at the Albuquerque Museum when he was overwhelmed by a case.

That wasn't Carbonne's style. He changed into his oldest clothes and went to the picnic bench by Building Two at the VA Medical Center in Albuquerque. The homeless men there were good listeners. They seldom asked prying questions and didn't expect conversations to be logical. Moreover, their problems—like where they would sleep tonight and where could they get decent cheap food—made his search for clues seem trivial. Even so, he had trouble focusing on the conversation of the two homeless men who he treated to a tasty chicken dinner at a nearby Golden Pride restaurant.

Carbonne's mind kept returning to Sara and to Lurleen's murder. He liked Gil's suggestion to set a trap for any gang members who might be watching Sara's house, even if Chuy thought it a waste of time. The new report from the lab was discouraging. The cloth gloves in the pot had Lurleen's blood on the outside and Kayla's skin cells on the inside. This new evidence along with Pete's testimony would cinch the case against Kayla. Maybe Chuy and Ulysses were right and it was time to accept that Kayla and Matt killed Lurleen. Mitzi was just a distraught mother trying to save at least one of her children and didn't deserve punishment for trying to protect Kayla.

Then he re-read Sara's latest email. Sara had given detailed instructions on where to look for the photo of Bug being baptized by Matt in Lurleen's home. When he read the message earlier, Carbonne had thought the viewing would provide answers and make the search for a photo and then the font in the chaos of Lurleen's house unnecessary. Sara could find the photo after she returned from India. Now he realized the DA might officially charge Kayla and Matt with the murder of their grandmother *before* Sara returned from India. Carbonne thought the kids deserved one more chance.

That meant he needed help tomorrow, and the FBI lab crew was too busy already. He called Chuy and requested help, without mentioning the new lab results.

***

Carbonne thought Chuy proved his administrative abilities when Barbara Lewis arrived at Sara's house at seven-thirty the next morning. Carbonne had worked with Barbara before and even gone to dinner with her a couple of times. She was Native American from the Acoma Pueblo. Unfortunately, her family was pushing her to start a family soon. That was definitely not part of Carbonne's plans, but she was a pleasant, smart woman.

Sara's photo albums were in chronological order. Many of the photos were dated on the back. Sara knew the baptismal incident had occurred six to ten years before. Barbara found the photo while Carbonne changed the timers on Sara's lights, opened the curtains in one room and closed them in another, changed the wreath on Sara's front door, removed a dead potted plant in her front yard, and made other adjustments to the property. He thought the house would look different to an alert observer driving by regularly.

As Carbonne and Barbara studied the snapshot, they realized the easy part of their search was over. Sara was holding a wet dog over a gray font with a brown font in the background. The woebegone, dripping dog didn't look like Bug, but Carbonne had only seen Bug with his long hair dry and fluffed. In the photo the dog's hair was wet and flattened against his head and body. A young boy, only four or five and grinning ear to ear was standing by Sara. The child didn't really look like Matt, except that he had light brown hair and light, probably hazel, eyes. Even so, Carbonne was sure this was the right photo.

The problem was the fonts in the photo were nondescript. The gray stone font—ugly and heavy with carved crosses—at the front of the picture looked like most of the ones Carbonne had noticed in Lurleen's house. The font in the background of the photo was brown. Sara had noted in her email that Lurleen had directed them to use another font after she murmured something about not wanting to get her "hiding place wet," but Sara had admitted she had no idea about the appearance of the special font—only that it would be in the background of the photo. Carbonne didn't remember seeing any brown fonts at Lurleen's house but thought the lab crew had listed one in their inventory.

He scanned the photo and sent it to the lab techs and asked them to enhance the brown font in the background. Both Carbonne and Barbara thought the font in the back of the picture might be made of wood. It seemed less sturdy than the gray stone one at the front of the photo.

The two investigators stopped at Sonic and picked up drinks before they headed to Lurleen's house because Carbonne doubted there were clean glasses there. They found the yellow police tape on the front door was untouched, but the tape that had sealed the back door lay on the ground. Carbonne emailed the lab crew and Chuy to see if they had left the site without replacing the tape. He doubted it and guessed someone had entered or at least tried to enter the house. The most likely candidates were Pete and Mitzi. Both had been warned not to enter the house without Mercado police present, and the locks on the doors had been changed with no key provided to Mitzi. Again, he felt pangs of guilt for trusting Pete too much.

Barbara used the computerized inventory prepared by the FBI lab crew to locate the box with a brown font. They rolled the box on its side and slid a brown marble font sheathed in packing paper out of the cardboard box. Carbonne looked for a secret drawer, and Barbara tried to rotate the top. They even checked the base., but it appeared solid. If this brown font had a secret compartment, it wasn't obvious. It was just another sturdy stone bowl with a thick stand.

Carbonne and Barbara opened more boxes that were three or four feet high and heavy, assuming many would contain fonts. They were discouraged after they opened almost twenty more boxes. They'd found only one more brown stone font and an oak font. The oak font wasn't really brown, but colors in old photographs were often misleading. The rest were gray or ivory stone fonts. As Barbara continued to open boxes,

Carbonne searched Lurleen's bedroom and closet. He reasoned she may have kept her hiding place accessible.

In the back of her bedroom closet, behind lots of clothes, he found a walnut font. He dragged it to the dining room where three other brown fonts stood. Then on a hunch, he went to Pete's workshop and found another heavy brown stone font in a closet. Carbonne located a dolly and was dragging it into the main house when Barbara screamed.

He left the stone font by the back door and rushed to the kitchen. Barbara stood over a box labeled *eighty-three*. It was shorter than most of the boxes she'd opened and only about thirty inches high. She held a wad of newspaper in her hands.

"Look." She pointed to two bloodied plastic gloves in the box. "I know I was only supposed to open boxes that were three or four feet tall because the fonts in the picture were at least three feet tall, but this box caught my attention. It was under four small boxes and two of them had already been cataloged because they were smeared with blood. When I moved them because I wanted to get at a tall box behind this stack, I noticed this box was sealed with blue tape and not the clear tape that had been used on the others. I thought it odd and noted my observation on the inventory before I slit the tape and pulled back the cardboard flaps. The smell of stale blood hit me. Another odd thing is the top packing material in the box is newspaper. All the rest contain standard packing paper, not newsprint."

Carbonne gaped at the gloves. "I knew they had to be somewhere, but I'd given up on finding them."

Barbara put clean paper on the counter and was ready to transfer the gloves. "Let's see what's under them."

Carbonne grasped her arm. "Don't touch them. Let the lab crew collect them as evidence and analyze them for DNA in the blood on the outside and the sweat on the inside."

He dropped onto the only empty chair in the kitchen. "Chuy and I knew the person who had made all the blood smears had to dispose of at least one pair of plastic gloves, but we didn't find them in the garbage here, Mitzi's car, or her home." He didn't add that they had not searched Pete's rental car for bloodied gloves. Carbonne would check tomorrow but knew it was too late to find anything significant.

Barbara examined the newsprint as he spoke. "You really lucked out. This page is from the *Albuquerque Journal* on the day before the murder." She pointed to the heading. "That's proof the gloves were sealed into this box around the time Lurleen was killed."

"You're good. If Chuy doesn't give you a raise, I'll recruit you to the FBI." He didn't add that her recruitment to the FBI would earn him a bonus. Ulysses Howe and the FBI in general were frantic to recruit women and Native Americans, and Barbara was a "two-fer."

She blushed.

Carbonne was glad he hadn't told her that she was a two-fer. "I'll call the lab and tell them to complete the search of this box. Note on the computer inventory what you told me. Then we'll drag the font I found in Pete's lair to the dining room and seal up the house. I'm too tired to figure out how to find a secret hiding spot in those brown fonts, but I'm pretty sure one of them contains what we're looking for" He winked at her. "Where do you want to eat? It's my treat."

CHAPTER 27: Sergeant Chuy Bargas Worries

All hell broke loose after Lurleen's weird funeral. Mitzi called the mayor of Mercado who demanded Chuy appear in his office immediately.

Chuy knew that a number of citizens had appealed police decisions to the mayor over the last few years. Gil had cursed about the wasted time, but he seemed to handle the issues easily and quickly. Chuy found his time in the mayor's office nerve-wracking.

The mayor—a Harvard-educated Hispanic businessman turned politician—listened politely as Chuy summarized the Lurleen Jansen murder investigation. Then the mayor made several observations. "I wish Gil was leading this investigation. He knows how to handle emotionally unbalanced citizens, and Mitzi Jansen's comments seem irrational. Another problem is our police force is understaffed, particularly with Gil on leave of absence."

Chuy felt these comments suggested the mayor doubted his abilities, especially when the mayor stood and pulled a page of notes from a file by his phone.

"I've talked to the Sandoval County district attorney. He admitted this case was complicated by jurisdictional issues because the apparent perpetrators are minors." The mayor smiled. "He thinks you've done a great job so far on this case. Unfortunately, Mitzi is threatening to file suits against Pete Jansen, Dr. Piaget, the court-appointed psychologist, and our police department for collusion. She claims that together you are depriving her of her parental rights, and in doing so, are endangering her life and that of her daughter Kayla."

"It's not true."

"Doesn't matter—it would make bad headlines. Can't you assign more of your staff to find the needed evidence and put this black eye behind us?"

Chuy felt defeated and hopeless. If he didn't succeed in solving this case, he doubted he'd ever become the permanent chief of the Mercado Police Department. What made it worse was he thought he could have more quickly solved the case a year ago, before his injuries. He knew his physical and mental reflexes were slower. All he could do was beg the mayor for another day or two before he asked the DA to comply with Mitzi's wish to charge Matt and close the case.

Chuy thought his luck might have changed when Carbonne called him at home around ten that night. He also thought he could do Carbonne a big favor. That man spent too much time alone or with homeless men on the street. He needed a girlfriend. While most women were turned off by Carbonne's often unkempt appearance, Barbara Lewis of the Mercado police force seemed to find him interesting when they worked together on a previous case. She might also be desperate to get away from her clannish family on the Acoma Pueblo.

***

Lurleen's house was a beehive when Chuy arrived at one. Two technicians wearing masks were bent over a large box in the kitchen. Chuy believed movers would call it a lamp box. One of the techs recognized Chuy. "Barbara deserves the credit for this find. We gave up a couple days ago after we processed over sixty boxes. This is box eighty-three." She waved to a large tray. "So far, we've found two pairs of bloody gloves and a gold chain with a pendant engraved with *ZI* in this box. I guess we would have found this evidence eventually because someone would have noticed the stink emanating from the box."

Chuy looked into the box. It was hard to be sure but it looked like a blue towel soaked with blood in a plastic bag would be the next item to be retrieved. He pointed to the newsprint. "Is this the newspaper Barbara mentioned when she called? The one from the day before Lurleen died?"

"Yup. If we can find DNA in the gloves, this case may be about solved." The technician giggled. "That is if the genius crawling on the floor in the dining room can find the secret compartment in a baptismal font where Sara thinks Lurleen left a note or something about her suspicions."

Chuy saw Carbonne sitting on the floor and staring at five brown baptismal fonts. One was reddish brown sandstone with crude carvings on its thick stem and around its octagon bowl. One was polished brown marble with carved lacy scallops on the pillar supporting a fluted oval bowl that looked like a giant clam shell. The oaken one was modern and looked like a thick post with a pyramid on top. The walnut one had a slender stem with a silver lid on top. Barbara sat on a chair, as tapped the octagonal supporting column of another brown font, and listened with a stethoscope.

J. L. Greger

Carbonne stood. "Found a compartment in the oak font." He pushed the pyramidal lid and it pivoted to reveal a space for a bowl. Then he pushed the section of the font below the bowl space and it also pivoted. A small compartment was visible under the second movable section. He pointed to the dining table. "That yellowed note was in the compartment. Probably been there a long time, but Sara said Lurleen had kept many of the fonts around her indoor swimming pool in her home in Michigan. The chlorine would have yellowed the paper quickly. So, it could be one of Lurleen's notes and not some vestige of church history."

Chuy felt his Adam's apple bobbing in his throat. Discoveries like this made him nervous because they were easy to misinterpret, especially when police were so desperate for answers. "What did the note say?"

"Paper's brittle and I didn't try to unfold it. The lab can do it better."

Chuy felt calmer because Carbonne appeared to acting rationally. "Probably nothing."

Carbonne said, "Agreed. Sara said Lurleen was agitated on the drive to Chimayó because she'd just discovered something. That means the note will be new. Besides, the oak font was in a box and it was difficult to get to. I think the note will either be in the walnut font, which I found in her closet, or the octagonal brown marble one, which I found in Pete's backyard retreat." Carbonne motioned for Barbara to steady the octagonal marble one, as he tried to slide or pivot various segments of the font.

Chuy nodded. "What about the ugly reddish brown sandstone one? Was it in a box too?"

Carbonne bit his lip. "No, it was in the laundry room. Looked like Lurleen used it to collect safety pins, buttons, other things that fell off in the wash. We couldn't find any pivot mechanism in it." His phone emitted a ping, and he read his new message. "Damn. The lab enhanced the fonts in the photo of Bug being baptized. It's definitely not the walnut font or the fancy marble font with the shell-like basin. The stem of the brown font in the photo is sturdy and probably stone, but the photo is lousy. We may not have found the right one yet."

Chuy yawned. "Why not ask Pete? He might not have enjoyed his wife's collection, but I bet he knows a lot about it."

Chuy thought it was strange how Carbonne grimaced and said, "Barbara, why don't you check out other boxes by your box eighty-three. Chuy and I will get out of your way and talk in Pete's workshop."

As soon as Carbonne closed the door to Pete's retreat, he said, "I didn't want Barbara and the technicians to hear me. I've been thinking that maybe we, actually I, biased this whole case. I accepted Pete's comments as true because…"

"Why not? The phone tower transmission, the gas receipt from Gallup, the receipt from the Frontier all were consistent with his story." Chuy sat down at the game table. He was glad Carbonne had suggested they move to Pete's lair. He found the chaos in Lurleen's house unsettling, even before the technicians had started opening boxes. The neatness of Pete's area made it seem calmer. He also didn't want anyone to hear comments that might support Mitzi's claim of collusion among Pete, the police, and the psychiatrists.

"Yes, but he could have driven much faster than I estimated." Carbonne continued to pace. "All he needed was an extra fifteen minutes and he could have been the murderer."

"I doubt it. As you said initially, he too neat to have generated such a messy murder scene." Chuy pulled out his phone. "What made you doubt yourself?"

"I talked to Lurleen's divorce lawyer. Should have done that sooner. Seems Pete was willing to give her the house, its contents, and about two million dollars in retirement accounts."

"New Mexico is a community property state. She should…."

"Yes, but Pete's inheritance was set up to avoid application of community property laws, at least to the funds in the trust. Also, Lurleen thought Pete had for years placed part of the money he earned on overseas assignments into secret foreign accounts in the Caribbean, but her lawyers couldn't locate the accounts. They also hypothesized he was deferring payments for his current work until the divorce was finalized."

"So, the divorce was less friendly than his words at the funeral viewing suggested?" Chuy shook his head. "Knew that show seemed fake."

"After telling me all of that, Lurleen's divorce lawyer indicated although the size of the settlement annoyed Lurleen, it wasn't the sticking point. The key point of argument was Pete, as the sole trustee of his parents' trust, had enacted a clause in the original trust agreement. Seems the trust stipulated a trustee could restrict payments to a child and his or her parents if the trustee deemed the requests as unreasonable or illegal. Pete decided a month ago to limit payments to any child or parent to fifteen years. That means Mitzi would get payments for caring for Matt and Kayla for only a couple of more years. Then Mitzi has to go back to work."

"No wonder she's frantic. She gotten her full support from her grandparents' foundation for years."

"He's definitely squeezing Mitzi. Wonder why?" Carbonne drummed his fingers on the table. "I watched him at the viewing. He knows how to manage a room and lie smoothly and convincingly."

"When did he lie?"

"To Kayla. He knows she's capable of murder and told me so." Carbonne stared intently at his phone as he searched for a file. "Found it." He nodded as he scanned a file. "Checked his work history and talked to his colleagues. He's testified in court many times for his employers. Evidently, he's good at it. They say he knows 'what to leave unsaid' and how to phrase his comments so they 'aren't technically lies.'"

"Okay, but his comment about believing in Kayla was a white lie. He was responding as Dr. Piaget had instructed him to behave when he comforted her." Chuy closed his eyes. "But I have my doubts about him, too. He was too manipulative at the viewing. Too sure of himself." Chuy feared that Mitzi's claims of collusion were sounding more reasonable.

"Lurleen's death saved Pete a lot of money and bother. And if this case is resolved as expected, Pete can shed his responsibilities to Mitzi, Kayla, and Matt easily... honorably." Carbonne stared at his phone. "I can't even blame him for wanting to distance himself from Mitzi and her adopted kids. They're money pits that give him no satisfaction."

"You're being too cynical. However, I think the DA would agree with you. I had a long meeting with an assistant DA this morning."

Carbonne looked startled. "Why?"

"The DA is scared. He thinks it could take years to sort through all the allegations Mitzi is making against Pete. Basically, Mitzi claims he's trying to alienate her children from her by placing them in the expensive private psych unit. She also claimed Pete bribed Dr. Piaget to get the reports he wanted."

"Has the DA seen any evidence?"

"Pete has paid Dr. Piaget's fees directly for more than eight years, ever since Lurleen discovered a dead cat in her backyard at La Bendita. Pete also insisted Dr. Piaget send him reports on Matt semi-annually. Mitzi's lawyer provided supporting documents."

Carbonne pulled his hands through his hair. "Irregular but not proof of a bribe."

Chuy gulped. "Agreed. I called Dr. Piaget. He admitted that he'd allowed the court-appointed psychologist to see Matt's file because he felt he was acting in the boy's best interest. Then he said something interesting. 'The testimony of a court-appointed psychologist is generally considered more unbiased that that of a personal psychiatrist in court.' That means we do have the appearance of collusion among Pete, Dr. Piaget, and the court-appointed psychologist."

Carbonne tapped his fingers on the table. "Okay, but making charges of collusion and delaying the closure of the case is not in Mitzi's best interest if she really wants Matt locked away. Maybe she's more afraid that a key piece of evidence will be revealed if the investigation continues. 'Evidence' is probably too strong a term. This… this gem is probably hearsay and maybe something Matt overheard." Carbonne smiled. "If it incriminated Pete, Mitzi would want it well known. That suggests to me she's trying to protect herself or Kayla by suppressing this bit of info."

"You're assuming Mitzi is acting logically. The assistant DA said Mitzi's lawyers hinted she had stepped off the deep end, but of course they would never say that publicly."

Carbonne drummed his fingers on the table. Chuy wondered whether Carbonne had picked up that mannerism from Ulysses Howe.

"Maybe that's Pete's intent to push Mitzi to a breaking point—but why?" Carbonne smiled. "I think I'll quote Sara now. She always says she thinks best when she relaxes and forgets a problem. So, I'll relax now and read the sound technician's notes to you." He cleared his throat. "Bill said at the casket, 'Did you hate her that much?' That's not my idea of helpful, and his comments at the back of the room were unintelligible. I figure one of us needs to grill Bill because I agree with Pete that his son knows something."

"What about Mitzi's comments?"

"At the casket, 'Too bad the makeup hides so much.' And to Kayla, 'Shut up!' and 'I'm the only one who loves you.' right before Kayla shouted no."

Chuy shook his head. "I'm surprised the mikes picked up so much of Mitzi's comments."

"I'm not. Pete somehow convinced Kayla to wear a mike."

Chuy gulped. Pete was trying to subvert Mitzi's children, or at least Kayla's loyalty to her mother. "No wonder Mitzi unleashed so many legal accusations and actions against Pete." He pulled a folded sheet from his pocket and pushed it toward Carbonne. "The funny thing is Kayla made no accusations against Mitzi this morning when she talked to the court-appointed psychologist, but the girl named her lovers."

"More than one? I figured Josh Ahrens." Carbonne studied the page. "Explains why neighbors saw her in the orchard so often. You know one of them might…."

"Already considered that one of them might have helped Kayla kill Lurleen." Chuy didn't add that the assistant DA had already indicated he didn't want to pursue statutory rape charges against the two young men because the cases were unwinnable. It was doubtful the neighbors would testify against the young men on a rape case if they wouldn't even admit what they'd seen in regard to Lurleen's murder. Furthermore, the assistant DA thought Kayla would not generate much sympathy from a jury.

Carbonne studied Chuy. "You don't bluff well. Poor Kayla—the DA doesn't want to prosecute anyone on rape charges, does he? And he knows that's out of federal jurisdiction. So, Kayla gets raped again."

"The court-appointed psychologist is much more sympathetic to Kayla now, and I'll try to bluff the boys into confessing by suggesting they could be charged with abetting murder."

"My friend, you are a good man but a lousy poker player. Get Gil to talk to the boys."

Chuy knew his Adam's apple was bobbing in his neck as it always did when he was nervous. "I'll try."

CHAPTER 28: Sara at the Taj Mahal on Day 9

It was six-thirty in the morning. Sara poked Sanders as the bus passed families huddled around small fires near the road. Tents and sheds were nearby. He squeezed her hand but seemed to be in his own world. She wasn't surprised. He'd gotten more sleep last night than the night before because he had liberally consumed medications from their combined pharmaceutical store, but he still looked pale and tired.

The bus pulled into an open lot on the shore of the Yamuna River. The guide said it was an archaeological site called Mehtab Bagh. It had been a pleasure garden in the time of Shah Jehan and was believed to be the perfect site for viewing the Taj Mahal across the Yamuna River. The guide intimated that Shah Jehan had planned to build a larger mausoleum for himself in the garden area but had been stopped when he was overthrown. His family had interred him in the Taj Mahal instead.

The guide promised the group a spell binding view of the Taj Mahal and hurried them off the bus. Sara was skeptical. She could see the gray Yamuna River with yellow mists above it and mud flats next to it. Scraggly greenery and rubble from buildings or walls filled the area between the bus and the river. She guessed the guide's claim might be exaggerated because only three other buses were discharging tourists. Sara figured at least she wouldn't be jostled during this viewing of the Taj Mahal and grabbed Sanders's arm as soon as he alighted.

They strolled along the river. Women in brightly colored saris were washing clothes on the rocks at the water's edge. Gradually the yellow mist lightened to gray and the outline of the Taj Mahal in a darker gray became visible. Sunlight hit the dome and it began to whiten and shimmer.

Sanders put his arm on Sara's shoulder and guided her to a low wall. "We need to talk. Yesterday everything was so crowded and noisy. This is quiet but it looks...."

"Like the banks of a river that overflows it banks regularly?"

"Yes, but I expected it to be more refined and romantic." He fumbled in his jacket pocket.

She realized he wanted to propose and might even foolishly go down on one knee in the mud. That would be a mistake—a funny one. She remembered a quotation from Oscar Wilde: "Nothing spoils romance so much as a sense of humor in the woman."

She pulled his hand from his pocket and stroked it. "Yes, we should talk but why not after we go back to the hotel for breakfast? We can sit on a comfortable bench in the garden behind the hotel. It will be empty and quiet this morning"

He coughed. "I can't eat. My gut...."

"I know. We can sip tea and eat a little toast or rice and then relax in the garden by the hotel. The tour doesn't resume until this afternoon when we go to the Agra Fort. That garden will be more private than here."

He nuzzled her ear. "Glad you understand. You know I love you not just because you're bright and interesting but because you understand me."

She nuzzled him back. "Love helps us see the best in ourselves and others."

"Let's not make a scene here." They held hands as they walked back to the bus.

Sara was relieved. From the beginning of their discussions of this trip, she'd thought she wouldn't find India romantic and she hadn't. The stark reality of the poverty, pollution, and overcrowding aroused her mind more than the beautiful sites aroused her heart. And Sanders was much sexier and romantic when he was being his real self—a smart determined man who wanted to make the world a safer, better place.

The guide was more relaxed than usual as they drove back from the Yamuna. Sara guessed that was because the tour was ending tomorrow. He tried to be funny. "We have a joke in India. If you're driving down the road and have to choose to either ram into a crowd of people or a herd of cattle, what should you do?" He studied the tour group.

Sanders whispered to Sara, "Perhaps our advice to tell jokes was a mistake."

The guide smiled. "Hit the crowd of people. You'll be sentenced to less time in jail."

There were a few titters. Mostly groans. Sara felt sorry for the guide and announced loudly, "It's not easy to explain your culture to Americans. We appreciate how hard you've tried." She clapped.

Soon everyone on the bus was clapping. The guide blushed, bowed slightly, and said, "Namaste."

***

As they walked in the garden holding hands, Sara mentioned the erotic performance of the snake dancer. "Don't deny it. I wasn't the only one turned on."

He smirked. "It was… stimulating. Though neither of us have the flexibility of the lead dancer. Her fluidity was hypnotic."

As soon as they sat on a bench almost surrounded by pomegranate trees, Sanders pulled out a box and then another from his jacket pocket. He opened the first box quickly. "Don't say anything until I've had my say."

Sara had mixed emotions. Like any woman, she was pleased an interesting, bright man was about to ask her to marry him. However, she doubted their partnership would be improved by marriage. Sanders had agreed with her until his dalliance in Cuba became apparent. That bothered Sara since a legal document wouldn't have prevented his mistake. Her continual presence might have, but she knew she would grow grouchy if she had to be always watching him. She'd gone to enough diplomatic receptions and events with him to know the most successful, no *happiest*, marriages among ambassadors and their spouses were flexible. Ones where a spouse was "guarding" their partner from temptation devolved into bitterness.

Sanders leaned over and kissed Sara lightly. "I love you and feel you love me. I also know that the legality of a marriage license isn't necessary to guarantee love or fidelity. But I'm proud of you and of our relationship. I'm asking you now to marry me."

Sara must have squirmed because he quickly added, "No interruptions. I doubt you'll say yes, so I had this ring…" He pulled out a gorgeous gold ring. White and yellow gold were intricately spiraled in the band. He grabbed her right hand. "I had this ring sized to fit your right hand. That way you don't have to consider the ring as an engagement ring or wedding ring and wear it on your left hand. Consider it as a symbol of my commitment to you as you wear it on your right hand."

"I love you and the ring is perfect."

"Wait." He dropped her hand and opened the other box. It contained a second similar ring of twisted white and yellow gold. "I also had a matching ring made for myself. I want you to put it on my finger." He shoved his left hand forward.

"Honey, I know you hate to wear jewelry. You don't have to wear a ring."

A tear was dripping from the corner of his eye. "Yes, I do. I trust you, but know you… and I… we both know I need a small reminder of your love." He leaned over and kissed her deeply with his tongue exploring her mouth. After a long embrace, he pulled away. "Put it on my left hand. It's more comfortable there than on my right hand."

She slid the ring on the fourth finger of his left hand. "May this ring be a permanent reminder of our love."

Sanders pulled Sara to her feet and let the boxes clatter to the ground. He started by letting his tongue flick her left ear and cheek and then let his arms move slowly down her back as he pulled her tighter to himself. Sara felt a warm flush move up her body as his tongue found her lips and his hips swayed. After only a moment, or at least it seemed too short a time, he pushed her away. "Perhaps we should go to our room."

Sara was overcome by emotions she hadn't expected and began to sob uncontrollably. "This was perfect."

CHAPTER 29: FBI Agent Carbonne Gets Help

Carbonne figured if he asked Bill Jansen for an interview, the man would refuse. Bill had replied, "I don't know," to all of Carbonne's questions at Lurleen's viewing.

Accordingly, Carbonne and two FBI agents were waiting for Bill when he arrived at the Albuquerque airport almost two hours before his flight. Carbonne had guessed Bill would arrive early as the airlines suggested because he appeared to be an extremely organized man who was fastidious about details—a typical engineer. Carbonne watched Bill get out of Pete's rental car, stiffly shake his father's hand, pick up his bag, and walk toward the flight arrival and departure board.

As Bill stood in front of the large display, he pulled his ticket from his pocket, and smiled. He stared upward at the old painted wood vigas across the ceiling of the airport as he rode the escalator to the departure level. Carbonne noticed Bill's gait was different when he stepped off the escalator than it had been during the last few days. His shoulders were now back, and his arms swung slightly as he walked to the security check area. His lips were no longer strained thin lines but seemed relaxed and fuller.

As was prearranged, Bill was guided to a special aisle in the pre-flight security check area. Carbonne greeted Bill as he emerged from the body scanner.

Bill looked stunned. "I don't know anything."

"Bill, I respected your desire to avoid a scene at the service for your mother. I even understood you didn't want to make any statements in front of your father or sister. But we both know, and so do your sister and father, that you know why Lurleen was killed."

"I don't." Bill looked nervously at his ticket. "I've got a flight to catch."

"You've got plenty of time to make your flight, if you tell me everything."

Bill hunched his shoulders. "Nothing relevant."

Carbonne guided Bill to an interview room. "I heard you say, 'Did you hate her that much?' at your mother's casket."

Bill's face turned white. "How?"

"Your father arranged for us to have mikes and cameras around the room. I also saw how you tensed when your sister entered the room."

"Everyone tensed. She was rabid."

"Bill, if you tell me what you suspect and why, I will try to keep your answers confidential. I suspect it's something that happened years ago." Carbonne motioned to the door of the tiny room. "There are two other agents with me. You know why they aren't in here?"

Bill shook his head.

"Because if you don't talk, I'll tell your father that you had a lot to say about him. And it wasn't an attractive picture."

Bill laughed. "Go ahead."

"You're right that was a bluff, but now I'm not bluffing. If you don't talk, I'll tell your sister that you had a lot to say about her, especially when she was a teenager…" He noticed Bill didn't flinch. "…and when she was a child."

Bill gasped.

Carbonne guided Bill onto a chair. "If she and Kayla are not detained, they will track down you, your wife, and your daughter. You've seen what Mitzi and Kayla can do."

Bill supported his head in his hands as he leaned over a small table. "I don't know anything about Kayla. Only what Mom and Dad told me. They suspected she was raped by older boys about a year ago. And that wasn't unexpected. Mitzi was so… I don't know how to explain. She wasn't a reasonable mother. One minute she was dressing Kayla like a Barbie doll, and the next she was ignoring the girl because Mitzi had a headache."

Carbonne was disappointed. Bill had only confirmed what others had already said about Mitzi. His comments about Kayla's sexual partners might be useful to scare Josh Ahrens and his friend, but the information was hearsay and wouldn't hold up in court. "What about your dad?"

"When I was a young child, Dad and Mom bickered about everything." Bill paused. "I guess the real knock-down-drag-out arguments started about the time Mitzi started school and I entered junior high. Mitzi wasn't a good student like I had been, but that wasn't the problem. Before she went to school Mitzi used to hit my arm repeatedly when she wanted attention. Mom and Dad ignored my complaints, but they couldn't ignore the almost daily calls from teachers and other parents once Mitzi started school. I'll give Mom credit—she quickly broke Mitzi of her bullying."

"How?"

"She placed Mitzi in a room with only a chair and a table. She made Mitzi print bible verses for hours whenever she heard about Mitzi bullying others. Sort of 'tough love' time out periods. Dad thought Mom was too severe. His approach to bad behavior was to keep you busy with outdoor activities."

"You said their arguments were intense. Were they physical?"

Bill winced. "Of course not. Just loud and long."

"None of the current neighbors reported hearing your parents argue. Do you know why?"

"Sure. Dad stopped arguing with Mom and started taking overseas assignments almost continuously about the time I entered high school."

"So, you didn't see your dad much?"

"No, I did. Although he was seldom home for more than a week at a time, he took me along on his trips during summers and holiday breaks. Often he arranged jobs or mini-internships for me at the various sites." Bill now studied his hands folded on the table. "He knew Mom's nagging bothered me. So, he encouraged me to graduate early from high school and helped me pick a college as far from home as possible. I went to MIT." He shrugged. "I guess he never took Mitzi along on his trips. At least, that's what she claims now. I don't know."

Carbonne realized Bill hadn't told him anything he didn't already know about Pete. He hoped he'd get more on Mitzi. "Now it's time to talk about Mitzi as a child and a teenager. Was she like Kayla?"

Bill blinked. "Are you kidding? I thought you found my mother's collection of baptismal fonts. Mom preached fire and brimstone to Mitzi. For all I know, Mitzi was a virgin until she met the guy she married, poor fellow. Gail and I were surprised the marriage lasted even a couple of months. Mitzi claimed he was rough with her, but I think the guy would have admitted anything to escape." Bill looked at the ceiling.

"Stop stalling. You've got a plane to catch. What was your sister like as a child? What do you suspect?"

"Mitzi was a tattletale and generally a pain for an older brother." He sighed. "But there was one incident that happened the spring before I graduated from high school. Mitzi, who was about ten, convinced Mom to adopt a fat tabby cat." He snickered. "It wasn't fat but pregnant. Mom complained a lot about all the kittens but Mitzi seemed to love them. She kept dressing them up in her doll clothes. Dad had come home because he wanted to be present at my graduation. After watching Mitzi play with the kittens, he told her to stop. He thought she was damaging their shoulders and hips when she pulled their legs into the sleeves of doll clothes. Mom disagreed. As they screamed, I saw my sister trying to tie a bonnet on one of the kittens. It bit her. She tightened the strings on the bonnet around the cat's neck, tighter and tighter. The cat clawed at first and then went limp." Tears streamed down Bill's face.

Carbonne decided silence was best at this point.

"I looked at Mitzi and expected her to scream or cry. She just scowled. I quickly untied the knots in the ribbons. It was too late. I knew Mom would scream if she saw the kitten, and Dad might leave and never come back. I'm not proud of this...." He looked almost searchingly at Carbonne. "Remember, I was only sixteen. I said, 'You must never do this again, but I'll help you this time.' We buried the cat together in the fruit orchard in our backyard in Michigan. I skipped my high school graduation and went with Dad to Africa the day after my last exam. He was consulting on a water project in the Sahel region."

"And?"

"At the end of the summer, I returned home, packed everything I owned, and went to MIT. Mitzi and I never exchanged more than short conversations ever again. I never returned to my parents' home for more than a week, although I traveled with Dad every summer in college. I've never told this story to anyone, but I suspect my wife Gail guessed."

"That's it?"

Bill stood. "Nothing usable in court, but as I told the cops in Omaha when they questioned me right after Mom's death my sister is capable of anything, but I can't prove it. Now keep your promise and tell Mitzi and my Dad that I knew nothing, except that my parents argued a lot and it bothered both Mitzi and me."

Carbonne ordered the other agents to escort Bill to his flight and to make sure neither Mitzi nor Pete followed him onto the flight. Carbonne knew this precaution was silly but he agreed with Bill—Mitzi was capable of anything.

He closed his eyes. He'd wondered all along whether Mitzi could have been the other person with Lurleen and Kayla that Pete saw in profile through the shade. But Mitzi's psychological profile had been wrong. No one—social workers, psychiatrists, psychologists, physicians, fellow teachers during the two years she'd taught, neighbors, Pete, Sara—

ever mentioned she was physically abusive to children or animals. Although most hinted her erratic behavior might engender psychological problems in her children. Both Dr. Piaget and the court-appointed psychologist had reiterated the dogma that violence to animals was a damaged child's, not an adult's, behavior pattern.

Of course, Bill's story didn't mean that Matt or Kayla hadn't killed animals, only that Mitzi had done so as a child. He and Chuy still had the same problem: Matt, Kayla, and Mitzi might all be capable of Lurleen's murder. Moreover, Kayla and Matt feared Mitzi too much to testify against her. That meant box eighty-three was the key to the case. One thing was certain, if Pete's DNA wasn't found inside the bloodstained plastic gloves, he could be eliminated as a suspect.

That box wouldn't have been found if not for Barbara Lewis. Carbonne smiled. Barbara was special. He thought of Sara and Sanders. Their relationship started with great professional respect, which broadened and deepened over time. He and Barbara were more like them than Carbonne cared to admit—bright loners who had never quite fit into society's norms. Maybe he and Barbara might have a future together? Starting a family might be better than trying to move up in the administration of the FBI. He certainly didn't enjoy administrative duties. Then again, this particular case was not an advertisement for parenthood.

J. L. Greger

CHAPTER 30: Sergeant Chuy Bargas Struggles

Chuy was having trouble hearing the assistant DA of Sandoval County on the phone because of the uproar in the outer office of the Mercado Police Department. Two teenagers had been arrested last night as they broke into a music shop in downtown Mercado. The argument between their parents and the shop owner was unnecessary. The secretary at the front desk hadn't planned ahead and had allowed the shop owner to bring an amended list of damages to the department at about the time the parents had agreed to pick up their sons. The boys had been arrested several times for minor offenses during the last six months. Last night their parents had decided a night in the Mercado jail might be a good dose of reality for their sixteen-year-old sons. However, the parents took offense when the shop owner called their sons "delinquents."

When Chuy asked the assistant DA to repeat a comment a second time, the assistant DA said, "Sounds to me like the Mercado Police Department is out of control without Gil Andrews. I told you yesterday to make the investigation of Lurleen Jansen's murder your highest priority. Instead, this morning I got complaints from two sets of parents. You and two other officers spent two hours harassing their sons yesterday over the allegations about the sexual assault of a willing girl. I'm told you have no witnesses to substantiate her claims."

Chuy choked. He should have taken Carbonne's advice and asked for Gil's help, but he tried to keep his voice from squeaking. "Excuse me sir—you are misinformed. We have several witnesses who claim the young woman was having sex in her grandmother's backyard. The victim's only thirteen and by definition that means the sex was not legally consensual. The young men are nineteen and twenty."

The assistant DA roared, "Her lawyers can file this case anytime during the next year. Meanwhile, the lawyers for Mitzi Jansen called again and reiterated their claim you were harassing their client. You've got to prioritize things."

Chuy was glad the assistant DA could not see his hands were shaking. "I did. The minor female is Lurleen Jansen's granddaughter. If we take her complaint seriously, the court-appointed psychologist thinks she's more apt to testify on what happened the night of the murder. We found more evidence yesterday, but we need her testimony."

"Oh? Tell me about the new evidence."

"We found bloody gloves, towels, and jewelry. All the samples are at the FBI lab awaiting analyses."

"Keep me informed." The assistant DA hung up.

Chuy figured the assistant DA was another underpaid, stressed local authority. He was being bullied by constituents, who had reason to be worried, and he was passing his frustration along to someone lower in the chain of command. That didn't change the fact that assistant DA was right. Chuy knew that he needed to prioritize, but he had no idea where to begin.

The noise in the outer office was now at a dull roar level. Chuy thought it safe to get a cup of coffee. He called Barbara Lewis who was at Lurleen Jansen's house.

Barbara was in a bubbly mood. She and the two FBI technicians only had about twenty more boxes to check. They'd found nothing interesting in the boxes they'd opened today. The lab had not analyzed any of the items found in box eighty-three, but they had unfolded the yellowed note, which Carbonne found in the oaken font yesterday, and sent Barbara copy.

"It's dated 'June 1989' in the top corner Barbara read:

Lu,

Smile when you find this.

Pete

Chuy groaned. "That's not useful, except it confirms Pete's comments about once loving Lurleen."

"Mmm. The technicians and I think Pete knows about the secret compartments in the fonts. We emailed Carbonne and suggested he talk to Pete, but Carbonne's off the grid and didn't respond."

***

An hour later, Dr. Piaget called and suggested Chuy join him, Matt, and Kayla for lunch in the private psych facility where the children were being held. "I think Kayla may be more willing to talk now because we got good news from a juvenile court judge this morning. The judge said it was rare when a psychiatrist for a client, officials at the CYFD, and a court-appointed psychologist agree on interpretation of events. Accordingly, she accepted our advice."

"What does that mean?"

"Although we thought it likely Matt was present when Lurleen was killed, we don't believe he participated in her murder. We have two reasons. First, we all doubt he has the knowledge to locate and slice Lurleen's jugular vein. Second, his so-called confession was devoid of all details. He always recounts it in the same manner, as if it was rehearsed or suggested to him by someone else. In other words, his confession meets all the criteria of a false memory. We're beginning to believe the same is true for all his confessions of animal abuse. Accordingly, Matt won't be transferred to a facility for juvenile, criminally insane patients but will remain at this facility for psychologically damaged children."

Chuy knew this was good news for Matt, but it didn't help him solve the crime. "Didn't Mitzi and her lawyers protest the judge's decision?"

"We foresaw her objections and noted Mitzi was incapable of providing the guidance Matt needs. An assessment of Matt's developmental skills indicates, he has regressed under her supervision during the years since his adoption. Accordingly, the judge ordered Mitzi could only have supervised visits with Matt."

Chuy thought about Carbonne's comments. Maybe Carbonne was right—Pete Jansen had demonstrated again that he was good at understanding complex systems and making them function as he wished. "What does that mean for Mr. Jansen?"

"First off, Pete is ultimately responsible for Matt unless Mitzi regains custody of him. Pete told the judge that the family trust would pay his grandson's expenses while staying in a private facility until he was an adult, if necessary. The judge thought this was the best option, provided Pete accept he too could only have supervised visits with Matt."

Chuy wondered whether Pete really cared about his grandson or had done this to rile his daughter. Chuy thought he'd worked too much with Carbonne and was beginning to think like him. "So, Pete's happy but nothing changes for the children?"

"Not true. That's why I want you to have lunch at this facility. You won't believe the difference in both of the children. I think Kayla will answer simple questions now about what she and Matt were doing at La Bendita after Lurleen's murder. Matt might even say intelligible words."

"You know Kayla will eventually be charged with Lurleen's murder if Matt didn't do it. She was present, per Pete's testimony, at the site. Her sweat was inside the bloody cotton gloves found on the patio."

"That's why I want you to give her one more chance to tell her side of the story."

***

Chuy was surprised as he pulled up to the private juvenile psych facility. It looked like another large home in the upscale residential area. The operators must have paid big money or been good at schmoozing to get a group home located in this neighborhood. He wondered how Pete had located it.

The electronic system at the entry was sophisticated. The security officers within were thorough, but their uniforms weren't standard issue. They wore pastel shirts and no ties. Every other aspect of the reception was also child-friendly. Someone had liked pink, soft greens, pale blues, and yellow. The walls were painted to look like fantasy clouds in those colors and the light wood furniture had practical, sturdy, denim-like upholstery.

Dr. Piaget quickly appeared and escorted Chuy to the dining room. It was a sunny space, containing six practical tables with an adult dressed like the guards at each table. Matt and Kayla sat with their backs to the door at a table by the window. The woman at the table left as Chuy and Dr. Piaget sat down. Matt barely looked up from his plate as he shoveled macaroni and cheese into his mouth with a plastic fork. Kayla stopped drinking milk from a yellow plastic glass.

Kayla looked at Chuy. "Dr. Piaget said you wanted to talk to me. What do you think of this bubblegum world? Everything here is color coded with pink, blue, green, and yellow." She smirked. "Kinda silly but Matt likes it. All the good little boys and girls are coded with pink and blue. See—Matt's name tag is blue. I'm coded yellow like a warning light."

Dr. Piaget pulled his napkin to his mouth. Chuy thought to cover a groan.

Matt stopped eating long enough to say, "Food's good." He then forked a couple of green beans.

Kayla shrugged. "I'm too old for this, but he's right." She stared at Chuy. "Let's get the questions over. Save your breath and don't ask about Grandma Lu's murder."

Chuy could see Kayla hadn't lost her grittiness If anything she was more vocal than before. "I want to understand what happened on the night we found Matt at La Bendita." Chuy decided it best not to mention her previous alibi that she'd been shopping at Walmart. "Why did you leave Matt inside La Bendita when you left?"

"Oh that." She chewed a mouthful of green beans slowly. "We… I needed to get to Walmart to shop. Matt doesn't like shopping."

"Are you sure? Sara Almquist—you know her and her dog Bug— saw someone about your size in a dark green hoodie." Dr. Piaget had warned him not to suggest Kayla was doing anything wrong. So, he hadn't said "following her" or "throwing a stone at her window."

"Oh, yeah. We…" She frowned. "I was playing a game of…"

Matt didn't even look up. "I like hide and seek."

Chuy was amazed at Matt's improved diction.

Kayla blinked. "Yes, I was playing hide and seek."

Chuy frowned. "But you were alone then and you scared Sara and Bug. Why didn't you talk to them?"

"It would ruin the game." Kayla began to eat rapidly.

Dr. Piaget pulled her plate away. "Kayla, this isn't a game. You said you'd rather talk to Sergeant Bargas than to the dirty policeman."

"I'm not a baby like Matt."

Matt whined but kept eating.

Kayla continued, "I know the other one is FBI. I'm thinking."

Dr. Piaget pushed the plate back toward Kayla. "Think less and just tell him everything you remember."

"I bicycled to La Bendita. Left the bike outside the back gate and crawled over the wall." She paused. "Often did it when Grandma Lu lived there. She told me to go to Sara's house and look for her but not let Sara see me."

Dr. Piaget had warned Chuy not to refer to Mitzi. Thus, Chuy didn't ask who "she" was but only said, "Why?"

"She and Matt would be joining me at La Bendita."

"Did she plan to talk to Sara?"

Kayla gulped her milk. "I don't know." She glanced at Dr. Piaget. "Really don't know. She said she had a surprise for Sara." She wrinkled her face. "She was mad at Sara because Sara had helped Grandma Lu get the mud."

Dr. Piaget beamed. "Good. When you met Matt at the gate, what did she do?"

Kayla frowned. "She told me to give Matt his medicine while she visited Sara. Sara's okay but Bug is great. Wish we had a dog like him."

Chuy thought the last comment was strange for a child who killed and dismembered dogs. He didn't even want to think about Bug that way. He remembered the scene when he found Matt. "What did you give him?"

Kayla looked surprised. "His usual medicines. He didn't want to take them and muttered, 'Not again.'"

Dr. Piaget frowned and patted Matt's shoulder. "Did he often fight with you over his medicine?"

Kayla shrugged. "Sometimes." She looked at Chuy. "Are you through with your questions? She doesn't like me to talk about her."

Chuy thought a bit. He needed to avoid mentioning Mitzi. "How long did you and Matt wait for her?"

Matt said, "Long time."

Kayla nodded.

"Why didn't Matt leave with you two?"

Kayla shrugged. "She told me to walk back to Walmart while she and Matt talked."

"About what?"

"Don't know. Never understood their conversations."

Matt pointed to his clean plate. "More?"

Dr. Piaget looked concerned. "You don't need more. If you eat more, you'll be too sleepy to play in the yard."

Kayla chuckled. "You mean you don't want him to get fat."

Chuy looked at his watch. This lunch had been a waste of time. He had gained only a little new information. "Did your..." He stopped. "Did she join you right away?"

"No. Oh, I forgot—I was told to wait for her in an empty lot not far from the Walmart parking lot. I was sitting there when she ran up and wanted to play games. She shoved our old ugly hoodies in a bag and promised we'd get new prettier ones. It was chilly, but she wanted to go into the auto repair place on the far side of Walmart."

CHAPTER 31: FBI Agent Carbonne Discovers More Problems

Chuy should have gotten back to him by now. When he and Chuy had divvied up the remaining tasks, Chuy had reluctantly agreed to have Mercado police officers check on Sara's house twice a day. Just to be sure, Carbonne decided he'd stop by Sara's place after he left the airport.

Nothing looked different when he parked at the La Bendita clubhouse and walked to Sara's nearby house. Everything in the front yard was as he'd left it. He walked to the backyard and stopped suddenly. There were footprints in the sand of Sara's Japanese-style garden. The prints, especially by her bedroom windows, looked as if they were from two different types of shoes. He'd raked the sand carefully yesterday to make it look like Sara had returned from India and cleaned up her yard. There definitely were no footprints in the sand when he left yesterday afternoon.

A couple of months ago Sara had installed Japanese-style raked sand gardens around her patio and under her bedroom windows. If anyone snooped, they'd leave footprints. Carbonne didn't know whether the raked sand was her idea or something Gil or Sanders had suggested. She hadn't said much about it except she had complained it complicated her gardening. He didn't want to step in the sand so he took quick photos of the footprints. He guessed Chuy hadn't warned the Mercado officers not to step in the raked sand.

Inside, the house looked as he left it. He decided to check the feed from the cameras at the front and patio doors before he called someone from the FBI lab to analyze the footprints in the sand. He replayed the tape from the front door in fast forward mode. No one had entered or neared the door. Carbonne didn't even see any shadows. Damn—that meant Chuy had forgotten to have a Mercado police officer monitor Sara's house. That was a problem, especially since Ulysses had left him another note reminding him that if Lurleen Jansen's murder was never solved it would be "unfortunate," but it would be catastrophic if anything happened to Sara before she testified at the trial of the gang leaders. He had ended his note with the single word. "Prioritize."

Carbonne had reiterated to Chuy yesterday how important monitoring Sara's house was. Heat was now rising up Carbonne's neck as it often did when he was angry. He took off his jacket and pulled a diet soda from Sara's refrigerator. She wouldn't care, and he needed to cool off before he talked to anyone. The feed from the camera by the patio door required more attention. Dogs and rabbits trotted through Sara's backyard. No humans appeared on the tape until about midnight. He saw a hooded image peering at the edges of the patio door. Then the figure tried to look around the edge of the drape pulled across the patio door. Carbonne wished he'd installed a camera at the bedroom window. He guessed judging by the size of the footprints outside and their varied impressions that two men—not children—had cased out Sara's house last night.

***

Barbara and two FBI technicians greeted Carbonne eagerly when he arrived at Lurleen's house. They began with their bad news: The lab had only been able to identify Lurleen's DNA on the bloody towels and in the blood smears on the boxes. If one of the killers had cut themselves or shed a few skin cells, their DNA would be almost impossible to find in the large volume of Lurleen's DNA. It also appeared all fingerprints had been wiped from the pendant found with the bloody towels.

Their good news compensated for the bad. The cover page of the newspaper found in the box had partial fingerprints besides Lurleen's. The prints appeared to be similar to Mitzi's and not Kayla's. Rapid DNA analyses indicated the DNA inside the plastic gloves was Mitzi's. Carbonne gave a silent prayer of thanks for the department's new rapid DNA analysis capabilities. However, he ordered the lab to do the full DNA analyses because these results would be crucial in a trial.

Carbonne also breathed a sigh of relief. He hadn't botched the case by trusting Pete initially. He could now charge Mitzi with evidence tampering and abetting Lurleen's murder. However, a jury might not convict her of murder based on this evidence alone without testimony from Kayla and Matt.

As he debated how to elicit helpful comments from Kayla and Matt, he barely heard Barbara's final announcement of good news. They only had only fifteen more boxes to check. She and the technicians had found more fonts, but only one was brown. They'd placed it with the other brown fonts in the dining room.

After he congratulated them, he said, "I'm afraid I have bad news. A more urgent situation has arisen. You two technicians have to take photos of footprints at Sara Almquist's house and look for fingerprints around the windows. Barbara will have to complete the task of opening and cataloging the last boxes alone." He started to leave and then added, "Oh wait—go to Pete's lair and scoop up a pair of his shoes. They won't be the shoes he's been wearing, but at least we'll know his shoe size."

***

An hour later, Carbonne walked into Ulysses Howe's office. "Sorry to interrupt, but I think the gangs are waiting for Sara's return. I found footprints in the sand in Sara's backyard and fingerprints around Sara's patio door and bedroom window. I've already eliminated Pete Jansen and Mitzi Jansen as suspects on the basis of shoe sizes. We know the two children were in a secure facility. The footprints suggest the culprits were men under six foot. One wore gloves. The other didn't or at least not all the time. One good print and several partials match those of a small-time gang member we have on record as living in Mercado. I've got agents looking for him now."

The three FBI agents with Ulysses looked annoyed. Ulysses didn't and he shooed them out of his office. "Have you called Sara and Sanders or the U.S. marshals yet?"

Carbonne waited until the door closed behind the last agent. "No, wanted to alert you first. It's three in the morning in India now."

"And?"

"The marshals will be steamed. This is the day Sara and Sanders leave India. They won't have much time to make changes in their flights. However, I checked and their flight isn't due to leave until eleven at night. There are plenty of earlier flights on Air India but none on U.S. carriers from Delhi to east coast cities. At least one U.S. flight leaves Delhi mid-afternoon for Los Angeles. We must get the details worked out quickly if we want to get Sara and Sanders from their Agra hotel to a flight from Delhi. Thought you could call your buddy Elmo Sanchez at the marshal's office in Albuquerque."

"You can call Sanchez. I'll call Sanders's boss at the State Department. She's an assistant secretary of state that I met on a case I worked with Sara. The secretary can help us arrange things with the embassy in Delhi and get Sara and Sanders back to Delhi fast. Before I make the call, tell me why didn't you report this sooner?"

Carbonne looked at his feet for a moment. "My fault. I interviewed Bill Jansen this morning at the airport and depended on others to check Sara's house."

Ulysses grimaced. "You're learning to prioritize the hard way. Get anything useful?"

"Yeah, the brother is sure Mitzi killed her mother because Mitzi started abusing pets as a child. He can't prove the murder charge, though."

**

The next hour was a nightmare.

Elmo Chavez had a temper. He didn't ask who had dropped the ball, but assumed it was Carbonne. However, he agreed with Carbonne that Sara should not use her reservation on the flight from Delhi to Newark tonight. An earlier flight under an alias would be better. Elmo was relieved to learn Sanders was Sara's traveling companion because he had dealt with Sanders before. "He's one of the best at arranging covert removal of Americans from overseas sites. Have you talked to him yet?"

"He's my next call. Ulysses Howe is on the phone with Sanders's boss, an assistant secretary of state, now." He saw Ulysses give him a high sign. "He'll add you to his connection with her." Elmo Sanchez didn't say thank you.

**

Sanders answered the phone in Sara's hotel room. He sounded wide awake but Carbonne knew Sanders was a pro at taking emergency calls in the middle of the night.

Sanders's reaction to Carbonne's message was worse than Elmo's. His voice was sharper and his phrasing more staccato than usual as he said, "You were lax. Now her life is in danger." He quickly elected to be connected by another phone to Ulysses's conference call.

Carbonne felt the acid in his stomach rise up his esophagus when Sanders handed the phone to Sara. She had reason to he hysterical and angry, but she wasn't, or she hid her emotions.

"I heard enough of Sanders's comments to know my vacation is over. While Sanders and Ulysses make the big arrangements. I guess you and I have to take care of the details. I'm packing our cases as we speak. We can be at the front door of the hotel in five minutes. We both have only carry-on luggage, but I have no disguises like wigs or caps to hide my hair. Don't suggest a sari. I tried...."

Carbonne kept himself from snickering. Sanders had included a picture of Sara in a sari with one of his earlier emails to Ulysses. He'd subtitled the picture: "Not her style." Ulysses had shared the picture with Carbonne. He thought it looked like the intro to a strip tease routine and the sari hung precariously on Sara's hips. He banished the thought from his mind. "When will the tour director miss you if you disappear?"

"We're in luck. We don't have to have our bags out until one in the afternoon and the bus leaves at one-thirty. Up to then, we have no planned activities." She changed the topic before Carbonne could reply. "I figure this lapse occurred because you depended on Chuy Bargas. He's easily distracted and is too trusting of others. It would be best if you didn't tell him about this glitch, just in case there's a leak in the Mercado Police Department. I know Gil was always cautious.

CHAPTER 32: Sara Returns Home on Day 10

Sara had zipped her suitcase closed and was standing at the door by the time Sanders completed his phone conversation. He kissed her cheek lightly. "We're traveling as embassy personnel who because of an emergency have to get back to Washington fast. No one should ask for details. The embassy will have a local driver meet us in front of the hotel. Let's roll."

Sara could tell the plans were incomplete because Sanders seemed more nervous than usual. He was chewing gum. Something he rarely did. He also gave no explanations in the car and she knew better than to ask. Thus, she was surprised when the car pulled up not to the entrance of the commercial terminal but to the gate of the Indian Air Force complex at the airport. Sanders told the driver to say, "Captain Edwards and Sergeant Hollister are here."

When they alit from the car, a young U.S. Air Force sergeant rushed them to a military cargo jet with its engines already roaring. As soon as the they entered the jet, the door to the cargo hold closed behind them.

Sara saw a beat-up jeep and lots of decrepit equipment in the large bay as the sergeant led them to the cockpit. He pointed to two uncomfortable looking jump seats, strapped himself into a standard seat behind the pilot, and said, "Ready."

The pilot gunned the engines and the plane began to taxi down the runway. Sanders looked at his watch and whispered into Sara's ear. "This plane was supposed to leave at four-thirty. It's thirty-one minutes after four now. Pretty good all things considered."

Sara nodded. "I've heard the horrors of long flights on military cargo planes. I also heard you say 'she can do it' earlier. Is this flight going to Delhi or directly to the U.S.?" She thought she knew the answer.

He squeezed her hand. "This was our best option for getting out of Agra. It's almost a four hour drive from Agra to Delhi. No commercial flights were available but this military cargo plane, which had delivered repair parts for jets and new equipment to the Indian Air Force Base in Agra and had picked up Pakistani equipment captured in Kashmir by the

Indian army, was scheduled to leave for Joint Base Andrews in Washington, D.C."

"You didn't answer my question."

"We will land in Delhi to pick up another passenger and an official packet."

"Okay—the details are above my pay grade. Am I Sergeant Hollister? Is she a real person?"

"That's the beauty of our plan. Edwards and Hollister are in Delhi and were scheduled for this flight from Delhi to Joint Base Andrews. They were delighted to learn they could instead use our business class tickets to return to the U.S."

"What about our passports and the fancy biometric checks the Indian government uses?"

Sanders winked at her. "Remember we were waved through those systems when we entered India because so many older women had no usable fingerprints. The American embassy in Delhi will issue the real Hollister and Edwards temporary passports as us. We won't officially enter the airport in Delhi so our credentials won't be checked carefully, especially after our official packet is delivered."

Sara sighed. "I get it. We'll be traveling with a diplomatic pouch made possible by your rank in the State Department. Does Hollister have a first name?"

"Yes, my first name will be Ed. Yours is Nora, but no one will ask for identification unless we face unforeseen problems."

"What about the other person we're picking up in Delhi?"

"A real military attaché already scheduled for the flight. Let's get some sleep."

"Wait—will I be able to get off in Delhi and stretch my legs and get some food? If we get to suggest food choices for the fifteen-hour flight to D.C., please order McDonald's cheeseburgers for me. I'm sick of Indian food."

He shook his head in mock disgust. "You're bad." He leaned forward and consulted with the sergeant.

Sara closed her eyes and willed herself to sleep, which wasn't hard at four-thirty in the morning. Besides, she'd learned to save her energy for emergencies. At this point, there was nothing useful she could do.

***

She awoke as the cargo plane bumped on the ground, bounced a bit, and lumbered roughly down the runway. It made her appreciate commercial passenger jets and pilots. However, she had to admit the view of the runway was spectacular from the cockpit, even from the back row, which she alone occupied. Engaged in conversation, Sanders had moved and was seated behind the co-pilot next to the sergeant.

Sara's back hurt even though this flight had been less than an hour. There was no need to whine. A lot of people were breaking their backs to get her home safely and protect her until the first federal trial in a month. She wondered whether she had a future after the trials. If gangs leaders had commissioned lower level members to stake out her house as Carbonne believed, would they commission a hit on her afterwards for revenge? The U.S. marshals had already warned her that she might need to establish a new identity. That would destroy all the dreams she'd spun with Sanders. She and Bug would be alone again. Sara tried to think of a bright spot. There wasn't one, except she wouldn't have to worry about someone from Lurleen's family tracking her down. That wasn't much comfort because she trusted Carbonne to solve that case.

As soon as the plane lumbered to a stop, the cargo door opened. The sergeant bustled Sara and Sanders into a small sparse lounge. A dark haired man, who didn't bother to introduce himself but who she assumed was the military attaché, was waiting. He handed Sara a black passport and pushed her into line behind the pilot, co-pilot, and himself. An Indian official quickly glanced at her passport and stamped it.

She studied the new passport as she waited for Sanders and the sergeant to clear the immigration check. Somehow the embassy had found an old picture of her and created a passport for her as Nora Ellen Edwards. According to the passport, Nora was in her thirties.

After a pit stop, the crew and passengers tramped to the plane as a fork lift pulled away from it. This time the sergeant didn't rush Sara as she moved through the cargo hold. He pointed out a lavatory, a tiny kitchenette, and a refrigerator stocked with beverages and fruit. "You can microwave meals whenever you wish. I couldn't get you and McDonalds' cheeseburgers but you don't need to worry. This pilot dislikes what he calls 'foreign food'" so there are plenty of familiar snacks available. He also pointed to a closet with stacks of pillows and blankets. "After we take off, you can walk the length of the plane for exercise, but don't touch any of the equipment."

***

Sanders was busy during much of the flight. Actually, all five men either slept or worked during the flight. The sergeant, Sanders, and the military attaché were frequently huddled over one computer screen. Sara suspected they were planning how to hide her until she testified at the upcoming federal trials, but they seldom consulted with her. She interrupted their conversations only twice to say that she wouldn't go anywhere without Bug. Each time Sanders had groaned.

Sara tried to read a novel but couldn't concentrate. She caught up on with correspondence from USAID that she'd ignored over the last week. She wasn't like Sanders or most young executives who felt a need to keep up on work correspondence while on vacation. But this flight was no vacation.

No amount of work could stop her from thinking about witness protection. When the marshals had tried to protect her in Albuquerque, she had felt it was like being confined in a disorganized jail. It almost made her feel sorry for criminals. This time, they would quickly move her to a distant location. She doubted the arrangements would be disorganized, but, rather would seem like solitary confinement. They'd keep her there until the trial. After her testimony at multiple trials, she'd be moved to another location from which she'd never return.

There was no need to think about her future with Sanders. He'd assumed a distance, an *aloofness*, that she hadn't seen since she first met him in Bolivia. He had all but told her that she would be entering the witness protection program without him. She couldn't blame him. Of course, Gil Andrews, Carbonne, neighbors in La Bendita, staff and patients in pediatrics at the University Hospital and at the VA Hospital where she and Bug did pet therapy, and her co-workers at USAID would also soon be part of her past. They'd just be photos in a secret album stashed in a back closet if she entered the program.

Now was not the time to cry. So, Sara walked laps around the cargo hold and thought of Bug or slept.

CHAPTER 33: Sergeant Chuy Bargas Is Too Busy

Chuy read the email which Carbonne had sent four hours ago:
Must pull technicians out of Lurleen's house. Barbara will have to finish checking the last boxes alone. Will personally monitor Sara's house from now on.

Chuy was pleased because he figured Carbonne didn't have enough to do as an FBI agent. Carbonne didn't have to respond to angry calls from community residents caught in traffic jams as road crews resurfaced the main road into Mercado from I-25. Chuy frowned. Gil never took those types of calls either because he made the secretary at the front desk calm the callers with four standard answers encased in a plastic sheath kept by the phone. The current problem was that same secretary refused to follow this procedure for Chuy.

Barbara Lewis knocked on his door. "Sorry to interrupt your thoughts, but I finished cataloging the contents of all the boxes at Lurleen Jansen's house." She then embarked on a long explanation of the lab data.

The light on his phone began to flash because a caller was waiting. With his luck, it would be the mayor or Mitzi's lawyers again. "I'm kinda busy. What do you need?"

Barbara Lewis looked surprised. "I thought you'd want an update on the Jansen case because I have a new lead. I used a jeweler's loupe to check some of the fonts. I use the loupe when I help my sister-in-law make jewelry for fairs and thought it might be useful. Anyway, I saw two vertical cracks in the stem of one of the brown stone fonts. I don't think they're signs of age. They look like cut edges, but I couldn't open anything. I emailed Carbonne but he didn't answer. He usually does."

Chuy figured Carbonne either had gone undercover or was intensely involved in another case. That surprised him. He thought Carbonne was focused on only two cases now—Lurleen Jansen's murder and protecting Sara until the federal trial, which was no work while Sara was in India. Maybe Ulysses Howe had figured how little Carbonne had to do and gave him more administrative work.

He didn't have time to redirect Barbara, and she was obviously into the Jansen case. "Call Pete Jansen and have him look at the fonts."

Barbara frowned. "I don't think Carbonne will like that idea, but Pete Jansen did leave a note for Lurleen years ago in the oak font. You know the yellowed note we found?"

He must have given her a blank look because she began a long explanation. "I don't need the details now. Just get Pete to help you."

She looked alarmed. "But I should have someone with me when I speak to Pete Jansen, especially if I take him to Lurleen's house to examine the fonts. I don't want to invalidate any evidence. You know...."

He'd never noticed before how talkative Barbara could be. "Fine—take Martin Padilla."

"He's a rookie. I've never worked with him...."

"He's all I have."

Barbara stared at him.

Chuy picked up the phone and let the caller identify themselves. Barbara was still staring at him. He pointed at her and said, "Go."

CHAPTER 34: Mercado Police Officer Barbara Lewis

Barbara Lewis thought she'd been set up to fail as soon as she spoke to Martin Padilla. He immediately began to brag, "My amigo Chuy and I agree. We don't need the help of the FBI to know those two crazy kids killed their grandmother. Time to lock them up, and let their mother have a life."

She knew simple failure would be a good outcome today as she talked to Pete. He seemed gleeful when she asked him to meet her at Lurleen's—now—his house. In his excitement, Pete revealed that Carbonne had not only forbidden him from entering the house during the last week but had changed the locks on the doors to the house. Obviously, Carbonne didn't want Pete to see any potential evidence or be able to guess the FBI's progress on the case.

All Barbara could think to do was send an email to Carbonne explaining the situation and flag it with "EMERGENCY" in the subject line. She also texted the message to him and prayed he'd get back to her before she entered Lurleen's house.

***

Padilla couldn't seem to focus on Barbara's instructions as they drove to the house and kept bragging how he raided the lockers of middle school kids when he was a guard for the Albuquerque Public Schools. Finally, as they entered the house, she said, "If you say anything or touch anything without my permission, I guarantee your career will end today, even if Chuy is your pal. And if you aren't lucky, FBI agent Carbonne will also charge you with evidence tampering. Your job today is to record everything Pete and I say and do."

Padilla looked surprised.

"You'll do a continuous video and audio recording." Barbara reviewed with Padilla how to operate the camera and sound equipment. She knew it was demeaning because he claimed he already knew how to operate the equipment, but she couldn't take a chance that he was bluffing.

She also threw tarps she'd brought along over all the piles and objects in the kitchen and dining room, except for the brown fonts. When the doorbell rang, she ignored it and walked around the kitchen, dining room, and living room. Everything but the sink and appliances in the kitchen was covered. Padilla had the videotape running as Barbara greeted Pete Jansen at the door.

Pete's jaw dropped when he saw his kitchen and Padilla awkwardly pointing the camera at him. Pete started to touch the tarp on top of the kitchen island.

"Don't touch anything, unless I ask you to." Barbara knew she was being paranoid but she was not going to blow this case. Her professional and personal relationship with Carbonne was too important. She led Pete to the row of brown fonts in the dining room. She debated whether to admit she already knew how to find the hiding spot in the oak font. It could be a way to check his honesty. He obviously did know how to find the hiding spot because they had found his note. She decided to be honest and took the lid off the oak font and twisted the basin area to reveal the hiding spot. "We think there are hiding spots in the other fonts, but we can't find them. Please help."

He looked puzzled. "Why do you care?"

She debated her options and again decided honesty was best. "We know Lurleen had a secret hiding spot."

"How?"

Barbara tried to give a blank stare.

Pete laughed. "Oh, another hint from Sara? What did Lurleen keep there?"

"Not so fast. You want us to solve this case, don't you?" She fluttered her eyelashes. Carbonne had told her women detectives should use their wiles when interviewing men. She remembered how he had fluttered his eyelashes over lunch and said, "See it doesn't work for men." She had thought his black lashes and eyes were pretty interesting to her. She swallowed hard and told herself to focus on Pete and not on thoughts of Carbonne.

"The fonts were Lurleen's obsession. What makes you think I know anything about them?"

"We found a note in this one." She pointed to the oak font.

Pete choked. "So long ago... Most fonts don't have secret compartments, but some do. Lurleen liked those best. We scoured most of the Midwest and New England looking for church closings or remodelings. eBay didn't exist in those days, so finding fonts was more difficult." He sighed. "But we were happy then."

Barbara motioned to Padilla to move the focus of his camera to the last brown font they'd found and pulled out her jeweler's loupe. "I found two vertical cracks. I think they're intentional cuts in the stem of this stone font—take a look"

Pete knelt next to her. He didn't bother to look through the loop. "Could be a seam because the mason didn't have a large enough block of stone, but probably not." He slid his finger along the smooth edge. He stood and lifted the stone lid off the top of the font and placed it gently on the floor. He rubbed his finger around the uncovered bowl. "See this." He pointed to a small carved rosette at the base of the bowl. If I lift this rosette, we'll find a metal pull underneath. Like a stopper in a bathtub." He tried to wiggle the stone flower. "I'll need a small screwdriver or kitchen knife to lift it. I can get it from the drawer." He started to move toward the kitchen.

"No, you stay here. I'll get the kitchen knife."

As soon as she handed him a knife, he started to pry at the flower. "Got be careful. I don't want the metal to detach from the stopper. If that happens the drawer is much harder to open."

Barbara held her breath. Pete lifted the stone rosette an inch. A copper chain was attached to a loop in the stone underneath the rosette. Nothing in the stem below moved. As he lifted the flower further, a small latch, like a lobster clamp on jewelry, appeared. He carefully opened the clasp and a loop of chain was released.

He looked up at Barbara. "I recognize this as one I fixed years ago back in Michigan." He lowered the rosette into the basin and knocked gently along the edge of the seams in the stem. Nothing happened. He used the knife to pry into the seam in the stone on one side and then the other. A rectangular section of stone emerged from the stem about an eighth of an inch. "If I had some duct tape, I could stick it to the front of the drawer and pull it out. That's how Lurleen usually opened these stone drawers."

Barbara told Pete to move away from the fonts and told Padilla to keep the camera going as she looked under the tarps on the counters in Lurleen's kitchen. The one good thing about cataloging all the boxes was she knew there were rolls of blue duct tape somewhere in the room. The lab technicians and she had used blue tape to reseal boxes after they cataloged the contents. They'd left only brown fonts outside the boxes.

J. L. Greger

Otherwise the clutter in the house would have precluded even walking through the rooms. She could hear Padilla and Pete snickering as she peeked under the tarps. Two rolls of blue tape were under a tarp in the last place she looked.

Pete quickly formed loops of tape, applied them to the surface of the stone rectangle and pulled. He tinkered for a several minutes before he pulled a stone drawer from the stem of the font. Barbara put on gloves and pulled a slip of paper from the drawer. The blue ink had faded but was legible:

St. Mary's Church in Sault Ste. Marie, Michigan, about 1880. Replaced when church remodeled in 1980s. Restored by P. Jansen in 1989.

Barbara bit her lip. She'd been so hopeful. She thought of the ugly font found in the laundry room. The one Lurleen had used as catch-all for items found in the wash. "I'd like you to look at another font." She pointed to the original reddish brown stone font. "I think there are seams in the stem."

Pete smiled. "This one was Lurleen's favorite because it was the first one she found with a secret compartment." He knelt by it as he repeated the process he used on the last one. Only the button at the bottom of the basin was easy to pry out. The clasp opened easily, and the drawer slid out smoothly with the tape pulls.

Barbara was feeling hopeful. Lurleen must have used this drawer regularly. There was a full sheet of paper folded repeatedly in the drawer. She knew she should call the FBI lab before touching the document but she was wearing gloves. The paper was not yellowed and wouldn't flake. Just in case, she put a clean sheet of brown paper on the dining table and unfolded the white page over it. One look was enough for Barbara to know that Lurleen had provided important new details about Mitzi and her "friends."

Barbara didn't want Pete to know what the note said. He might try come back to steal it. She had no backup to protect it, and she thought Padilla was enough of a blowhard that he might tell the wrong people. Worse still, Carbonne suspected leaks in the Mercado Police Department, even though he hadn't been specific. He only said, "Gil Andrews kept a lid on the problems in Mercado. Not sure anyone else can."

Barbara knew now was the time to bluff. Lying was counter to her Indian culture, and she doubted she could lie without stuttering or turning red. She decided this was the time to remember how she had acted in her senior play. She would try to act like Carbonne. He'd be all business, but try to distract Pete with some trivia. She shook her head. "Not much, but I'll take a photo of it and the other note." She pointed to Padilla. "Take Pete to the car while I take the photos. Why don't you two prepare a statement that says you…" She pointed to Padilla. "…video recorded this search and Pete knew he was being video recorded."

She took the photos, but waited until the front door closed before she fiddled with her phone and texted both photos to Carbonne and the technicians in the FBI lab with a note:

> URGENT—*Breaking protocol. Necessary to remove Pete from site. Not sure of my backup—Martin Padilla. Document important. HELP.*

Barbara joined Padilla and Pete at the car. "I guess I wasted your time. I hope Carbonne will find the notes interesting, but I doubt it."

CHAPTER 35: FBI Agent Carbonne Creates a Plan

Carbonne knew the assignment of tasks had been fair, but he felt like he'd drawn the short straw. Sanders would direct the extraction of Sara and himself from India. The U.S marshals stationed in Washington and Elmo Sanchez would find a place to house Sara until the first trial. Everyone thought it best if Sanders had no contact with Sara after the flight because gang members would be watching him, and he might inadvertently lead them to her. Carbonne would be the key person in the FBI checking leads to determine which defendant in the upcoming trial had ordered Sara to be followed and threatened. He had insisted Sara be given a special email account for communicating with him because he knew she could be helpful. The marshals in Washington, who didn't know Sara, had argued with him, but Elmo Sanchez, as the ranking U.S. marshal on the case, and Ulysses Howe had supported Carbonne's request.

Now he sat in Ulysses Howe's office outlining what had to be done. The fingerprints around Sara's window matched the prints of a small-time criminal who had done errands for gang leaders in Mercado. He called himself "Joe Smith." Carbonne had decided he'd learn more from having the man followed than by questioning him because according to his arrest record, he wasn't clever enough to know much. The federal prosecutor had agreed and gotten court permission for a wiretap of Smith's phones. So far, the guy had made no calls and only left his house to do deliveries for Hometown Pizza in Mercado.

The threatening call Sara had received in Washington on the day of her flight to India had provided few clues. FBI technicians had quickly determined the call was from a throwaway phone and was picked up by a tower in Florence, Colorado—site of the federal prison where the defendants for the upcoming trial were being held. Carbonne had gotten a list of all visitors to the federal prison in Florence for the day Sara had received the ominous call, the week before, and the day after. Only two lawyers had visited the defendants. The federal prosecutor doubted he could get a court order to allow wiretaps on the phones of the lawyers, even though one only worked on cases for two of the defendants. Accordingly, Carbonne had assigned an agent to track that lawyer a week ago. He groaned to Ulysses, "The net result is I have a very long list of probably useless leads."

Ulysses had perused his emails and appeared to only half-listen to Carbonne through his long dialog, now he said, "Talk to Jack Daniels."

"I don't think I have the patience or the time."

"Have Chuy talk to him, then."

"I'm no longer sure about Chuy."

Ulysses's eyes about popped from his skull. "What do you mean? You've not said anything about your new concerns."

Carbonne explained that Chuy had not only dropped the ball on security at Sara's house but also seemed inattentive about important details on the Lurleen Jansen case. "Barbara Lewis just reported to me that Chuy refused to give her adequate back up when she was checking an important lead on the case."

"His administrative load with Gil Andrews's absence must be unbelievable. His head is elsewhere."

"It's more than that." Carbonne paused and decided to explain his real concerns. "It's like we're not on the same team. He knows that I suspected Pete may have tricked us, and I didn't want Pete in Lurleen's house. Yet he ordered Barbara to invite Pete to the house to examine some potential evidence."

"So, you two have differing opinions?"

"It's more than that a difference of opinions. He knows Kayla will be more cooperative if he acts on the rape charges against Josh Ahrens, but he's all but refused to pursue those charges."

"I'll say it again, don't waste any more of your time on the Lurleen Jansen case. Let Chuy do the follow up on it. I think he's a good man, but he's in way over his head trying to step into Gil's shoes."

"Can't drop it—not yet. Barbara Lewis just found a letter Lurleen wrote on the day before she died." He flashed a triumphant smile at Ulysses. "In a secret drawer in one of the fonts you deemed a waste of time."

Ulysses drummed his fingers on his desk. "I've never doubted that you're a great sleuth. My point is you're too talented to waste your time on minor cases. Why's the letter important?"

"Lots of reasons, but one that will particularly interest you because it relates to Sara. Seems Lurleen thought Mitzi had developed an 'attachment to a loser called Joe Smith.' I think it could be the same Joe Smith who left fingerprints around Sara's bedroom window and patio door two nights ago. I want to interview Mitzi about her friend. Besides stalking Sara, Smith may have been present when Lurleen was murdered."

Ulysses snorted. "Get someone else who Mitzi's lawyers haven't named yet in their harassment suits to do the interview."

"Barbara Lewis fits the bill." Carbonne tried not to smile. "Why don't *you* tell Chuy that the FBI will pay Barbara Lewis's salary for the next couple of months until the first federal trial is underway? Tell him Barbara will work with our lab to tie up details on the Lurleen Jansen's murder and provide protection for Sara. Then Chuy won't have to know any the details of Sara's security, and he'll assume Sara is in the Albuquerque area."

Ulysses stared at Carbonne. "Are you setting a trap for Chuy and trying to shield Barbara?" He paused. "I guess he won't notice, but Gil Andrews might."

"I know. I'll talk to Gil after I've made a few calls."

***

Carbonne's first call was to Elmo Sanchez. The marshals had Jack Daniels in witness protection at an out-of-state location until he testified at the upcoming federal trials. Carbonne figured Sanchez would resist any attempt to interview Jack, especially since their unpleasant conversation earlier in the day. Instead Elmo said, "If police in the Albuquerque area were bribed to ignore threats against witnesses in the upcoming trials, Jack is apt to know, even though my marshals have tried to keep him isolated."

Carbonne's next call was to the agents tailing Joe Smith. Joe had delivered pizzas all day. One of his deliveries was to the Mercado Police Department. They noted the pizza had been ordered by Martin Padilla to be delivered to Chuy's office.

He called Barbara. She was pleased because Chuy had just told her she would be on loan to the FBI for a month or two to finish up the investigation of Lurleen Jansen's murder and to provide security for Sara. She was also annoyed. When she reported to Chuy's office, she found Chuy, Padilla, and another male officer wolfing down a pizza. She complained Chuy didn't ask her about Pete Jansen or the baptismal fonts. Instead, he said, "Padilla already told me your search for secret compartments in Lurleen Jansen's baptismal fonts was a wild goose chase. You'll find the FBI, especially Carbonne, wastes a lot of time on useless details."

Carbonne laughed internally. The detail he wanted now was to know what had been exchanged among Joe Smith, Padilla, and Chuy. He bet it was more than pizza.

First, Carbonne wanted to get Barbara out of the Mercado police station. She could be in danger if anyone guessed what she had hidden from Padilla and now Chuy. "Bring the videotape of your search of the fonts and the notes you found to the FBI building immediately. Doesn't sound like Chuy will care. Then you're going to become Kayla's and Mitzi's best friend. I think they'll both talk more freely to a woman. They certainly won't talk to me. Probably because I don't look like Prince Charming."

Barbara tittered. "I wouldn't know about that."

"Maybe we can have dinner afterwards? I promise it will be better than Hometown Pizza's food."

"That's not much of a promise. Hometown makes terrible pizza." She paused. "Wait—I didn't..."

He couldn't let her complete her sentence. Someone might be monitoring the call. He said the first thing that entered his mind. "The lab report on the plastic gloves is interesting. Seems only Mitzi's DNA—presumably from sweat and skin cells—was...." His phone beeped to indicate Jack Daniels was ready to talk via a video conference. 'Sorry—have to go."

Jack Daniels was his usual slimy self. He looked more unkempt than the last time Carbonne had interviewed him. Carbonne listened for five minutes to Daniels's self-aggrandizement. "Okay, Jack, we both know you're an expert on dirty cops." Carbonne didn't add "because you're the dirtiest one" because he needed Jack's help. "What do you know about Chuy Bargas of the Mercado Police Department? He was on the New Mexico Gangs Task Force for a while a year ago. He's been on sick leave for most of the last year. Do you know why so long? Does he have other problems?"

Jack snickered. "Is this a trick question?" He licked his lips. "You somehow have guessed Gil Andrews's poster boy developed a nasty habit while he was recuperating. I thought his whore, guess his wife now, read him the riot act and stopped his bad behavior. She's a real hard ass and an up-and-coming star on the Albuquerque police force."

"Jack, cut the build-up."

"Heard Chuy was dependent on painkillers."

Carbonne thought that wasn't surprising. Chuy had broken more than ten bones in his accident. He stared at Jack and didn't prompt him because he didn't want to lead the discussion. Jack would confabulate if he thought it would earn him more favors.

Jack scratched his matted hair. "Chuy spent some time at a rehab facility in Mexico. Didn't show on his record because the unit calls itself a weight loss spa." Jack smiled. "A real expensive spa. I heard his wife took out a second mortgage on the house. Surprised that was enough. He was at the spa, let's see, for several months." Jack stopped scratching his head and rubbed his thumbs against his curled fingers.

At first Carbonne thought Jack had found something in his hair. Then he realized Jack was requesting payment with his hand gesture. "Do you want me to send a case of your namesake beverage to the marshals for delivery to you?"

"Naw. They'd drink most of it. Have the FBI cut me a check." Jack chuckled. "You're an administrator now, you know how to transfer funds to a man with no name, like me. Enough for a sixty-inch..." He paused. "...or bigger flat screen TV."

Carbonne thought he'd gotten off cheaply. "Anything else you know about Chuy, Gil Andrews, or others in the Mercado Police Department?"

"Gil's old lady is dying, and you've got the hots for a young squaw on the force."

Carbonne bit his tongue. No wonder Sara found him so disgusting. "Anything else?"

"No."

"How about a rookie called Martin Padilla?"

"They were stupid to hire him. He's from a bad family with ties to gangs in Colorado."

"Details?"

"Don't remember. You can figure it out." Jack smiled and gave Carbonne the bird. The screen went blank.

Finally, Carbonne made the hardest call—the one to Gil Andrews. Gil quickly explained he couldn't talk long because his wife was having a bad day. He admitted he'd assigned personnel issues, mainly hiring, to Chuy when he returned to work part time several months ago.

When asked about Padilla, Gil said, "Martin Padilla worked security for Albuquerque Public Schools for a year after he completed police academy training. I'd heard rumors about his family, but Chuy figured Padilla was better than a raw recruit and wanted to give him a chance. I'm afraid I should have paid more attention to this hire because you're asking about him."

Carbonne heard the distress in Gil's voice and didn't want to cause this man any more pain. He considered Gil a role model as did everyone in Albuquerque law enforcement. "I'm asking because the FBI is always recruiting and in my new administrative role I'm looking for agents with his background."

"I wish I believed you. I won't tell anyone about this conversation." Carbonne heard a woman moaning in pain in the background before Gil disconnected the call.

CHAPTER 36: Sara in Romeoville, Illinois, on Day 24

Bug was like a puppy as he plowed through the piles of dry leaves at the edges of the Lewis University sidewalks. The grounds crew had blown the gold and brown leaves from the walks between the red brick buildings of this small university in Romeoville, Illinois.

After their walk, they stopped at a McDonald's and shared a cheeseburger and fries—Bug's favorite meal. It had all started when Sara took him to McDonald's after they left pet therapy visits in Albuquerque years ago. Bug was funny. He didn't like McDonald's burgers brought home to him. He liked to eat them in the car. The women marshals hated the McDonald's visits. They thought Bug might leave stains on the car's upholstery even though Sara brought along a large towel for Bug to sit on. She figured they were trying to be annoying because they knew Bug never made mistakes.

As she dangled a fry in front of Bug, Sara thought how she'd gotten into this uncomfortable situation. The U.S. marshals had decided while she flew back from India that she would blend in best in a midwestern town, but not a small community where everyone knew their neighbor's business. Romeoville was a stop on the Heritage Corridor of the Metra train system. In other words, Romeoville was a bedroom community for Chicago. Thus, Sara had been assigned to spend the month after her return from India in Romeoville.

At first, she'd thought Romeoville could be a pleasant location. She figured she could get to downtown Chicago in less than an hour. But the marshals wouldn't allow her to take the train alone and claimed they were too busy to chaperone more than two short field trips a week. Accordingly, Sara spent an hour twice a week walking Bug around the small college campus. The marshals assigned to her would have preferred she went to nearby shopping malls, but dogs weren't welcome at the enclosed malls. The only other facility nearby was Stateville Correctional Center—hardly an appropriate place for a person in witness protection to walk her dog.

The last two weeks had been hell for Sara. The U.S Marshal Service had assigned four women to be her primary guards. All four were in their late twenties or early thirties. Their cover was they were flight attendants and were living with their "aunt" until they could find homes of their own because it was an easy drive from Romeoville to O'Hare Airport. Only two of the women were present in the house at any time.

The disagreements between Sara and her guards had begun as soon as they entered the red brick, three-bedroom ranch house. Sara had given them a grocery list so she could cook as she had for herself and the marshals in Albuquerque. These marshals had said they preferred to eat salads and would provide her with food from carry-out restaurants.

Sara had called their supervisor Elmo Sanchez on her new throwaway phone. She had been told she should only use the phone in an emergency, but Sara felt being faced with nothing but pizza and other carry-outs was an emergency. After the call, one of the woman had gone on a grocery run, while the other one sulked as Sara set up her computer.

Even her use of the computer was problematic. Sara's guards provided her with computer games, which she ignored. She didn't want to waste her time. She was used to being productive, but that wouldn't be easy. Although she could use a computer to search the Web, she couldn't communicate with any of her colleagues in Bolivia, Cuba, or Washington, D.C., or with Sanders. Thus, Sara decided it was a good time to write the final report on her work with USAID in Bolivia. Besides, recent upheavals in the Bolivian government suggested the new Bolivian regime would respond positively to a new initiative by USAID in the country. She included lots of helpful insights in her report on Bolivia.

When she completed the report, her women guards refused to forward it because they feared it could be used to locate her. She pointed out that she had not ceased to be Sara Almquist yet. Gang leaders knew she was alive and would testify at the upcoming trials. Nothing in the report suggested her current location, but the guards were adamant. Again, Sara called Elmo Sanchez. He promised her a solution within a week

The next day one of the marshals took an USB drive with the report with her when she left the house. Sara believed, although she hadn't been told, that the marshals reported in to an office in the Chicago area on a daily basis. That was another problem. Previously, FBI agents and marshals guarding Sara in Albuquerque had communicated with her and she felt part of the process. These four women considered it inappropriate for Sara to know anything about her own protection.

This conflict with her new protectors made her think. If she accepted witness protection after the trial, Sara Almquist would cease to exist. She could not contact anyone or consult because her expertise would give away her identity even if she used an alias. She toyed with making soft sculptures, really elaborate woven textiles, as she'd done before the flu epidemic and her consulting for USAID. The U.S. marshals protecting her had told her to forget that idea. They weren't going to transport her looms from La Bendita, and they were sure no other marshals would be willing to transport her looms to a new location. Again, the looms and her work were too distinctive. Sara had reached the conclusion that the life the U.S. marshals were willing to provide her after the trial wasn't worth living.

The only bright spots in her life were Bug and her emails from Carbonne. The marshals complained daily about how her long walks with Bug were attracting the attention of neighbors. They also grumbled Carbonne's daily updates were preventing them from orienting her to her future.

Carbonne kept Sara apprised of his progress on solving Lurleen's murder and finding those who had stalked her and Bug. In the letter found in the brown stone font, Lurleen had noted Mitzi had acquired a questionable boyfriend named Joe Smith, apparently the same Joe Smith who had left fingerprints around Sara's bedroom window. Carbonne had guessed that Joe might have been the "muscle" when Lurleen was murdered, but he had an iron-clad alibi. Smith had been arrested in Colorado for disorderly conduct on the night Lurleen was murdered and spent all the next day in the Durango jail until he could post bail.

Sara sadly realized that meant he had not stalked her and Bug at La Bendita either. She hated to think Kayla and/or Mitzi had not only stalked her but thrown rocks at her patio door and broken the glass.

Carbonne had decided not to charge Mitzi with her mother's murder until he learned the importance of Kayla's role. Accordingly, Barbara met with Kayla daily to gain the needed information while Dr. Piaget tried to heal Kayla's troubled psyche. However, they'd only learned that Kayla was terrified by the thought of ever having to live with Mitzi again and felt guilty about Lurleen's death.

Matt was no help. He seemed to have blocked all memory of his life prior to being in the mental health facility and seemed unable to recognize photos of Lurleen and Mitzi. Pete spent all his time suing Mitzi for custody of Matt and Kayla even though the suit was a moot point. Both children would remain in the mental facility until Lurleen's murder was solved and experts judged the children not to be a danger to themselves or others.

Sara was surprised and annoyed that Carbonne didn't bring Joe Smith in for questioning, even though he had ascertained that Mitzi and Joe often met at a local bar. After several emails, Sara guessed Carbonne's reasons. He'd lost confidence in Chuy and feared leaks in the Mercado Police Department could derail his investigations. She then emailed Carbonne:

> *Chuy failed to provide protection for me in an earlier case. It was one of the times Gil Andrews had to rescue me with guns blazing. At that time, the FBI suspected Chuy of being on the payroll of drug gangs. Chuy quickly proved his loyalty but then had his horrendous accident. My assessment of Chuy is that he's basically a good man overwhelmed by his current responsibilities. He's also a bit naïve and might have trusted the wrong people.*

Carbonne responded:

> *Where would you look for leaks in the Mercado PD? Can't ask Gil. He's overwhelmed with his wife's care.*

Sara had thought for a day before responding:

> *I don't think Gil has scrutinized new hires carefully during the last six months. He had too many personal concerns. There could be a weak link in the group.*

After that email, Carbonne finally admitted a number of details to her. The most interesting was:

> *Martin Padilla, a recent hire in the Mercado PD, is Joe Smith's cousin. Their relatives in Florence, Colorado, are major figures in the drug trade there.*

At the end of a long email, Carbonne added:

> *The marshals protecting Jack Daniels think he is dangerously depressed and fear he may commit suicide. Even Jack doesn't deserve the isolation and hopelessness of his protective custody. I assume yours is better.*

Sara had responded she would endure the U.S. marshal's protection until the trials were over but doubted the life they would provide her afterwards was worth living.

***

The next day, right after Sara and Bug returned from their walk at Lewis University, Elmo Sanchez arrived at the safe house with two middle-aged women carrying boxes of groceries and packages. "I remembered the great meals you made for the marshals in Albuquerque. I convinced these two to come along by saying we were going to the best new restaurant in the Chicago area."

Once he was inside, he eyed Sara and sent the women to unpack the groceries. "I came here for several reasons. Your report was delivered to Sanders and he was delighted." He handed a medium size box wrapped in silvery pink paper to her and pointed to the bouquet of yellow and pink roses the women had placed on the kitchen counter. "The box is from Sanders. The flowers are from Ulysses Howe and Carbonne. I can give you a couple of minutes to open the package."

Sara rubbed her finger along the smooth paper and the satin bow. "No, I want to open it when I'm alone." She placed it on the counter.

"I've come to discuss your future. It's obvious this arrangement isn't working." He continued to stare at her. "What in hell happened to your hair? How did it turn gray in less than two weeks?"

Sara gasped. "So, it looks as bad as I thought."

Elmo continued, "The marshals at Joint Base Andrews gave you a short dark brown wig. What happened to it?"

"I liked it because in the cool weather of late October of the Midwest it seemed liked a cap. But my assigned guards insisted I dye my hair because I didn't wear the wig to bed. They chose a gray shade." Sara drew her hands through her hair. "They thought it looked natural." Sara frowned. "I think the dull gray shade makes me look twenty years older."

Elmo rubbed his lower face. "The federal prosecutor will have my hide if you show up for the trial looking like a frail old woman." He paused. "That didn't sound right. Why don't we cook dinner together? My wife has trained me to be a decent sous chef."

Sara beamed. "I'd be delighted because I'm tired of eating alone." She walked to the kitchen and looked at the containers in the refrigerator and on the counter. I guess you're hoping for lasagna?"

"Carbonne says your spaghetti is great, and your pot roast is to die for, but he likes the lasagna best."

As Sara prepared the lasagna and Elmo diced carrots, celery, and olives for a chopped salad, one of the mature marshals paced the house.

The other middle-aged woman marshal sat at the dining table and consulted with the young women marshals who had been staying at the house. "Why did you pick the dull gray hair color for Dr. Almquist? You know the federal prosecutor wants her to look like herself—blonde, bold, competent—when she testifies. Her appearance shouldn't be changed until after the trial. And then…" She studied Sara. "Judging by her gait and carriage, I'd try to pass her off as a carefree divorcee with red or maybe silvery hair with a purple streak."

One young woman snapped. "She's supposed to be our *old* aunt. Do you realize how hard she is to contain? She sits in front of the Memorial Union at Lewis University with that show-off dog and talks to students, asking them about their majors. And she wants to walk the dog three or four times a day. Not just around the block but one or two miles. When the dog is worn out, she carries him. We're sure everyone in the neighborhood knows about the crazy dog lady."

The other young woman pointed to Elmo. "As our supervisor, you warned us that there had been several shoot outs at her house in Albuquerque. We were scared."

Sara and Elmo had listened silently to the conversation. Now Sara interrupted, "I'd have been happier if you had housed me and Bug in a coat closet in the basement of any FBI building and let me work on cases during the day and sleep there on a cot at night. I need to be useful. Besides, I never gave my name when I was at Lewis University. I always said I was waiting for my daughter to finish her class."

Elmo shook his head. "It's my fault." He looked at the young woman marshals. "I warned you serious attempts might be made on Sara's life. I forgot to tell you that my marshals and the FBI agents in Albuquerque liked guarding Sara because she was a resourceful, pleasant ally. I thought you'd figure it out." He turned to Sara. "Both Carbonne and Ulysses Howe had warned me you'd need a lot of activities to keep you busy. I should have known something was wrong when the marshals didn't come laden with baked goods you made and all sorts of materials for Sanders when they reported in daily."

Sara smiled. "So, how are you going to correct the situation? Jury selection begins for the first trial next week. Maybe Bug and I can return to Albuquerque or at least to New Mexico?"

J. L. Greger

CHAPTER 37: Police Officer Barbara Lewis in Albuquerque on Day 27

Barbara saw a familiar scene. Pete was playing ball with Matt by the basketball hoop in the backyard of the group home. As usual, Kayla sat watching alone. The nurses at the front desk had said that Dr. Piaget had already made his daily rounds and noted no changes in either child.

Barbara pulled a small bag of caramel corn from her tote. "Kayla, I was in Buffet's—you know, the good candy store in Albuquerque?—and saw the caramel corn. When I was a kid, my mother would make caramel corn around Halloween. She said it was too much bother to make any other time. Want to share it with me?"

Kayla reached in the bag and popped pieces of the sticky corn in her mouth. "Mom always said it was bad for my teeth, but Grandma Lu bought it anyway." She winced when she said, "Grandma Lu."

"I don't think the guys need an audience. I know the nurses here took away all your makeup, but I bet they wouldn't care if I braided your hair. My mother used to braid my hair. And it always made me feel special when she wrapped the braids on top of my head like she did hers." She opened another bag full of purple, red, and yellow ribbons. "Maybe I can braid the ribbons into your hair. Let's see if the guys notice."

"They won't." Kayla stood and led Barbara to the craft room. "I like the purple ribbons."

Barbara quickly realized it was easier to braid her own thick dark hair than Kayla's thinner blonde hair. Kayla remained silent as Barbara combed, braided and unbraided Kayla's hair several times. When Barbara finished the first braid, Kayla seemed to relax and began to chatter about how her mother had once tried to braid her hair. Evidently, it hadn't been successful. After Barbara finished the second braid, she experimented with looping the braids around Kayla's head.

Kayla liked the braids best spiraled in buns behind her ears. "I'd look like an Indian princess if my hair was dark like yours." She touched Barbara's hair. "Then I could forget about all the dogs I buried for Mom."

Kayla had not mentioned burying dogs before. Dr. Piaget had cautioned her not her to ignore such a hint but not to push either. "Want to tell me about them?"

Kayla looked down. "No, but Dr. Piaget says I can't feel better until I admit what hurts." She studied her fingers. "Maybe we could manicure each other's nails next. I have some purple polish in my room."

Barbara glanced at her own nails. "My nails are too short to be worth purple polish."

"Like mine after I buried the dogs, but they've grown out."

Barbara tried to act natural as she pulled out her phone and recorded Kayla's halting story.

"Buried a lot…. Whenever Mom got angry… usually with Grandma Lu… or when she had a headache… she killed dogs… and cats… usually at night. Then she'd wake me. Claimed she couldn't bury them. She'd put them in a box. I'd find it in the trunk of the car… with a shovel. She'd open the garage door and I'd drive to the orchard… alone. Felt so sorry for the dogs…. Sang to them. Couldn't mark their graves…. Others would notice…. Finally, Grandma Lu did…. She kept asking: Why… why does Matt do this?" Kayla looked up at Barbara. "I couldn't tell her the truth."

Barbara hugged Kayla. "Anything else you want to tell me?"

Kayla nodded and continued, "When I came home, Mother would be in bed with Matt, whispering. Always touching his hair… combing it with her fingers… and whispering. Usually she'd have a candle lit in the room… a scented one… usually lavender. I went to bed alone." For the first time, Kayla broke down in tears.

Her sobbing was so loud, a nurse approached them. Barbara said, "Tell Dr. Piaget to get here fast and bring Carbonne. Tell them she confirmed Lurleen's letter."

Barbara continued to stroke Kayla's hair for the next fifteen minutes until Dr. Piaget clapped his hand on Barbara's shoulder. He whispered in Barbara's ear, "I knew you were the one who would ultimately make the breakthrough with Kayla." He sat down by Kayla whose sobbing had ebbed to soft moans. "Kayla, it seems like you might be ready to create your own future not haunted by your mom and dead animals." He lifted her chin. "Are you ready to tell us everything?"

Kayla sniffled as she rubbed her eyes with her fingers. "Last time I told my story… to Grandma Lu… I got her killed."

J. L. Greger

Dr. Piaget helped Kayla stand and pushed her forward "No one gets hurt this time. We're going to a conference room. Your Grandpa Pete will be there and so, will Mr. Carbonne."

Kayla stopped moving. "Grandpa?"

Dr. Piaget said, "Your Grandpa doesn't have to be there. I thought you might like his company, but it's your choice."

Kayla didn't move. "It might make Grandpa mad. It's my fault that Grandma is dead." She suddenly cocked her hip and assumed her tough girl swagger. "He can listen to the tapes." She turned to Barbara. "I know you taped our talk, but you do it nicer than Carbonne. I wouldn't want him to comb my hair. He doesn't comb his own hair."

Dr. Piaget nudged Barbara as Kayla strutted forward. "I hoped we'd be interviewing the child, not the tough teen." He rushed to catch up with Kayla.

***

Barbara was surprised by Carbonne's first question. "Kayla, your Grandpa Pete told me a story about some holy dirt that your Grandma Lu got in Chimayó, but he didn't seem to know big parts of the story. I think your grandma got the dirt on the day before she died. You just stop me whenever I say anything wrong. She had three containers of dirt."

"No, only two."

Barbara suddenly realized how thoroughly Carbonne planned to test Kayla with all sorts of interview tricks along the way.

Carbonne looked at his notes. "You're right. I had trouble reading my notes. He said your grandma painted crosses with the wet dirt on your and Matt's foreheads. Did she say anything?"

Kayla shrugged. "She just put it on Matt's forehead and I'm not sure what she said. Some type of prayer."

"What happened when your mother saw what your grandmother did?"

"You know the answer. She was angry, especially after stupid Matt tried to put the dirt on Mom's face."

"Anything else make her angry?"

Kayla fiddled with the bobby pin holding her braid in a spiral behind her right ear. "Grandma said that Mom 'needed a whole container of mud to make a face mask for her sins.' or something like that."

Carbonne nodded. "That was pretty insulting." He lowered his voice and moved closer to Kayla. "Do you know why your grandma insulted your mom?"

Kayla looked at her lap. "It was my fault. The day before... maybe two days before... late at night... I woke her... Grandma Lu... after I buried another dog in the orchard.... I told Grandma Lu that I was tired of burying pets in her orchard. I was tired of Mom screaming. I was tired of her telling Matt he killed the pets.... Poor, dumb Matt." Kayla began to cry.

When Barbara put her arm around Kayla's shoulder, she pushed Barbara away. "I'm tired of pretending. Matt never killed anything bigger than an ant when he stepped on it. But Mom would brush his hair and whisper in his ear at night. He'd cry and say the next day that he made another 'boo-boo.' She tried it with me, but I told her to stop."

Barbara found the next part of the interview frightening as Kayla explained how Mitzi had convinced Matt and Kayla to help her tie up Lurleen as part of a game of cowboys and Indians. Kayla admitted she had doubted it was game but didn't want to annoy Mitzi. She couldn't explain why Lurleen hadn't fought Mitzi, but noted that "Grandma Lu seemed awfully sleepy, until Mom started to stab her." Lurleen had evidently moaned "forgive" a lot. When she said, "Kayla and Matt forgive me. Didn't know," Mitzi had laughed and stabbed deeper. Then Kayla said, "Mom got more excited... Laughed louder... and louder. Blood... more blood."

Barbara almost gagged at one point. She was grateful when Carbonne asked her to bring lunches into the conference room. Although she was no expert, she thought Kayla's answers had confirmed and enlarged the evidence provided by Pete's, Matt's, and Sara's comments; Lurleen's letter; and the lab data. Throughout it all. Kayla denied ever killing an animal or stabbing her grandmother. However, she admitted she never tried to stop her mother because she feared what she would do when "she was in one of her moods."

The most poignant moment during Kayla's confession was when she grabbed Carbonne's hand and said, "Mom will hurt Matt and me if she finds out about what I've said. Can you promise me that she'll never be near us again?"

The interview after lunch focused on what happened after Mitzi had slashed Lurleen's throat with a piece of broken vase. Evidently, Mitzi's rage was spent, and she became organized. Kayla explained, "Mom always wants to clean everything after she kills a cat or dog. She was the same with Grandma. Ordered me to collect all the pendants, which Grandma gave us, wipe them clean, and pitch them in the bags with the bloody towels." Kayla bit her lip. "I liked my pendant. So did Matt. I unclipped his pendant as he slept on the bed in Grandpa's den. He didn't even wake up. I guess he was worn out and the house was finally quiet. Then I shoved the pendants and my chain in a pot on the terrace."

Dr. Piaget stopped her. "Why there?"

"I could get the pendants and chains from the pots anytime. Then I heard Mom screaming. She told me to put on gloves and take the bracelet off Grandma. I didn't want to do it but Mom yanked one pendant off the bracelet and threw it at me. I was scared and did what she said."

Carbonne interrupted. "When did your Grandpa Pete call?"

Kayla bit her lip and appeared to think. "About then and that upset Mom. I guess that was good. She forgot the bracelet and told me to bring Matt to the kitchen."

Dr. Piaget waited for Kayla to continue talking, when she didn't, he said, "What did Matt do?"

"Freaked out. He touched Grandma... and ran around the house touching things with his bloody hands. Mom started screaming, 'Get out!' I grabbed Matt and ran to the car. Mom drove."

Barbara was relieved when Carbonne asked Dr. Piaget to step out of the room with him. When they returned, Carbonne said, "Kayla, Dr. Piaget wants to talk to you more about your grandma, but first I need to know more about your visit to La Bendita. You told Chuy earlier your mom ordered you to follow Sara Almquist? Do you know why?"

Kayla frowned. "How am I supposed to know?"

Barbara interrupted, "Did your mom like Sara?"

"No. Thought she gave Grandma Lu bad ideas... like Grandpa."

Carbonne winked at Barbara. "What type of bad ideas?"

Kayla stood and walked to the door "I don't want to do this anymore."

Dr. Piaget guided her back to the chair. "Only a couple more questions today."

Kayla pulled the bobby pins out of her hair and the two braid fell to the sides of her face. "Don't tell Mom. They thought she was lazy and should go to work. That made Mom mad."

"Okay, I understand." Carbonne pushed a scribbled note to Dr. Piaget. "A couple of weeks ago, you told me that your mom left you with Matt by the back gate of Alegria after you followed Sara and Bug. Do you know where your mom went? Or what she did?"

Kayla closed her eyes. "I saw her talking to someone in a hoodie."

"You didn't mention that before."

Barbara almost laughed as Kayla displayed her tough side. "Give me a break. I was worried about Matt. He wouldn't take his medicine and that would make Mom mad."

"What did the person in the hoodie look like? Was it a man or a woman? How big?"

Kayla closed her eyes. "About Mom's size." She paused. "Hoodie dark." Kayla paused again. "Probably a man. He ran toward Sara's house as Mom walked toward me. Ran like a man." Kayla brought her hands to her face. "Can I quit for today?"

"One more thing—how did your grandma's bracelet get into a pot on the patio?"

Kayla assumed her tough teen mode. "What was I supposed to do with it? Mom would be mad if she knew I had it. Grandpa was already at our front door. So, I left it in my hoodie's pocket with the icky gloves and walked around with it all day. When Mom left with Matt for Walmart, I rode over to Grandma's on my bike and shoved it into a pot on the patio, but the pot tipped. And then another pot fell, too. I didn't have time to fix everything."

Carbonne smiled. "Your Grandpa says your favorite outing is getting ice cream sundaes with sprinkles. I couldn't arrange an outing, but I had five flavors of ice cream and several topping delivered here. Matt and your Grandpa are waiting for you in the party room. You can invite anyone you want to your party."

Kayla sashayed to the door. "I invite Barbara… and Dr. Piaget." As she left the room, Kayla smiled at Carbonne. "You can come too, if you comb your hair."

***

The party room was draped with purple streamers. Purple balloons floated about the room. Matt was playing with two other boys of his size. Two girls of Kayla's age sat at a table waiting. As soon as Kayla entered the room, Pete announced, "Matt and I are so proud of you. You get the first sundae. What do you want?"

As Kayla basked in the attention of the staff. Dr. Piaget told Pete the news. "She's not out of the woods yet. She's been forced to be an adult in Mitzi's warped world for a long time. Everything she said today was consistent with our evidence. I think the juvenile court judge and court-appointed psychologist will decide she's innocent of wrongdoing—

at least of murder, abetting murder, and cruelty to animals. Hence she can stay in this facility and not face detention in a criminal unit."

Carbonne nodded in agreement. "I'll recommend neither child face criminal charges."

Pete whispered, "What about their custody?"

Dr. Piaget smiled. "You should be able to get full custody soon. Of course, they will have to stay here until they're ready."

Carbonne frowned. "It might not be quite as simple as you think. There's no doubt that we should throw away the key for Mitzi, but the federal prosecutor will be willing to negotiate with her."

Pete Jansen frowned. "Lurleen's murder case will be handled in the state courts."

"But they won't fight the federal prosecutor. We have to know who Mitzi hired to threaten Sara Almquist. Otherwise, Sara in essence will spend the rest of her life in the equivalent of prison in the witness protection program. It's possible Mitzi was being manipulated by gang members. That's what I have to figure out and fast. Sara testifies at the first federal trial of gang leaders in a week. I'm sorry, but I may have to offer Mitzi the chance to see her children occasionally."

Pete grimaced. "I don't like it and neither will the children."

"Neither do I." Carbonne left so quickly, Barbara had to run to catch up with him.

CHAPTER 38: FBI Agent Carbonne Sets a Trap

Three hours after Kayla completed her long interview, Carbonne delivered to Chuy and the assistant district attorney edited versions of the video recording with all references to Sara and the mystery man at La Bendita deleted. He didn't bring Barbara along because he didn't want her to have to lie to her boss.

As Carbonne had expected, Chuy was hesitant to file charges against Mitzi. He didn't believe Kayla's statements would hold up in court and claimed premature charges might validate Mitzi's lawyers allegations that he was harassing their client. The assistant DA disagreed.

Carbonne was pleased because he'd now split Chuy and the assistant DA. He needled Chuy to investigate Kayla's rape allegations against Josh Ahrens and the other young man in the Jansens' neighborhood. The young assistant DA, who had previously thought the charges were unsustainable, now also pressured the reluctant Chuy to act. However, the assistant DA wanted to see Dr. Piaget's written statement regarding Kayla's rape charges and the videotape of Kayla remembering the rapes before he acted.

Carbonne had expected these requests and hoped his somewhat flimsy trap would work as he dramatically searched his phone's files. "The lab must not have logged them in, and I'm swamped. I could find them at the building in less than five minutes with help. If Padilla comes with me, I could send him back to you with copies of both. Believe it or not, that will be quicker than waiting for the lab to log them in, even though the techs would be able to transmit them electronically."

Chuy retorted. "Doesn't matter. I won't work on the rape charges until next week at the earliest."

The assistant DA protested. "You'll act on it as soon as I review the evidence. I'm tired of hearing Mitzi's lawyers claim she's being treated unfairly."

Afterward, Padilla accompanied Carbonne to the FBI building. During the drive, Carbonne decided Barbara had been kind in her comments about Padilla. He was not only a blowhard but a stupid one with a mean streak. One of his comments was, "Kayla got what she deserved."

Thus, Carbonne enjoyed turning the tables on Padilla. As soon as he was seated in a conference room in the FBI building, Carbonne told Padilla that the FBI planned to charge both him and his cousin Joe Smith with intimidation of a federal witness and racketeering."

Padilla laughed. "Prove it."

Carbonne pointed out that Joe Smith's fingerprints had been found at Sara's house.

Padilla laughed. "You've got nothing on me."

Carbonne pulled out a copy of the duty roster for the Mercado Police Department for the week of Lurleen's death. "You were assigned to the unit that circled La Bendita six times a day about a month ago. I'm told most officers don't like that assignment, but you requested it."

"It's easy." Padilla didn't laugh this time.

"The senior officer assigned to patrol La Bendita wanted to reduce the evening patrols on the day of Lurleen's murder because the department was so shorthanded. You volunteered to patrol La Bendita alone." Carbonne knew it wasn't much but it was all Barbara Lewis could locate without raising suspicion. He tried to increase the impact of his words by snickering as he stared at Padilla.

"It's a good thing I did. I got a car directed to the emergency gate. That's where they found the boy. Remember? I was with Chuy at the gate when you arrived."

"Yes, but you ignored the emergency call from the Almquist house."

"The boy was in bad shape."

"Were you ordered to ignore the emergency call from the Almquist home?"

Carbonne in one sense wanted Padilla to say yes and accordingly implicate Chuy. But, he more strongly hoped the answer would be no. He didn't want to believe Chuy had been bribed.

Padilla shrugged. "What do you want me to say? I was confused."

"Doubt it. And you don't lie well—your ears turn red. Why didn't you answer the emergency call?"

Padilla rubbed his earlobes. "I want to talk to my union rep."

Chuy checked his phone. "Are you sure? I believe your rep is Barbara Lewis and she doesn't like liars."

Padilla's shoulders drooped.

Carbonne's phone buzzed and he squelched a smile as he studied the text. He'd tricked Padilla into following him through a patch of raked sand as they entered a back door of the FBI building. The lab crew had photographed their footprints, and the message confirmed Carbonne's suspicions:

Padilla's footprint, including the extra wear on his right heel, match the file photographs from Sara's house. A judge granted me a search warrant.

Barbara

"Before you make any decisions, you should know Barbara Lewis just got a search warrant for your apartment and car. As part of that warrant, I'm claiming your shoes now for more photographs."

"What?"

"We can prove you and Joe Smith snooped around Sara Almquist's house two weeks ago. He left fingerprints around her bedroom window and patio door; you both left footprints." Carbonne smiled. "We also know someone tried to intimidate Sara Almquist at La Bendita on the day Lurleen Jansen was murdered, and it wasn't Joe." Carbonne smiled. "Barbara Lewis is ready to talk to you now, but not as your union rep."

Carbonne strode into another interview room where Mitzi was waiting impatiently with her lawyers. He didn't bother to sit. "Mitzi Jansen, you will be charged the premeditated murder of your mother tomorrow by the Mercado police in collaboration with the Sandoval County district attorney. You will also be charged with at least twenty counts of extreme cruelty to animals. The lab data combined with your father's, brother's, and daughter's testimony make the cases air tight."

One of the lawyers raised an objection as Mitzi stood and howled, "Lies! Lies!"

Carbonne pointed at her chair. "Please sit down. I'm authorized to make you a deal. We know you collaborated to stalk Sara Almquist with someone who had plans to kill her. Unfortunately for you, Sara will be witness in several upcoming federal trials. That means you committed a federally punishable crime."

He paused as Mitzi alternately sobbed hysterically and screamed. Finally, Carbonne grew tired of waiting for her to calm down and said, "You don't want the man to come from behind that mirror." He pointed at the mirror. "He's prepared to charge you with racketeering, which means the case against you for the murder of your mother could be transferred from a state to a federal court." He sneered. "Who helped you try to intimidate Sara Almquist?"

"I don't know!" Mitzi screeched.

"You can do better. How and where did you meet him?"

Mitzi buried her head in her hands. "Don't know."

"Federal maximum security prisons make state prisons look pretty comfy. Don't doubt you will be convicted. The pictures of your mother will convince any jury that you should never get out of jail. Most jurors will wish they could send you to Texas for a death penalty trial." He glanced at her lawyers. "Federal prosecutors are willing to drop federal charges if you cooperate. I will let your lawyers explain this is the best deal you'll get." He was bluffing. When the lawyers saw Kayla's tape, they would realize that an insanity defense might work. "You have two minutes to begin cooperating."

The lawyers hunched over Mitzi. She screamed, "No!" several times and then whimpered, "Okay."

Despite warnings from her lawyers, she insisted on explaining at the start, "I never wanted to adopt Matt, but the juvenile court judge and Mother made me. Mother promised I could get support from my .grandparents' trust as long as Matt lived. But she lied and Dad was going to cut off my funds."

At that point, Carbonne sensed he could easily get Mitzi to admit she had intentionally overdosed Matt, but he decided to take Ulysses Howe's advice to prioritize. He focused on getting information on the stalking and attacks on Sara.

First, he focused on learning Mitzi's intent in regard to Sara. That was relatively easy. Mitzi wanted Sara dead because Lurleen had muttered about a letter describing Mitzi as a "killer of animals" while being tortured. Mitzi assumed Lurleen had sent the letter to Sara. Mitzi moaned, "If she knew my secret, she could take Kayla away from me. Kayla helps me with my little problems."

Second, Carbonne assessed Mitzi's relationship with Joe Smith. Mitzi gushed, "He's the first man who wanted to protect me. He told me he would eliminate anyone bothering me, but then he got arrested in Colorado and couldn't fulfill his promises." Carbonne probed more, and Mitzi admitted, "But he got his friend to help me." Carbonne kept asking for examples. Finally, she said, "I could never have managed Mother without his special medicine, and I could have never thrown a stone hard enough to break a window."

Third, Carbonne wanted to learn about Mitzi's knowledge of—and association with—the Mercado Police Department and gang members. Mitzi was unable, Carbonne thought unwilling, to identify anyone when he showed her pictures of Mercado police officers including those of Padilla and Chuy.

Thus, when Mitzi's lawyers finally forced him to stop questioning her, Carbonne still had no answer to four big questions. Was Joe Smith freelancing or working for organized gangs when he agreed to eliminate Sara for Mitzi? Did Padilla know all of Joe's and Mitzi's plans? Did Chuy hire Padilla in return for a bribe? It was difficult to believe anyone would have thought Padilla could be a competent police officer. And was the bribe from gangs being investigated in the upcoming federal cases?

CHAPTER 39: Sara in Albuquerque on Day 35

Sara looked in the mirror. With the help of a good hairstylist, her hair was now its normal ash blonde color. The hairdresser had called it "champagne blonde." Sara wished she felt as sexy and attractive as the color name suggested.

She had on her good black knit suit with the paisley shawl that Sanders had sent draped on her shoulders. Its subtle color scheme of peaches and beiges was exactly what she would have picked, but she'd been disappointed when she opened the box. The note said only, *Love*, written in Sander's handwriting. He hadn't signed it. She knew the U.S. marshals in Romeoville had refused to deliver anything to her that could be useful in tracing her location. She wished Sanders had not followed the rules this time. She fingered the ring on her right hand and wondered where Sanders's matching ring was now.

The last week had been pleasant because she'd been busy. She and Bug had spent most days in a tiny office in the FBI building in Albuquerque—the one she used previously when she was in danger and being guarded by the agents. There she could work with Carbonne and meet with the federal prosecutor because Ulysses Howe had more than a year ago put her on payroll as a special consultant to the FBI. Bug had seemed calmer in the familiar environment. He also liked his walks better because his long thick coat didn't get soaked as much as it had in rainy Romeoville.

Sara was ready to testify today. She expected her testimony would take less than an hour but the cross-examination by the defense could be much longer than that. They would try to disqualify many of her statements. Carbonne and Gil Andrews would testify tomorrow. Sanders would testify later in the week. Thus, she didn't expect to see the three men today because they couldn't be in the courtroom when she testified.

***

The marshals shepherded Sara into a back entrance of the federal court building in Albuquerque to avoid photographers. However, the courtroom was packed when she was sworn in as a witness. She saw familiar faces in the courtroom, but most were at the defendants' table, and they didn't smile at her.

The questions from the prosecution were easy because she was prepared for them. Those from the defense seemed tricky at times, so she replied slowly and carefully. The judge recessed the court for lunch after the defense had hammered at her for over two hours. She guessed the defendants' lawyers weren't getting what they wanted because they appeared to be prepared to continue all afternoon.

At least the marshal assigned to eat lunch with her was talkative. After the trials were over, Sara would be eating most of her meals alone with Bug in some yet-to-be-determined location.

Sara was surprised when she returned to the courtroom. The defense lawyers announced, "We have no further questions for this witness at this time." The judge noted Sara could be recalled for further testimony. The lead federal prosecutor had winked at her as the marshals led her away.

***

Sara worked with Barbara Lewis and the assistant Sandoval County district attorney at the FBI building during the next two days completing details needed to guarantee Mitzi's conviction for murder, two counts of attempted murder in regard to Matt and Sara, and twenty counts of extreme cruelty to animals. Once the federal prosecutor decided not to charge Mitzi with racketeering because she had provided evidence against Smith and Padilla, the Sandoval County district attorney had added the two counts of attempted murder because he agreed with Carbonne. Mitzi would kill again if annoyed.

The marshals seemed more relaxed on the second day and allowed Pete Jansen to bring Kayla and Matt to the FBI building after a juvenile court awarded him custody of the two children. The judge had declared Mitzi had no visiting rights unless the charges against her were dropped. He'd also ordered the children must continue to receive psychological counseling and general rehabilitation daily for six months. They would be reevaluated at that time, but it was anticipated they would require special counseling for years.

Sara was amazed at the changes in the children. Kayla still had a smart mouth but asked questions as Sara led the Jansens on a tour of the FBI building. Previously, Kayla would have pouted and called everything either "lame" or "boring." Matt talked—granted, in partial sentences— more than he had in years.

At the end of their visit, Pete pulled Sara aside and said, "Lurleen made many mistakes, but she was wise to have you go with her to Chimayó. I hope you'll see Kayla again. She needs a strong woman role model." He squeezed Sara's hand and rushed away with tears in his eyes.

***

Sara didn't see Carbonne and Ulysses Howe either day. She assumed they were testifying at the federal trial, until Barbara Lewis confided that Carbonne was trying to determine whether Chuy had been bought off by the gangs. Sara couldn't believe Chuy, who always seemed so earnest and sincere, would have participated in or knowingly allowed the gangs to plot her death. Barbara Lewis refused to be specific but noted that she didn't want to return to the Mercado Police Department if Gil Andrews retired.

The marshals surprised Sara again later in the day and drove her to the hospice where Jen Andrews was staying. Gil Andrews greeted her at the entrance. "After Carbonne realized the seriousness of the threats against you, he and Ulysses Howe convinced me that Jen and I would be safer here. They brought Jack Daniels here, too. Then the federal prosecutors office let it slip to the defense lawyers that Jen and Jack were in dire straits and might not last until the end of the trial. That gave me an excuse for staying here at night under the watchful eyes of marshals." He smiled. "As you'll see, Jen is responding well to her new round of immunotherapy. She doesn't want me to retire. Says I'd be a pest around the house all day, every day."

"How's Jack doing?"

"He seems to enjoy gossiping with hospice patients and he helps to serve their meals. So far, Carbonne has found no evidence of threats against me, or anyone testifying at these trials, but you."

Sara tried to keep smiling during dinner. This would probably be the last time she saw Gil and Jen because soon she'd be in some distant location with a new identity under the witness protection program.

***

The next afternoon, Sara was called to court late in the day. Just before she entered the courtroom, a marshal handed her a note:

It's over. Joe Smith and Padilla were not acting on behalf of gang leaders. The threats against you were all initiated by Mitzi and these two men hoping to get big money when Lurleen's will was probated. Chuy Bargas is no longer the acting chief of the

*Mercado police, but he will stay on the force and will not be
charged with any criminal activity.*
Carbonne
*P.S. That means you won't be under the thumb of marshals after
the federal trials are over. Ulysses and I could find a position for
you with the FBI, if you don't get a better offer.*

Sara felt a weight lifted from her shoulder. Her next two hours of cross-examination flew by quickly. Again, the judge warned her that she could be called back.

This time the marshals didn't whisk Sara away through a side exit. They slowly led her to the door at the back of the courtroom and allowed her to turn as she was about to exit. The next witness had entered the courtroom. It was Sanders. He lifted his left hand—with the matching ring on his fourth finger—up to his lips and smiled before the bailiff swore him in.

THE END

THE SCIENCE AND HISTORY BEHIND THE STORY

The theme of this novel is that water is essential for life and is considered holy in many cultures but it is also often polluted. It's a theme especially appropriate for a novel set in the arid regions of the American Southwest and in India.

- The Food and Nutrition Board of the Institute of Medicine recommends adult males and females ingest 3.7 liters and 2.7 liters, respectively, of water in food and beverages daily. (*Dietary Reference Intakes for Water, Potassium, Sodium, Chloride, and Sulfates*. The National Academies Press, 2005) Thus, the potable water needs of eight billion people in the world and trillions of animals is staggering.

- Most religions associate water with life in their teachings and include purification rites involving water. Semantics aside, water is, or at least can be, holy if it's clean. The Old Testament and the Quran specify rules for the disposal of human wastes ostensibly to prevent contamination of water sources. Yet, one environmental group listed three rivers with religious significance (the Ganges, Yamuna, and Jordan) among the eleven most polluted rivers in the world. (https://conserve-energy-future.com/most-polluted-rivers-world.php)

- The major sources of water pollution are agricultural and industrial wastes and human sewage.

- Improved sanitation is a first step in reducing water pollution, especially in Asia, Africa, and South America. Sixty-percent of the people in the world do not have access to safely managed sanitation. (https://ourworldindata.org/sanitation#access-to-safe-sanitation)

- To conserve this essential resource, everyone needs to shift their view of wastewater management from "treatment and disposal" to "reuse, recycle, and resource recovery" (*Wastewater: The Untapped Resource*, UNESCO, 2017, https://reliefweb.int/report/world/2017-un-world-water-development-report-wastewater-untapped-resource)

There are a number of other scientific issues mentioned in this novel.

• India is believed to have some of the most polluted air in the world. As noted in the novel, air pollution is the worst in October and November when farmers burn crop residues to facilitate crop rotations. (*Science*, 9 August 2019, Vol. 365: 536-8)

• Chronic kidney disease in agricultural workers in India (as noted in Chapter 18) is probably just another example of a malady exacerbated by pollution. In this case, the core problem is hypothesized to be chronic dehydration. (*Science*, 1 April 2016, Vol. 353: 24-27)

• India has no equivalent to the Social Security numbers used in the U.S. and has developed the world's largest biometric identification system based on fingerprints, photos, and iris scans. The system is used in all kinds of cash transfer programs and for passports. (*Science*, 20 January 2017, Vol. 355: 244-5) However, the author, like Sara in the novel, was unable to use the system when she entered India because of 'weak' fingerprints.

• Researchers have shown that it is possible to implant false memories in susceptible individuals and this phenomenon has led to false confessions to police. (*Science* 14 June 2019; Vol. 364:1022-1026) Matt Jansen, the mentally impaired boy, in the *Dirty Holy Water* is a good example of an individual who could be coerced into confessing to crimes he didn't commit.

• At least one of the security problems that Sanders dealt with at the embassy in Havana is based on real world events. U.S. government personnel serving at the embassy in Cuba reported neurological impairment in 2016 and 2017. Two potential causes for these symptoms are: "direction audible and sensory phenomena" of unknown cause (*Journal of the American Medical Association*, 20 March 2018; Vol 319: 1125-33) and fumigants used to combat the Zika virus. (*Science*, 27 September 2019; Vol. 365: 1356).

• Traveler's diarrhea probably affects 40 million people each year but its impact is seldom considered in reports of the effects of poor sanitation on community health. (*Archive of Gastroenterology and Hepatology (NY)*, February 2011; Vol.7: 88-95)

Many of this novel's scenes in India reflect the author's actual experiences in that country. The historical events are related as accurately as a non-historian can explain.

ABOUT THE AUTHOR

J. L. Greger is a biology professor and research administrator from the University of Wisconsin-Madison turned novelist. She lives in New Mexico with Bug, the prototype for the dog of the same name in her mystery/thriller novels. Greger includes tidbits on science, the American Southwest, and her international travel experiences—including those in India—in the novels of her Science Traveler Series.

- *The Flu Is Coming* In the first book in the series, a woman scientist traces the spread of a deadly new flu virus among the frantic residents of a quarantined New Mexico community. (New Mexico/Arizona Book Award Finalist)

- *Murder...A Way to Lose Weight* A dean in a medical school helps police discover whether an ambitious young "diet doctor," disgruntled patients, or old-timers with buried secrets are killers. (Winner of the 2016 Public Safety Writers Association [PSWA] contest and New Mexico/Arizona Book Award Finalist)

- *Ignore the Pain.* A woman scientist learns too much about the coca trade and too little about a sexy new colleague while on a public health assignment in Bolivia.

- *Malignancy* A woman tries to escape the clutches of a drug lord and accepts a risky assignment as a science consultant in Cuba. (Winner of the 2015 PSWA contest)

- *I Saw You in Beirut* A woman's past provides clues for the extraction of a nuclear scientist from Iran. The author's experiences as a science and education consultant in the United Arab Emirates and Lebanon are featured.

- *Riddled with Clues* A homeless man and a woman scientist are targeted by drug gangs after she listens to the strange tale of an undercover drug agent about his war experiences. The memories of an actual CIA agent in Laos during the Vietnam War are featured. (New Mexico/Arizona Book Award Finalist)

- *A Pound of Flesh, Sorta* Police and a woman scientist can't decide whether a package contaminated with the bacteria that causes the bubonic plague is a plea by a whistleblower at a meat packing plant or a threat from gang leaders awaiting trial.

- ***Dirty Holy Water.*** A woman who usually serves as a science consultant for the FBI learns there is a thin line between being a victim and being a villain when she find herself as the chief suspect in a bizarre murder case.

http://www.jlgreger.com

CPSIA information can be obtained
at www.ICGtesting.com
Printed in the USA
LVHW040528231120
672447LV00005B/336

9 780960 028580